There Comes a Moment...

A Haunting In Highland

By
Andrew Carmitchel

iUniverse, Inc.
New York   Bloomington

Copyright © 2009 by Andrew Carmitchel

All rights reserved. No part of this book may be used
or reproduced by any means, graphic, electronic, or
mechanical, including photocopying, recording, taping or
by any information storage retrieval system without the
written permission of the publisher except in the case of brief
quotations embodied in critical articles and reviews.

This is a work of fiction. All of the characters, names, incidents,
organizations, and dialogue in this novel are either the products
of the author's imagination or are used fictitiously.

iUniverse books may be ordered through booksellers or by contacting:

iUniverse
1663 Liberty Drive
Bloomington, IN 47403
www.iuniverse.com
1-800-Authors (1-800-288-4677)

Because of the dynamic nature of the Internet, any Web addresses or
links contained in this book may have changed since publication and
may no longer be valid. The views expressed in this work are solely those
of the author and do not necessarily reflect the views of the publisher,
and the publisher hereby disclaims any responsibility for them.

ISBN: 978-1-4401-4266-6 (sc)
ISBN: 978-1-4401-4269-7 (hc)
ISBN: 978-1-4401-4268-0 (ebook)

Printed in the United States of America

iUniverse rev. date: 06/02/2009

Chapter 1

There comes a moment, inevitably in every one of our lives, when stark, unmitigated fear suddenly captures us completely. It is almost always when we least expect it, is always uninvited, and is characterized by a totally inexplicable paralysis that captures us, body and soul. When it comes, whether it lasts a long time or is blissfully short, we know somehow a fiber of it will always remain with us for as long as our contentious journey lasts here on this beleaguered, but still stubbornly blue planet.

It is a moment of blind terror when every cell is consumed with total fright; an emotion that brings, in a millisecond, a panic so intense that it robs us of all reason. It can come in a thousand ways, and at any time, but this terror freezes us in every way, and is unforgettable to the survivor. It is usually momentary, thankfully, but it stays lurking in the nervous system forever, waiting for the next time. And it will come again, you can be assured.

It may come in the split second before a perceived life-threatening accident or assault or, if we're lucky, as the result of a horrible, if ultimately harmless, nightmare. It may come with an unexpected sound in the dark, an unexplained rustling coming from right behind us as we walk, from a wayward rodent running over a foot, or even sometimes, as the unintended result of a well-meant surprise from a loved one. We don't know where, and we don't know when…but it's out there somewhere, waiting. For all of us.

Just such a "moment" came to Jonathon Parker in the first milky white light of dawn on what should have been an unremarkable summer morning in July. Jon's clear blue eyes snapped open, wide open, from what had been a dead sleep, and stared near uncomprehendingly at the clock at his bedside. It said 5:23. Something had happened, he knew. He was afraid to breathe, but didn't know why. He was perspiring, trembling slightly, and his mind was struggling fiercely to understand, to make sense of this, or even, in those first few seconds, to have a coherent thought. The clock turned to 5:24. He stared at it, his head still on his pillow, as afraid as he had ever been in his life.

Then the scream came. It was the second scream, he instantly realized. A woman's scream. A jarringly loud, piercing scream that somehow seemed to contain all the fear and grief of the world. And it seemed to be coming from right outside his bedroom window.

Jon bolted upright in his bed, and in those first few panicked seconds he wished, albeit irrationally, that someone was lying there beside him; a lover, or even just some girl he'd hooked up with the night before, or a place to run to, like the safety of his parent's bedroom long ago. Anyone. Someone.

The scream stopped. He threw off the sheet, and tried to get up, as it happened, too fast. He over swung his legs while trying to jump out of bed and stand at the same time and tumbled to the floor, hitting his head hard on the nightstand in the process. It was a blow that dazed him, and under normal circumstances he would have spent the ensuing minutes regaining his senses, and nursing himself in the bathroom, but he knew there was no time for that now. The paralyzing fear was still there, even if it now carried a bruise with it. If anything, it was greater now that there was silence outside. He struggled to his feet, took a deep breath to try to stabilize himself, then reached for his jeans.

Still dizzy, he almost fell again, but grabbed the nightstand to keep himself upright. Then he sat back on the bed, and after taking a moment to right himself, began struggling to get his pants on.

Moments later he was in full sprint down the hallway toward his kitchen when the screaming started again. He was further away from it, so it wasn't quite as ear-shattering, but now that he was fully awake, it was perhaps even more unnerving. He entered his still half dark kitchen, found the light switch after two quick tries, and then, with badly shaking hands, picked up the phone and dialed 911 for the first time in his life. An operator answered on the third ring.

"You have dialed 911. What is the nature of your emergency?"

"There's a woman screaming, right outside my house! Please send someone...now!" Jon said.

"Please calm down sir. What is your name, sir?"

"Jesus Christ! You're kidding!!" Jon screamed. He couldn't believe this. He'd heard some of these inane 911 calls played on TV before, but now it was him, and now he needed help. "Just send someone to 335 Devonshire Court... I'm begging you! I'm at the end of a cul-de-sac. Hurry up!"

"We're responding right away sir. Please calm down, and try to answer my questions. Is the woman hurt, Mr. uh... what was your name?"

Jon hung up the phone. He stood for a moment, still shaking, and tried to think clearly. As is almost always true in situations such as these, his first, primal thoughts were for his own safety. Had he locked both his doors last night? Had he closed the garage door, for sure?

He reached a hand up to wipe the sweat he felt dripping down his forehead, and when he pulled it back down, he saw that it was blood, not perspiration. "Great. Just great," he said aloud as he rushed over to the kitchen sink to wash himself. Temporarily, he thought only of himself. But as soon as he began to run the water, there was a scream again, shorter this time, and more guttural, as if the woman was in grievous pain. Rape?

Ashamed of himself, Jon shut off the faucet and looked around the kitchen quickly. He needed a weapon. He didn't own a gun. He saw the carving knife set his mother had bought him when he had first moved in. He'd never used them. He grabbed the handle of the biggest one, pulled it out and looked at it for a moment and then ran for the front door.

He had indeed locked it, and nearly cut himself again in his hurried effort to open it. He finally succeeded, swung it open wildly, and ran off his short front porch and through the cold, dew soaked grass in his bare feet to the side of his house that the screams were coming from.

He saw her immediately, as she was standing in the pale light almost precisely on the lot line between their two houses, and more toward the street than he would have guessed by the sound. Barb Ellsworth, the cute little blonde from next door, wearing her fashionable jogging clothes and pristine white running shoes, was standing over what looked at first like a big leaf bag, with her hands held up to her face as though trying to cover her eyes, and she was sobbing convulsively.

Jon sized up the scene as he slowed to a jog and then a walk, relieved beyond measure that Barb was not hurt, but only, apparently, terribly frightened about something. He lowered the knife to his side as he approached, not wanting to hear that scream of hers ever again. "Barb," he said as gently as he could with the breath he had left, "Barb, what's the matter?"

Barb appeared to be oblivious to his words or his presence, even when he got to within a few feet, and right across the bag from her. He saw that her trembling hands were actually on her upper cheeks, as though she was trying to pull her wide open eyes even wider as she stared down.

"Barb," he said a little more forcefully. "What is it?"

And then he looked down. It was hard to make out what

he was looking at, at first. To be fair, an eyeless, hairless head of a corpse that is almost the exact color of the grey dawn is not something one expects to see on one's safe, suburban lawn first thing in the morning. At least not most mornings. Jon bent closer to get a good look, and at once the overpowering smell of death, and the recognition of what had recently been a human face hit him. He jumped back, emitting an involuntary, almost effeminate scream of his own.

Jon's scream had the effect of violently retrieving Barb from her state of shock, and she looked up at her bloodied, bare-chested, bare-footed, knife wielding neighbor…and fainted, right on the spot.

Jon stood paralyzed, now several safe feet away, staring first at the wax-like head sticking out of the body bag, and then at his fallen neighbor, whose face was lying perilously close to the corpse's. He stood gasping for breath, and trying to comprehend what had just happened. He heard, but only vaguely, another neighbor yelling and coming on the run, and the distant sound of sirens in the early morning

---

Pete Vanderberg lived on the other side of Jon, the west side (the Ellsworths being the first house to the east), at the end of the Devonshire cul-de-sac. Pete was already awake, had had a cup of coffee, and was in the middle of shaving when he heard the distant scream. He turned down the news program on the radio he had on at the same time each morning and, face still half lathered, listened intently while staring at his tired, gray visage in the mirror in front of him. He heard nothing, so he continued his shave, but with the volume down. When the scream came again he heard it clearly, and it startled him enough to cut himself slightly. He swore out loud, but quickly wiped off the blood and remaining lather from his face, and then walked hurriedly toward his living room and front door.

His wife Margie came out of the hallway to their bedroom at the same time, and they almost ran into each other.

"Did you hear that?" she asked after she stopped just short of him. She was close enough to him for Pete to catch a whiff of sour morning breath, and between that and the wild sagebrush look of her hair, and the old tattered robe she insisted on wearing that made her look like a hefty homeless woman, along with the fact that she had scared him half to death with her sudden appearance from the hallway, all combined to make Pete answer her far more irritably than the situation called for.

"Go back to bed, will ya!" he snapped. "I'll handle this!"

Margie drew back in surprise at his tone, but said nothing. There was no screaming at the moment, and she was still half asleep, so she shrugged and turned to pad back down the hallway, while rubbing whatever dream or nightmare she must have been having out of her eyes.

Pete, towel still in hand, headed to the front door. He unlocked and opened it, stepped out onto his front porch into the grey, new dawn, and had just taken his first breath of the humid July morning air when he heard his friend Jon Parker scream. He had no idea it was Jon though, because the scream was short and high-pitched, unlike the one he had heard while shaving. It was the yell of someone temporarily frightened out of their wits, like a victim of a scare on a Halloween night. He couldn't tell if it was a man or a woman. It made him jump, and because it was early morning, and not Halloween, he knew then for sure that something was very wrong. He started out on the run toward the noise he'd heard.

Pete didn't have to go far. He saw the shadowy scene between Jon's and the Ellsworth's houses when he was only a few feet away from his porch. And then he saw someone, or something collapse to the ground. It was then that he yelled out, "Hey, what's the matter over there?" while racing over to see.

He recognized his neighbor Jon first, and saw the knife he was holding right away. The knife, and the dazed way John was standing there made him slow up considerably before getting too close. An image of Jon as a crazed murderer flew through his head, but didn't hold. Jon killing an intruder, maybe? But, in Highland?

"What happened here Jon?" Pete asked as coolly as possible, from what he judged to be a safe distance from the knife.

Jon stared at the bodies in front of him for a few moments more before slowly turning his head toward Pete. Pete saw that Jon's face was more frightened than frightening. That, along with a groaning sound from the ground gave Pete assurance enough to take his eyes off of Jon (and the knife), and look for the first time at what was lying down there. He saw Barb Ellswoth, the girl in so many of his illicit dreams, on the ground, rolling her head back and forth as though she was having a dream of her own, and he saw a large black bag next to her. Now Pete was even more confused. This scene made no sense. What about the screams?

"Pete, go look at the open part…the part up there," Jon said suddenly in a cracking voice. Pete took a step back instead, and shifted his gaze back over to Jon, who was standing right where he had been, but was now looking at, and pointing his knife with a shaking hand at, the top of the bag. In the growing morning light, Pete could now see the blood running down Jon's forehead and temple. He took another step back. He became conscious of the sirens then; sirens that were getting steadily louder. He knew they must be coming here. They were probably two minutes away.

"Go look, Pete! Right here in the yard!" Jon's voice sounded close to hysterical now. Pete studied his neighbor. He was trying to think calmly, but there were so many possibilities here. Should he keep backing up, and wait for the police? What if they weren't coming here?

"Look Jon," he finally began while easing backwards, "why don't you get rid of that knife, OK? Then I'll go look at the bag." Jon looked slowly down at the knife he was holding, and then at his friend. He looked to Pete as though he didn't quite understand. "Throw the knife down buddy. We've got to help Barb out, right?" Pete asked.

Jon looked at Pete for a long moment, then turned his head slowly back toward Barb and the bag. Then, finally, he took an audible, shaking breath, and threw the knife, hard, back toward his own house. Then he put his head down in resignation.

Barb raised her head up as Pete moved quickly over to her side. She looked confused, as though she had just woken up from a long beauty sleep, with her aimless look, mussed blonde hair and lack of make-up. Pete helped her to her feet while whispering that everything "would be all right," even though he still had no idea what had actually happened. The loud wail of the first police car turning into their cul-de-sac made all three of them turn and watch its approach. The sound raised the hair on Pete's neck, made Jon feel like running away…or sitting down, he didn't know which, and it appeared to make Barb more dazed and confused than ever.

As the first car screeched to a halt at the curb in front of them, a second car fishtailed into the entrance of the cul-de-sac, then gunned the motor and wailed down the street toward the first. The three stood mesmerized, and as still as the fourth one lying there, as the police officially arrived. Now, up and down the cul-de-sac doors swung open, and neighbors came out onto their porches and into their yards in pajamas and bathrobes, squinting into the new day's first sunlight, trying to see just what had happened down there at the end of Devonshire Street.

Officer Darrin Crandle was the first to arrive at the scene. Though he was the newest member of Highland's Police Department, and just 23 years old, there was no other officer more ambitious or enthusiastic about his chosen life's work.

In fact, the whole department combined couldn't match his boundless energy, and being a rookie, this added up to much hidden resentment, open teasing, and even jealous mockery from the mostly cranky, veteran staff. Officer Crandle was young, conspicuously bright, ridiculously good looking, and very single and free - all things that caused, understandably, envy and resentment in the rest.

The reason he was first on the scene is in some ways an illustration of this. Darrin knew the sprawling, growing suburban town like the back of his hand, even though he'd been a Highland resident for only five months. He studied it day and night, on duty and off, and he knew every street and alley (and almost every garbage can in those alleys) better than, or at least as well as anyone ever had. He also studied the people, the traffic patterns, and everything else he could think of that might some day benefit him in the line of duty. To some, he was too good to be true.

When he heard the call toward the end of his shift to proceed to 335 Devonshire he knew right where it was. The map in his head told him. The officer in the other car, who was also finishing up his night shift, knew about where it was too, but not as precisely as Crandle. He would arrive, therefore, a few seconds later. Once again, in second place to the kid.

Crandle was already walking up to the three frozen figures on the lawn when Officer Jim Melrose's car came screaming up to the scene. Melrose was trying to make up the time, but a little too fast. His car skidded to a stop, but not until it had hopped the curb and turned up some considerable ruts some twenty yards into the Ellsworth's lawn. When he finally stopped, Melrose looked over sheepishly to see Crandle and the other three people looking over at his car in alarm, so he immediately took the only option left to him. He got out of his car quickly and as nonchalantly as possible, to give the impression he had driven up there on purpose. He also said a silent prayer, asking

God to make sure this was a serious enough incident to make his wayward parking irrelevant.

Officer Crandle, after seeing that Melrose was all right, turned briefly to look at the ruts in the yard, shook his head in disgust, then continued the walk the slight upgrade to the people on the lawn. "What seems to be the problem here folks?" he said in calm police talk as he approached. He saw blood streaming down one man's face, and another man with a little blood on his chin with his arm around a pretty woman, and a lawn bag or something in between them. It looked like some sort of domestic dispute; maybe some jealous husband thing, and he put his hand down to his gun just in case. Raw emotion could be unpredictable and dangerous. He had seen it before. At least a few times.

The three remained motionless for a moment, and then the woman broke the silence. "He's dead!" she said, pointing to the bag. Her voice was overly loud and jolting, and carried the promise of hysteria.

Officer Crandle hadn't really looked at the bag. He had been studying the three, especially after spotting the blood, trying to measure the dynamics of what he'd assumed was some sort of incident between them. Now he looked down at the bag, saw instantly that it was not designed for lawn refuse, and ordered everyone to "Stand back!" as he pulled out his gun.

Everyone indeed took a few steps back at his command, and Darrin Crandle walked carefully up to the bag. He felt a bit numb, but tried to think professionally. He looked down and saw the exposed face, or what was left of it, eyeless sockets seeming to stare vacantly at him, and it made him involuntarily, and visibly, shiver.

"What is it Darrin?" Officer Melrose asked. He hadn't heard clearly what the woman had said, but had seen the reaction of his fellow officer as he looked at the bag.

Crandle looked up at Melrose as he backed away from the body bag. He looked pale, and uncharacteristically shook. "Call it in Jim," he said as evenly as possible. He looked toward the bloodied Jon before continuing, "We've got a dead body here. Call it in."

Officer Melrose looked at Officer Crandle in confusion. "What did you say? Dead body? In the bag?"

Darrin looked back at him with irritation. "Yes. Call it in!"

Jim Melrose looked at the bag, then took a long look at each of the three people standing around it. His prematurely bald, hatless head caught a ray of the rising sun perfectly, giving him an ethereal look that would have been funny on another occasion. "Just what the hell happened here?" he asked.

"CALL IT IN JIM!"

The command in Darrin's voice startled him, so he continued to walk backward toward his car, to make it look like he meant to jump. It didn't work, and as the meaning of all this began to sink into him, he turned and ran the last few steps to his car, and radio.

"OK, I don't want any of you to move from where you are, until you're told to…until help arrives." Darrin said. He slowly put his gun back in his holster as he talked. "We're going to stay right here for a few minutes, OK? " He looked at each of them. The two men made eye contact with him, and nodded yes. The woman was looking down at the corpse, and was crying softly, and shaking. "Suppose that one of you tells me what the hell happened here, as calmly as you can, while we wait. OK?" he said, again trying to act as calm as possible.

Darrin knew that procedurally, at a crime scene like this, he should do things differently. But this whole thing was as confusing as it was horrific. The parts didn't fit. An apparently long dead, mutilated corpse. Two men, both bloodied. An almost hysterical woman. All apparently unafraid of each other, gathered in shock around the body. It didn't feel like there was any imminent threat here at all, at least that he could see. His first big crime…or was it? He had to get a hold of it, somehow, before help came, and Melrose came back, to find him knowing nothing. He had to take charge here.

When none of them spoke, he turned to Jon. The stunned, bloody man looked like the one to keep an eye on. "How did you hurt yourself sir?" Darrin asked. "And what's your name?" That was sloppy, he thought.

Jon was looking down at the eyeless skull, and only after a few moments reluctantly raised his eyes to his questioner. Darrin thought he would have to repeat his questions (in the right order), but Jon finally spoke up before he could begin.

"Jon Parker. Jonathon Norman Parker," he said in a soft monotone. "I live right here," he said as he half-turned toward his house and nodded in its direction. "I hurt myself when I fell out of bed. It was when Barb screamed…I was trying to hurry."

Darrin, relieved at the seeming logic and soft tone of Jon's answer, turned toward Barb. Officer Melrose was walking up to rejoin them, and several sirens could be heard in the distance. "Ma'am…Barb," Darrin began, "did you discover the body? Do you know how it got here?…And what is your full name?" "Idiot!" he thought to himself.

Barb looked at him with soft, teary blue eyes that made him (would have made anybody) want to comfort her. Her chin was quivering. Pete still had his arm around her, and he gave her a little squeeze of support after the officer's questions.

"I was going out to walk!" she blurted out. Her voice was unnatural, and at the wrong volume considering the closeness of the parties. It also held an edge of panic that alarmed all who heard it. She took a deep breath, as though she was trying to regain her strength from her first outburst, then stuttered on, "I…I saw that bag, and I walked over to see…"

"Oh God! Oh no!" Officer Melrose shouted. He had walked over to satiate his curiosity about the bag that Darrin had ordered the others to stay away from. His shout made them all look over, and caused Barb to emit a squeaky mouse call of surprise. They turned in time to see Officer Melrose stagger a few feet away from the corpse and then vomit the entire breakfast he had eaten on break just a half-an-hour before. Then, in perfect choreography, the four heads turned away from the sight simultaneously, all with the same wrinkled expressions of disgust on their faces.

"Oh man…" Pete said. He let go of Barb to bend over and put his meaty hands on his knees. He hadn't even looked at the corpse, but the reaction of the others, and all the alarm, along with the sight and sound of a policeman vomiting made him sweaty and nauseous. "I'm afraid I'm gonna puke too," he warned the others. And he did. As he gagged, he hoped that Margie wasn't looking out the window at him, and that somehow, Barb, who he was still right next to, wouldn't notice.

Darrin watched all this with increasing frustration. The situation was getting ridiculously out of control. He had a hysterical woman, two weak stomachs and a dead body on his hands. And the one person who had made any sense at all was all bloody from not being able to get out of bed right, if he was to be believed.

Neighbors were beginning to move toward the scene, and an ambulance and two more police cars were turning onto Devonshire and roaring toward them. Darrin looked over at Officer Melrose, who was leaning up against the siding of Jon's house to steady himself. He was looking back at the black body bag.

"Officer Melrose?" Darrin said. Melrose kept staring at the corpse. "Jim?" he said a little louder. Melrose looked over at him reluctantly. "If you're all right, we're going to need some crowd control here, OK?"

Officer Melrose looked past Darrin and saw the other police arriving, and people in pajamas and bathrobes coming up the street toward them slowly but steadily. They looked, he thought, like the zombies in "Night of the Living Dead." He straightened himself up though, took a deep breath, and headed toward the street. "OK, everyone stay back!" he yelled while waving his arms in a "stop now!" gesture.

The first people to arrive stopped upon his order, and he soon felt like a professional again.

Chapter 2

By the time the sun had fully risen the police had successfully cordoned off the area around the body with their ubiquitous yellow "crime scene" tape (which is always a crowd pleaser and attraction in itself), and no one without high authority could get within thirty yards or so of the decaying body. The lack of anything to really see, along with the normal weekday demands of getting ready for work and various appointments to make disbursed the unnerved neighbors remarkably quickly, considering the apparent gravity of the scene. Soon enough, garage doors began opening, cars began backing out of driveways, and the people who lived on Devonshire began reluctantly leaving their little cul-de-sac for their appointed rounds, though carefully checking their rear-view mirrors all the way down the street before turning right on Coventry Street, to rejoin the normal world.

Soon enough, only the children without summer camps or Bible school assignments, along with Jon and Barb, were the only residents left. The children were all ordered by worried parents, in one fashion or another, to stay in their houses or yards. Most of them ignored this, of course, and as soon as their parents were gone, they creeped back out to watch the crime scene proceedings as best they could from a distance. They were joined in those early hours only by a young, frustrated reporter from the local Highland Newsleader, who stood outside the marked perimeter with them, looking for all the world like a

Scout leader with his restless charges, not knowing quite what to do.

Barb did not work. Her husband was on a business trip in Chicago. She always got to just stay home, which was a source of jealousy and some speculation among certain female neighbors.

Jon was a high school English teacher with the summer off, which of course also inspired jealousy.

The local police and even the paramedics who first arrived on the scene could be described as both excited and confused. In general, they all tried to keep calm themselves and act professionally, though this was a unique experience for most of them. At first, with no one present who had clear rank over the others, there was some initial confusion. There had not been a murder, if this was one, in their picturesque suburban town in more years than any of them could remember. Now, given a decaying corpse and stunned bystanders in the early morning sun on what should have been a peaceful summer morning, it was difficult to know exactly where to begin.

Officer Darrin Crandle, though lowest in seniority, was the closest to taking charge; because he had arrived first, and truthfully, because he was the most competent. After some argument back and forth, he convinced the paramedics that what was in the bag was quite dead, and to therefore leave the body alone until at least the coroner arrived. Then he suggested (rather than ordered) that Officer Blackwell, who had arrived just a few minutes before and was a policeman that Darrin knew, and himself take statements from the three "witnesses," separately. He asked the unfortunate Officer Melrose to keep an eye on the reporter and kids, and asked another young Officer named Cribbs to make communications with the County Homicide Unit, etc. The truth was, all the people who needed to be there were already on the way, but Darrin thought that it was best for everyone to have something to do.

Darrin talked to Barb, and Dick Blackwell took statements

from Pete (first, because he had to go to work, and he appeared to be the least involved) and then Jon.

Darrin thought it would be best to get the still shaky Barb away from the scene, so he asked her if there was some place they could talk. Barb looked at him quizzically for a moment, as though she didn't understand the question, but finally batted her big blue eyes a few times and snapped out of her stupor long enough to invite him into her house.

The front door of the Ellsworth house was only about 50 feet away from where the body was discovered, Darrin noticed. When he got to the front door, he turned and saw for himself how easily she could have spotted it first thing, even in the weak light of dawn. He also noted, for the first time, how the body was lying right on the property line between and toward the front of the two ranch style houses. He could tell because the Ellsworth lawn was freshly cut, and Jon Parker's needed cutting.

His first thoughts upon following Barb into the house were that everything seemed to be some shade of green, and that Ms. Ellsworth had a nice ass. He was ashamed of himself for the latter observation, but couldn't help noticing as she swished her way through the living room and into the kitchen with the ever observant policeman in tow. It also led him to his first question when seated across from her at the kitchen table, after politely refusing the obligatory offer of coffee.

"Where is your husband Ms. Ellsworth?" he asked. He had noticed the wedding ring.

"He's in Chicago. And you can call me Barb." Darrin noticed that she seemed transformed now that she was in the house. She seemed almost completely calm now. This was a good move… and he loved the way her hair on the one side was tucked behind her ear.

"Tell me what happened, Barb. How did you find, uh, the body?"

She took a deep breath, then looked out the patio door. She

had a gorgeous profile too. "I was going out for my morning run. Actually I walk more than I run, but I do it early every morning." She looked back at him with what he thought were breathtaking blues, even without make-up. "I opened the front door, and went out to my front yard to stretch before I ran. I always do that. And I saw the…the bag, right away."

"What was it that made you want to go over and check it out? That's what you did, right?" Darrin asked, perhaps a little superfluously. He silently told himself to shut up and let her talk.

She looked out the window to the back yard again. "I don't know," she said dreamily. "I wish I hadn't." She paused then, and moved her eyes from the back yard to her own hands that were folded in front of her on the table. She had pink nail polish, Darrin noticed. He wondered if her toenails were the same color. (He also had to quit thinking about those kind of things). He wanted to ask another question (not about toenails) but remained silent. He was determined, now, to just let her talk.

Eventually, she looked up at him and said "I guess I thought at first it was something that Jon, that's our neighbor, left out in the yard.…but…it didn't look like…oh, I don't know. Something just made me want to go over there and see what it was. Bruce had just mowed a couple of days ago, and he's so proud of his yard. I didn't want anything to make a spot on the grass."

"Bruce is your husband?" Darrin asked, breaking his own rule.

"Yes," she smiled. What a knockout! Couldn't be much more than 30, Darrin thought. Why didn't he ever meet someone like that?

But her smile disappeared quickly, and she looked vacantly past him at the garish green and gold kitchen wall with a pained expression. It was an astounding transition. Darrin knew that it was understandable that she was still struggling with what had just happened, but he also sensed that she must be a moody one. Hard to handle, maybe. That's a sexist thought, he thought.

Then after sighing deeply, she said "I unzipped the bag because I wanted to see if it was something to throw away, or…I don't know." She put her hands up to her face as though she was trying to rid herself of the memory of it all, and then she began to cry softly.

Darrin felt terrible for her, and felt like he should try to comfort her somehow, but checked himself. She put her head down on the table and sobbed. It was then that he thought that he had better intervene.

"Look, I'm sorry, so sorry about all of this. I just have a few more questions I have to ask, OK? Then I'll be done."

Her head stayed on the table, but she managed to get out a sobbing, "OK, "and then "I'm sorry."

She sounded to Darrin like she was revving up for a bout of hysteria, so he tried to hurry. "Did you hear any strange sounds before you found the body? Any cars going by? Any voices? Anything strange or unusual?"

"No! No." She answered quickly.

"When you unzipped the…body bag," be careful here, he told himself…"did you, uh, recognize who…"

"NO!" she shouted, startling Darrin. This gal was all over the place, he thought. He wanted to get out of there.

"OK, OK," he said, trying to be soothing. "Was your neighbor, uh, Jon was it? Did he get there first, or that other fella, Pete, did he come to help first?

"It was Jon, I think," she said; with a voice a little more moderate. "I'm not sure. I don't know."

"I understand." Darrin wished she would raise her head up, or something. "This, this is hard stuff, I know. But, uh, there was no one else out there, not those two guys, or anybody else, when you first saw the bag…"

"No!" she cried.

Her high-pitched answer startled him. This gal was a

strange one. That was enough for him. He stood up and slid his chair back, but she remained at her place with her head still down, now fully crying again, and seemingly oblivious to him or anything else.

"Look, I'm sorry this happened. That will be enough for now. Thank you Miss, Mrs. Ellsworth. You…try to get some rest now." He said this last line as he walked away through the living room and toward the front door. He wanted to get back out to the scene quickly now. As he was reaching for the door handle, he thought of one more thing he'd better tell her. He turned and saw her still in the same position at the table. She looked so pathetically sad there. Not so dangerous from a distance. "Mrs. Ellsworth?" he said in a voice loud enough that she had to hear, "There will probably be more questions. There'll be a detective coming."

She didn't answer. Was she asleep?

"Mrs. Ellsworth? You'll be home today, right?"

There was no answer.

"No, I didn't hear anything, until the scream. The screams woke me up," Jon said. And then he waited. Officer Dick Blackwell was nothing if not thorough. Although he had been asked only to give the initial interview to two of the apparent witnesses, to just get some basic information, he insisted on writing every word down. He didn't trust just notes.

Jon looked around at the scene in his yard. More and more police were arriving. He saw a state police car, a few more locals, and two men in suits were the latest on the scene. One of the suits was the Mayor of Highland, Jon recognized. He had been a policeman himself in the past, and had a habit of showing up when there was a big bust, or something else going down where he might get his picture in the paper. Jon thought he was a good mayor though.

"Jon, did you see anyone else, anyone at all, besides Ms. Ellsworth, when you came out to investigate the screams?"

"No," Jon said. He thought the officer would appreciate his brevity, but he kept on writing. Was he recording his questions too? Jon looked away again. He saw a couple of the neighborhood kids gawking at him from behind the tape. He was still shirtless, and beginning to feel conspicuous about it. He reached up nervously to touch the bandage again, the one that one of the paramedics had put on his head.

Blackwell suddenly jerked his head up to ask a question.

"Tell me how you hurt your head again, Jon."

"Look, Officer…Blackwell," he said after reading his name tag thing, "I don't…"

"Call me Dick," the suddenly smiling officer interrupted. He was trying to befriend the witness. Unbeknownst to Jon, Officer Blackwell had done a lot of reading about gaining the confidence of suspects. They made more mistakes that way.

"Look, Dick," Jon began. He was getting irritated, which was probably a good thing. He'd been in shock, and unfazed by anything, for close to an hour now. "I've told you twice. You wrote it down, Dick. I'd like to go in and put a shirt on OK? Unless you have any questions there that you haven't already asked, Dick."

The smile slowly died on Officer Blackwell's face, and a grimace took its place on the last "Dick." Jon noticed that he needed a shave, and that he looked Italian. He thought he looked like somebody in one of the Mafia movies, but he couldn't think of which one. Fredo from "The Godfather," maybe?

"Look, I'm just trying to do my job," Dick said. His voice was surprisingly reasonable and calm, considering the serious face he was displaying. "Just answer the question, please."

So Jon starting telling him how he fell out of bed again, but half-way into it, without any apparent reason, he saw vividly in his mind the skull of the dead man again, just as he had at dawn earlier, and the fat fly that had crawled out of one of the eye sockets. It caused him to pause mid-sentence, and Dick to look up from his writing to eye Jon suspiciously.

"Hey! I found a knife! Over here!"

This call came from a very excited Officer Jim Melrose, who had become bored with guarding the perimeter from kids and the skinny guy from the Newsleader. He was still trying to deal with his squeamish and embarrassing reaction to the dead body, and he wanted desperately to help, so he had begun aimlessly scouring the perimeter, trying to at least look busy. He spotted the carving knife under an undernourished rosebush that was trying to grow too close to the steaming bricks of Jon Parker's house. "It's over here!" Officer Melrose yelled again.

Everyone on the scene stopped what they were doing to look Melrose's way. The brief freeze melted only when the man in the other suit, the one who wasn't the mayor, yelled "DON'T TOUCH IT!" which made everyone look at who was yelling, and then back to Melrose, who, sure enough, was bending over to grab his prize evidence. Then they all saw him pull his arm back as though it had been snake bitten, and look back red faced, and embarrassed again.

The man in the suit (who was the much-anticipated homicide detective who happened to be close to Highland when the call came to him) and Darrin Crandle, who had just escaped the Ellsworth residence, both hustled over to the new find before the hapless Melrose could soil it. Everyone else, even those carefully working with the corpse, watched silently. A new, alarming dimension seemed to have been added to the proceedings.

"That's my knife," Jon said quietly.

Officer Blackwell turned his grizzled face toward Jon and asked "What did you say?"

"It's my knife. I brought it out here because I didn't know if I needed a weapon, and I…"

Officer Blackwell hadn't seen the corpse. He had only glimpsed something while trying to look around others when he had first arrived on the scene. He wasn't aware of its advanced state of decay, or that it was eyeless, and when Jon, the recently bandaged, bloodied Jon, casually took responsibility for what seemed undoubtedly to be the likely murder weapon, a chill ran through him. He knew what to do.

"You are under arrest sir!" he said firmly. He took a step back and almost tripped and fell as he fumbled for his handcuffs, and his gun, at the same time.

Chapter 3

Detective Gus Foster had a way of being bored and condescending about everything that was taking place around him, no matter what the circumstances. It's a posture that can be often found in many "I've seen this all before" veterans of almost any profession. We've all seen teachers like this, along with postal workers, business owners, bartenders and nurses. Especially nurses. It's as though they're a little bit smarter than everyone in the room, they know it, and they're trying to be patient with the rest of us, but they can barely manage it. After all, they know how it's all going to turn out. They've seen this scene.

So it wasn't long after Detective Blackwell finally got his handcuffs to work right, while he was frantically trying to give the struggling, protesting Jon Parker his right to remain silent, that Blackwell felt Detective Foster's meaty hand on his shoulder. The hand grabbed him and spun his slight frame around easily, and the puzzled policeman found himself suddenly facing the graying, obese, 6'2", 300- plus pound homicide investigator.

"What the hell do you think you're doing," (he quickly read the name on his chest), "Blackbeard?"

Dick Blackwell gulped but said nothing. Foster had him almost by the throat now, and his first instinct was not to answer, but to slide his eyes to the left, then the right to see who might be watching his embarrassment. Everyone was.

"I, uh"

There Comes a Moment...

"We don't make arrests until I say so, Blackbeard," the beefy man said as he gripped Dick harder. He was literally spitting out his words, and the specks of saliva landing on his face added to the well-meaning patrol officer's humiliation.

"But…he said that the knife was his!" Blackwell blurted out. "He could be the murderer! Or suspect, or…"

Despite the awkward phrasing, this caused Foster to hesitate a bit. He slowly released his grip on Blackwell's neck and shoulder and but still looked at him menacingly, and straight in the eye. Gus Foster relied on this look. He was aware that everyone was watching, and he was committed now. "Take the cuffs off him, Officer Blackbeard!" he spit out as he lowered his hand.

Dick, in an instant, hated this man so much that his whole body trembled with rage. There was no reason for this. He had done nothing wrong. Yet, he would probably never live it down. He looked quickly around to see who had witnessed the scene. Everywhere he looked, people looked quickly away as though they were back to work on something else. The exceptions were two dumbstruck kids outside the tape, who stood staring with their mouths open, and Jim Melrose, who was still standing by the knife, but now with a big grin on his face.

"Blackwell," Dick mumbled as he moved off angrily to un-cuff his prisoner.

"What?" Foster roared, sensing insubordination. Everyone's head snapped back to the two of them.

Officer Blackwell, now a safe five feet away, stopped and turned toward the homicide detective in a wholly unnecessarily confrontational manner. His pride had been devastated. "I said my name is Blackwell! Officer Blackwell, sir!"

Foster looked at angry young man he was humiliating to establish his authority. He felt just a little bit bad, but also couldn't help smiling a bit. Then he turned dismissively and headed back to the knife. "That's what I said, Blackbeard," he said over his shoulder. There was some muted laughter at that.

Investigator Foster, pleased with himself, walked back over to where Crandle and another investigator were carefully bagging the carving knife. He glanced back over his shoulder upon arrival, to make sure Blackwell was doing what he'd ordered. He was, but without taking his eyes off his tormentor.

"I doubt if you're going to get anything useful from that," he said, nodding downward toward the blade. The men stopped what they were doing, and both looked up at the burly detective. "Bag it anyway though," he continued. "Looks to me like the kid brought it out here for self-protection. He didn't know what the hell was going on. Am I right?"

Darrin looked up. "That sounds logical, I guess."

'Course it is, boy," Foster said. "Anybody can see that that corpse was killed a long time ago. Maybe weeks, who knows?" He spit a long streak of tobacco juice that landed dangerously close to the now-bagged knife. It caused both of the other men to jerk back. "We better question these suckers anyway," he said, ignoring the reaction of the other two by turning around and looking purposefully around the neighborhood.

"We've been doing that sir, Officer Blackwell and I," Darrin said as he rose to his feet.

Foster turned to find that he was looking at a man that was actually taller than he was, which was unusual. Taller, but a hell of a lot skinnier. "And just who did you talk to?" he asked.

"I talked to the woman that lives in that house," Darrin said, pointing. "Her name is Barb Ellsworth. She's the one who discovered the body. Blackwell talked to the other two; the two who were out here when we arrived."

Detective Foster looked at the house that Darrin pointed to, then back at him. "And what did this lady tell you?" he asked with unmistakable (and oddly misplaced) sarcasm.

"She was up early to go jogging, saw the bag, got curious, and went over and unzipped it. That's when all hell broke loose, and she started screaming. Then the other two neighbors came running out. At least that's what I know so far. I haven't had a chance to confirm that with Blackwell. He questioned the other two."

Foster looked away again. This young cop bothered him, for some reason. "You mean old Blackbeard over there?" he scoffed. "I think you should have done the questioning yourself." He looked over at Blackwell, who was still staring at him. "I can tell you right now, and I always have a feel for these things, Blackbeard's a dick."

"Yes sir, he certainly is!" Darrin replied immediately. He didn't understand the Detective's open venom toward someone he knew and respected, but that wasn't going to stop him from jabbing back. When Foster turned back to look at him, Darrin was smiling. "He certainly is, sir. A Dick, that is, sir."

Foster was confused, and quickly looked away from the smiling taller man. He launched into his all-knowing detective mode. "Obviously, somebody picked a nice, quiet little street to dump a body," he said, reaching for control again. "A cul-de-sac, even better. No traffic. Everybody asleep. Too easy." He walked a few paces over toward the corpse before continuing his lecture. He also wanted to get away from the tall, skinny cop. "If my guess is right, and it usually is," he turned here and looked right at Darrin for emphasis, "…this guy was killed a long time ago. Not here, of course. Probably in St. Louis, in one of your ghettos." Then he remembered that the corpse appeared to be white. "Or by the Mob," he added quickly. He then pointed at Darrin, which seemed to him to be an odd gesture. "Mark my words," he continued, "This cat was up to no good, and he's as bad as the guys that killed him," he said definitively, as he rotated his pointing arm slowly from Darrin to the general direction of the corpse, while keeping his eyes glued to the young cop for emphasis.

"Who's up to no good Gus? You talkin' 'bout me?"

Foster turned to see that he was pointing directly at his old partner, Mayor John Bander, who was standing there at the end of his outstretched arm. Foster didn't want to explain himself, or turn back to see the young cop smiling at him again, so he said "I've got work to do here, John" and brusquely moved by his old friend.

Jon was asked to provide a fingerprint, which he was surprised that they could do right out there in the warming sun, and very soon after a short conversation with a seemingly bored Detective Foster, he was finally told that he could go into his house and clean up. There would be more questions later, he was assured.

He went right in to a long, hot shower. He washed off the dried blood and sweat, and when he was through scrubbing, he just stood there and let the water tumble onto his head, bandaged wound, and body. He tried not to think of anything in particular, but was aware of an overall numbness that he had felt only a few times in his life before. It was a bit like the feeling he'd had when his father died, when his high school sweetheart left him, even the day when he was very small and his puppy got run over by the garbage truck. It was that same numbness, the same lack of balance that all came back to him there under the steaming water. Even though he didn't know, and would never know, the corpse out there on the lawn, discovering it seemed to be right there with all of those life-changing events.

Twenty minutes later, as he toweled himself dry, he found himself staring at his own reflection in his bathroom mirror, trying to get a grip on it all. The bandage made him look rugged, he decided. It went with his short blonde hair, blue eyes, and dimpled chin. A little overweight… but a hunk, he decided.

Jon didn't make a habit of giving himself internal pep talks in front of the mirror, but this morning was an exception. He had been struggling already with guilt feelings almost every day. He had made the bold decision, for him, to not work during summer vacation for the first time since he was a kid. Instead of cleaning floors down at the school for extra cash, he was taking the summer off to write a book. At least that's what he had told everyone. But he'd found that the writing was coming hard, some days not at all, and it was July and he had almost nothing done really. His mother, his friends, the neighbors, even the girls he asked out occasionally all asked him how the novel was going, all the time. He always said "fine," but he was failing. His self-concept was taking a beating, and it hadn't been much to begin with.

And then there was this morning. He'd been too slow to go outside, and then he'd been no help at all. He had panicked. He'd frozen up, and then he had to stand around bleeding and with no shirt on, feeling dumb and emasculated, for what seemed like hours. And then he'd been handcuffed, albeit briefly, in front of the neighbor kids. It was nothing to be proud of.

He was having a hard time admiring himself for anything.

And someone had dumped a dead body in his yard.

He pulled on some jean shorts and his *HARVARD* t-shirt, strapped on his favorite sandals, and went into his kitchen to make coffee. A few minutes later he took his cup to the living room window to see what was happening. He saw two parked police cars, and nothing else. No police, no police tape, no body bag, nothing. He was surprised and relieved. The police hadn't taken that much time, really. As traumatic as it had been, it was obviously what the fat detective had announced to anybody who would listen: a body dumped randomly, if unfortunately, on Devonshire. The luck of the draw.

He went back in, grabbed his cell phone, and headed out to his back deck to make some calls. He had some pretty exciting news to relate.

Jon's deck was his pride and joy. Jon and almost anyone else who got to see the view from there, thought it was not only the best place in the cul-de-sac, but perhaps the best in the subdivision. Being at the end of a cul-de-sac, especially this one, had its privileges. Instead of looking at another subdivision, the deck in his back yard looked out (right beyond the farmers fence bordering his yard) onto a grassy, hilly farm pasture that swept down and then dramatically up until it met woods that, from that view, seemed to go on forever. There were no other houses in sight. It was just nature, in the form of wildflowers, long grass, trees, and the occasional deer, turkey or other wildlife. It's what had sold Jon on the place six years before, and where he could be found most of the time, weather permitting.

Jon pressed the speed-dial for his mother's phone number as he slid the glass door open to step out onto the long, two-tiered deck, but by the time he had closed the door behind him, he had also closed his phone. Out there in the farmer's field were two policemen, about 50 feet apart from each other, walking slowly and looking down at the ground as they carefully proceeded. Even given the morning's events, it was a shock for Jon to see them, or anybody, walking in what was usually undisturbed pastoral delight. It seemed like a violation, somehow.

The policemen seemed to be concentrating hard, not speaking, and, obviously, were looking for something as they tromped methodically up the first hill of grass.

Jon watched, and as he did so he began to hear, intermittently, someone talking. He could hear the voice, but couldn't make out the words. It was coming from somewhere to his left and not very far away, and so after listening to the garble for a minute, he walked to the other end of his deck in that direction to see who or where it was coming from. By the time he got to the deck's edge, he could see.

It was the fat detective who wore the suit. He was standing by the fence that divided Jon's yard from the field, right on the other side of an oak tree. His hands were on his hips, and he appeared to be talking to himself as he watched the two policemen walk the field. Jon stepped off his deck and into his yard to get closer, and within a few feet he saw who the detective was talking to. The kid reporter from the Highland newspaper was leaning back against the tree with one leg up to hold his notepad, on which he was furiously scribbling down everything the fat man said. The kid was getting his story.

    Jon looked out to the field at the two policemen walking in the tall grass on a hot July morning, and wondered what the hell they could be looking for.

Chapter 4

After calling her husband Bruce to tell him everything that happened in a tearful, sobbing, one-sided conversation, Barb decided to lie out in the sun for a while. Upsetting Bruce had, in a way, calmed her down. It always did. She put on her yellow bikini and brought her sun lotion, a Cosmopolitan magazine and a couple of bottled Dasani waters with her to her fenced in back yard to try to relax for a while. Bruce was flying in from Chicago later in the afternoon, and she wanted to be tanned and perfect for him when he arrived.

Bruce could not have been more shocked and upset when he heard what his half-hysterical wife relayed to him, and his first reaction was to fly home to St. Louis immediately, but he was assured by Barb that the police were on the scene, and he had only one more very important meeting in Chicago that day, so he satisfied himself with worrying senselessly about what he could not control, and wishing time would pass more quickly.

He did make one phone call. His next-store neighbor, Jon Parker, was a good friend. It wasn't that he didn't trust his lovely wife's version of events, but she did have a real penchant for exaggeration. She had mentioned that Jon (whom she detested because her husband spent so much time with him) and Pete (whom he detested because he was always ogling his wife, and whom she rather liked for the same reason) had both been on the scene shortly after she had discovered the dead body. So while waiting for the big meeting, he called Jon who, he knew, would be at home.

"It was bad, man," Jon told him. "A dead body right between our two houses. And, and this guy, if it was a guy…I think it was a guy…he's been dead for a long time. His eyes were gone, Bruce."

"Did the cops give you any idea, how…how that could happen? The body ending up there, I mean?" Bruce asked.

"Not really. The old cop said something about how the body was probably dumped here, because we're at the end of a cul-de-sac, and it's quiet here, and all that. But…I guess it's too early. It shook me up, Bruce. I'll admit it. Did Barb tell ya that they handcuffed me for a few minutes?"

"No, she didn't," Bruce answered. Jon wasn't making him feel any better. "Look, go over and check on her for me, will ya? I'll be home tonight, but…just go over there and make sure Barb's O.K., will ya?" Bruce knew his friend well enough to know he wouldn't be writing any book today anyway, and would probably just be moping around worrying about things. He'd be even more restless than usual, and would be looking for something to do.

"Sure," Jon answered, "Sure buddy. She was pretty hysterical. We all were. I'll check to make sure she's OK. I've gotta tell you Bruce, it was…"

"Thanks Jon. Gotta go. See you later."

Bruce hung up to go to his very important meeting.

Officer Darrin Crandle could not get to sleep. His normal routine after working the night shift was to eat a big breakfast at the "8th Street Café," head back to his apartment to shower and listen to the news, then hit the sack for 6 to 8 hours before beginning his day at about 4:00 in the afternoon. Today it wasn't working.

First, he had worked almost three hours of overtime, between crime scene duties and the obligatory report he had to write back at the station. Then, by the time he was done, breakfast was no longer being served, and he had to settle for a patty-melt and Coke. And finally, the pictures from the crime scene on Devonshire kept running through his mind when he tried to get some rest, and though he was loathe to admit it to himself, they bothered him. Here he was, a professional, supposedly, trying to sleep, but instead seeing visions of everything from a dead man's eyeless stare to Mrs. Barb Ellsworth's swishing rear end, whether his eyes were open, or closed.

And the questions were driving him nuts. Why would anyone pick a lonely cul-de-sac in Highland, Illinois to dump a body? They were 30 some miles from St. Louis, if that's where the body came from, as Foster had said. Why drive that far, when there were a thousand country roads and closer cul-de-sacs to dump a body? Why take the time to place the body between two houses, up in the yard, that far away from the street? In all the excitement, did they do everything right? Did the guys who took over get written statements from the witnesses?

And why the hell can't a guy get breakfast in this freaking town if he happens to work overtime?

Eventually, after what for him was a record amount of tossing and turning, he got almost 45 minutes of rest. He woke up with a start though, and was reaching desperately for his weapon in his last moments of sleep. The dream he had had, whatever it was about, made him wake up sweating and alarmed.

This time, he was awake for good.

═══════════════

The clock couldn't move fast enough for Pete Vanderberg. He had never wanted to be home so much, since, well, since he was first married so many years ago. He had thought about calling in sick that morning, especially after throwing up, but this was no time to be missing work at Wicks' Organ Factory. With a national recession settling in, orders for organs, even the very best organs made in America, were significantly down. Lay-offs had happened that spring, and more were expected any day. The boss, who Pete admired and thought was an honest and forthright guy, had told them so. Even though he had been with the company for so many years, no one could tell for sure what jobs would be safe. Some of the younger guys were better, and faster than he was. It was also a non-union company.

Besides all that, a bad bout with the flu had cost him 6 sick days in February, and he didn't have many left.

But leaving the neighborhood that morning had been tough, what with leaving poor Barb, and for that matter Jon, out there with the body and the cops. It was such a horrible thing, but, in a sick kind of way, in his secret heart…exciting too. He couldn't remember feeling so alive, as he did that morning.

But the damned clock said 5 minutes after 11:00. He'd been late for work, and had spent most of the first hour telling everybody that would listen what had happened. And now there was just work; work that was boring and monotonous, especially today. He wanted to go home and talk to and comfort his neighbors.

After all, nothing like this had happened before. Not in his town. Not on his street.

He paused to look up at the big clock. It was 8 minutes after.

Detective Foster pushed his plate away and belched out loud with satisfaction. "That was one damn good burger," he said to the waitress who had given his guttural outburst a sharp look of disapproval while passing by his table. She turned away, ignoring the compliment from the stranger.

Foster started to reach for his chewing tobacco, but realizing that there was no good place to spit, went for one of the colored toothpicks on his table instead. He chose a green one, and had just burped again and put it in his mouth when his cell phone rang. As always, it startled and angered him. He had never learned how to adjust the volume, and the whole restaurant turned and watched his clumsy attempt to locate and open the damn thing, so that its jarring call would stop. He finally succeeded, but not before nearly falling off his chair first.

"Yea? What?" was his greeting.

"Detective Foster? I just wanted you to know that we've got the report all done…all the statements." Foster said nothing. "…And the corpse. The med. guys are doing the tests for you…and the dental records are going to be tough because…"

"Who the hell is this?" Foster demanded.

There was silence for a long moment, and then "It's Sergeant Wilson, down at the station. The Chief said to keep you updated on everything…"

"Call me when you know something, will ya? I don't need to know what you're doing, just what you find out! Got it?" He closed up his phone. He looked around the restaurant and saw that nearly everyone was watching him, but all hastily looked away when he met their glances.

When he was satisfied that everyone had been intimidated, he reached for his wallet, and mumbled "Damn idiots," which caused the green toothpick to fall from his mouth onto his huge belly, and then to the floor.

He left the scowling waitress no tip, but then again, he never did.

Barb was taking a sip from her water bottle when the doorbell rang, and it startled her. She jerked the bottle away from her lips and spilled the icy liquid down her chest on onto her bikini top, and she screamed from the cold shock of it.

Jon heard the scream from the Ellsworth's front porch, and an equally cold chill ran down his spine. It instantly brought the horror of a few hours before back to him. This time, he didn't hesitate. He tried the doorknob, but it was locked, so he lowered his shoulder into the wooden door and tried to push his way in. After several tries, he resorted to trying to kick it in instead. The kicks made a thunderous sound, but the door didn't yield. After his third kick he paused and tried to catch his breath, with his right shoulder and foot already aching. He was about to run around back to see if he could somehow get in back there, when he heard the door unlock. Barb Ellsworth, who had already looked to see who it was through her living room window, opened the door, and suddenly was standing before Jon in a daring yellow bikini with a wet top.

"What the hell are you doing, Jon?" she yelled at him.

Jon's astonished eyes went right from her scorn-filled face to her wet, erect nipples, and stayed there for too long. Only when Barb reached her hands up to half cover her breasts did he think to look back up at her face. He stood there with his mouth hanging open, knowing he had just compounded his error, but said nothing.

"I said, what the hell are you doing!" she screamed again. Her accidental exposure, on top of the fright he had given her, made her so angry that she was shaking.

This last bellowed demand was enough to shake Jon out of his stupor, at least partially. "I…I am supposed to check on you. I'm sorry…"

"Check on me? Check on me? Or check me out? You almost broke my door down! Who told you to check on me?" She was practically spitting out the words.

"Bruce did. I heard you scream. I'm so sorry…" Jon was pleading.

Barb stood for a moment, staring at his face, completely

absorbed in her anger, trying to think of the worst thing she could say to him. Instead, she brought down her hands, took a step back, and slammed the door as hard as she could, leaving Jon with a last unwanted image of her wet, shaking breasts.

He stood there for a minute, trying to think of what to do. He had only been trying to help, trying to be brave…and he had apologized. But she would have none of it.

Eventually, with his mind stuck somewhere between lurid arousal and a slow burning anger at her utter intolerance, he decided to just walk back home. There was nothing else he could do. He'd explain it all to Bruce later.

"Bitch," he mumbled angrily as he cut across the yard and over the spot (though not realizing it at the moment) where the mutilated body had been lying just a few hours before.

Chapter 5

It had turned into a blisteringly hot summer afternoon, with the unbelievably high humidity that only a St. Louis mid-summer day can provide. Jon was at his usual mid-day spot, in his deck chair with his feet up under the table on the chair opposite him, shirtless and sweating out the beers from the night before, while nursing his second cold one of the day. Usually he read, or listened to classical music or blues on his satellite radio, with his legal tablet and pen on the table as he gazed out at the pasture and woods, waiting vainly for inspiration. But today he just sat in the relative silence of his backyard paradise, with only the neutral hum of the neighborhood air-conditioners and the occasional chattering of squirrels or birds in the background to hear. After a while, he even put one bare foot up on the table and leaned back in his chair as he thought through what had happened that morning, again and again. Being an English teacher, he was soon lost in thought as to what metaphoric meaning this could all have for his own life.

It was in the depths of this reverie that he received the same shock he had given his neighbor Barb. His doorbell rang, and it was like an electric shock. The involuntary jump he made caused him to drop his beer can, as well as lean way too far back in his chair, and he tumbled over backwards, landing with a sharp enough thud to send any and all nearby birds to flight.

"God damn it to hell," was the first thing he was able to say after catching his breath, but he said it in a matter-of-fact way.

Once he realized he was OK, he thought it as more humorous than anything else. It would be a funny story to tell.

The doorbell rang again, and he rolled over and grabbed his now half-drained beer can, then struggled to his feet to go answer the door with a fuller appreciation of the shock he had given his neighbor.

In fact, he hoped it was his neighbor, whose wet, jiggling breasts flashed through his mind as he cut through the kitchen and into the living room as quickly as he could. He did not want it to ring again. His nerves were about shot for the day.

It wasn't Barb. Instead, when he opened the door he had to swing his eyes from breast level to slightly above his own head level to meet the face of the dark-haired, handsome young man who was standing there in jeans and a white t-shirt with black letters that said "Police Academy" on the front.

The two men stared at each other awkwardly for a moment before the young man spoke. "Excuse for interrupting your day," he said. "I'm Darrin Crandle, Officer Darrin Crandle. I was the first cop here this morning. Remember?"

"Of course," Jon replied, though he hadn't until just then. "Come on in. It's hot as hell out there." He stepped back and opened the door wider so that the lanky officer could enter.

"I don't mean to bother you," Darrin said obligatorily as he stepped in to the air-conditioning. "It, it's my day off, as you can see," he made a disparaging gesture toward his casual clothes, "and, well, I couldn't sleep after all that, and I wondered if we couldn't, you know, talk about it a little bit."

Jon stood looking at the officer suspiciously for a moment, then said, "I'm not a suspect or anything, right?"

Darrin did his best sheepish grin to nullify Jon's suspicion, "Oh, I think that's a little 'way out there,' don't you? That body has been dead a long time, right?" Jon didn't look convinced, and stood waiting him out. "Look, I'm just a beat cop. I'm not the big shot who will be investigating this. I just…I just thought we could throw some ideas around. Like maybe you saw a clue, or something, and you were too shook up to realize it at the time. Know what I mean?"

Jon held his gaze on Darrin for a few more seconds, trying to make up his mind. Then he shrugged his shoulders and held his hand out to shake. "You probably think I never wear a shirt, don't you?" he asked. Darrin smiled. "Do you drink beer?" Jon asked.

An hour later, with six empty beer cans on the kitchen table, and a fresh one in front of both of them, they were still talking. They were hitting it off so well that it frankly amazed Jon. They had talked about themselves, their jobs, their ambitions, and a little about the sexy Barb Ellsworth, more than they had about the events of the morning. Jon was pleased that he was actually striking up some kind of friendship, which as introverted and self-doubting as he was, he almost never did. This guy wasn't like he thought a cop should be like. He was smart, funny, and not pushy. Though younger than himself, there seemed a commonality there, on almost every subject. They just plain hit it off.

It was Jon himself, after a long pull on his just-opened fourth beer, who eventually steered the discussion back to the mysterious corpse in his yard. "How the hell do you think it happened, Darryl?" he asked.

"It's Darrin, asswipe," he answered. They both laughed.

"Darrin. Right. Sorry."

Darrin took a drink, and then gave his new friend a long, mock-serious look. "Well, Joan…" They both cracked up at this, as only late afternoon inebriated people can, finding hilarity in the obvious, and the innocuous.

When they recovered, Jon tried again. "I…I just don't get it, ya know? I mean, why would anyone do that? Why here?"

Darrin looked out the glass door that led out to the deck,

and to the pasture and woods beyond. "What's out there? I mean past the trees. What's way out there?" he asked.

Jon turned to look out there too. "It goes on for quite a ways. Half a mile, maybe. Maybe more." he said. He looked back at Darrin. "I walked it once. I finally came to a road that ran up to an old sewage plant, or at least that's what it looked like. Nobody there. No equipment running or anything."

"Who owns the land back there?" Darrin asked.

"You know, I'm not really sure. I think the real estate girl who sold me this place told me, but that was years ago, and I can't remember. I wanted to make sure nobody was going to develop it. This view is why I bought this place."

"Let's take a look at it. I can only stand air-conditioning for so long," Darrin said.

"A man after my own heart," Jon answered, and then immediately regretted it because he thought it sounded Gay. He got up from the table and led the way to the door.

Outside, it felt like they had just walked into a blast furnace, but it felt good to both of them.

"God damn, feel that sun!" Jon said.

Darrin went to the rail of the deck and looked out at the pasture and woods. "So there's no way somebody could have lugged a body from that direction, right?" he asked.

"Your guys ought to know. That fat detective that had 'em take the cuffs off me had them searching out there for something this morning."

Darrin turned and looked at Jon. "He did?"

"Yea. Saw it myself. Two cops looked like they were searching for something. Seemed kind of silly with that grass being so tall, but who knows?"

Darrin looked out again at the pasture. "Must've been after they sent me back to the station to make my report. Maybe they were just looking to see if anybody else had been there. Maybe they were looking for flattened grass. Like you said, you never know." Then he looked at Jon again. "I'll tell you the truth, and I guess this could be a minor thing, or maybe not, but..." he hesitated, then said "Jon, why the hell would somebody take the chance of driving down the end of a cul-de-sac, then presumably get a body out of the trunk of their car... and then instead of just dropping it in the street, they place it up in a yard? I mean you'd have to carry it up there, right? You see where I'm going?"

Jon looked away from him and toward the end of the house where, just around the corner, the body had been. He felt a quick, icy chill, again, right out there in the 95 degree heat. "Well. I guess, I guess I hadn't...I haven't been thinking about it, like that," he answered, "I mean, are you saying that whoever put the body there, that they put it out there, on that spot, on purpose?"

"Look at that!" Darrin whispered fiercely, again unnerving Jon. He was pointing out toward the woods. Jon looked, and saw the deer, a doe and twin fawns, standing at the edge of the woods where the pasture ended.

"You don't have to whisper," Jon said. "They're quite a ways away. I see them all the time," he added, which was not really true but he wanted his guest to be impressed.

"Wow," Darrin said as he watched the doe nervously start to graze, "you do have a cool view out here. That's amazing."

They watched the deer quietly for a minute, standing there on the deck under the full blazing sun. Jon reached up, and wiped sweat off his forehead. He wanted to head back in and talk some more, but Darrin seemed to be fully captivated, and didn't even appear to be perspiring yet.

"So you think maybe somebody put that body on that spot, on Devonshire, on purpose?" Jon repeated.

Darrin kept watching even though the doe had disappeared back into the woods. The fawns were slow to get the message. "I don't know," he said. "It just seems odd to me, ya know?" He seemed reluctant to look back over to Jon and miss a second of his deer watch, but he finally did, and saw the worry on his new friend's face. "Hey, look, I'm just fooling around, theorizing, ya know? Doesn't amount to a hill of beans. I'm just…"

He was interrupted by the jarringly loud sound of a police siren. It roared only once, coming from the front of the house, and it startled both men into total sobriety at once. They looked at each other with widened eyes of shock for a long second, then both turned and ran off the deck, through the back yard and around to the side and front of the house where the body had been, and where the cul-de-sac ended.

There in the street, right by the rounded curve of the cul-de-sac, directly parallel to the property line dividing Jon's house and the Ellsworth's, was the enormous Detective Foster, smiling and leaning against the front of his car, with the red police siren still flashing on the dashboard behind him.

The two men stopped at once and looked at the grinning detective in disbelief. Then they looked briefly at each other. Jon leaned over and put his hands on his knees. He'd had just about enough for one day, and was trying to regain his composure, once again. By now, Barb Ellsworth was standing out on her front porch (this time fully clothed), and other doors were opening all the way up the street, as the newly alerted children, along with a few adults who had already gotten home from work, came out to see what new tragedy, or perhaps arrest, was occurring.

"What the hell?" was all Darrin could think of to say to Foster, whose face still evinced the pleasure he took in all of this.

Foster, with some effort, brought himself up to a standing position, then did a full circle to see just how many were answering his siren. He ended when he faced the two men in the yard again who were still the closest to him. "Too damn hot to be going door to door, ain't it?" he said in the booming, bullying voice that worked so well for him. He looked over at the cowering Barb Ellsworth, and then growled even louder. "I'm gonna talk to the knife man here first, darlin', then you.

Don't go anywhere, OK? In fact, come on over here…I don't have time to be traipsing around."

Barb nodded limply, and Foster, his face already flushed and perspiring in the heat, turned and started walking up the yard toward Jon and Darrin. "Don't you ever wear a shirt, boy?" he asked Jon, who was now standing, but with a glazed look about him. He didn't answer the question.

"Well. Let's go into your house, unless you want to sit in a nice air-conditioned police car in front of the whole neighborhood, son."

Jon still didn't answer, but nodded an O.K. as he turned toward the house.

Foster took a few steps toward the front door before turning to give a frowning look at Darrin. "Don't I know you, boy?" he asked.

Chapter 6

When the unfortunate Jonathon Parker woke for the second time on that forever memorable day, he thought it was morning again. Just like the first time, there was only a weak, half light in the room, and it being his habit to sleep lying on his right side, he awoke facing the digital clock at his bedside, just like the first time. The clock said 8:35.

He also knew that something had just happened; something that he couldn't identify. But the pure panic he had experienced that morning wasn't there. He was just confused, and when the doorbell rang again, he merely sat up and stretched, and quickly put together that it was dusk, not dawn, and that he'd been sleeping for over two and a half hours, not twelve.

"Maybe I'm all panicked out," he thought to himself as he made his way out of bed (safely) and padded down the hall at a leisurely pace to answer the front door. He was more concerned about how sore he felt, all over, than about what surprise he might find on the other side of the door.

It was Pete Vanderberg.

"What's up Pete?" Jon said as he put his hand up to gingerly inspect the bandage on his head. He was feeling a giant headache coming on, from all the beer, or the accident, or both.

"A bunch of us are sitting out, ya know, talking about what happened and everything. Trying to figure things out. Come and join us, Jon."

Jon looked past Pete's shoulder and saw five or six people

in lawn chairs around a fire grate in the street in front of Pete's house. A couple of kids were trying to roast marshmallows in the gathering dusk, even though it was still hot out there.

"Sure, I'll be out in a bit. Especially if you offer me a beer. I drank mine out." Jon said this trying to sound more jovial and neighborly than he actually felt. He felt a hangover, and he felt beat up, but he wanted to drink down some aspirins with beer, not soda or milk.

"Sure, I got plenty," Pete smiled, "come on out."

It was a long running custom, for all those who wanted to in the neighborhood, to sit out around someone's fire (just about everybody had a portable grate) once every two weeks or so, and catch up with the neighbors. Usually it was on a Friday or Saturday night, or the night before a holiday, April through Halloween. It was a practice that Jon felt was one of the endearing features of this particular cul-de-sac. At least once at every "meeting," Jon, or sometimes another neighbor, but it was usually Jon, could be heard drunkenly saying "This is a great neighborhood," or, "Nobody else does this!" or some other similar self-congratulatory proclamation. And it was true that very few neighborhoods do that anymore; in Highland or elsewhere, in our increasingly digitally marginalized society.

This night was different, however, and not just because the gathering took place on a work-day evening. As Jon approached the circle of friends with his lawn chair in tow a few minutes later, he saw that only men were around the circle, including a couple that rarely made it. They were also uncharacteristically quiet, and seemed to be waiting for Jon's arrival. Besides Pete and himself, there was Bobby Benson, who lived on the other side of Pete, Jerry Closter, who lived on the other side of the Ellsworths, Fred Knotts, who lived down at the end of the block, and Bruce Ellsworth, who along with Jon was just joining the crowd.

"Welcome back Bruce," Jon said to his friend as he unfolded

his chair and got ready to break into the circle. "And I'll have that beer now Pete."

Pete reached into his cooler and pulled out a Bud Light. Jon noticed that Bruce just grimly nodded at him in affirming his welcome. Jon wondered how long he had been home, and what kind of nonsense his wife had filled him up with since then. "She probably told him I tried to molest her," he thought. "Bitch."

No one said much of anything until Bruce and Jon had comfortably ensconced themselves into the beer drinking circle. It was the portly Jerry Closter, who Jon knew was a successful independent insurance broker, and a hell of a golfer, who broke the ice. "Well, fill us in guys. They're not saying a damn thing on the news yet. At least anything we didn't already know."

Jerry's comment made Jon realize how self-absorbed, and distracted he had been all day. He hadn't even turned on the TV or radio. He hadn't even tried to get the news. And wasn't it odd that no TV stations had shown up with cameras? He'd only seen one reporter, and that kid was local. They were only 30 miles from St. Louis, for Chrissakes, he thought. A story is a story.

"Me and Jon and Bruce's wife Barb were the first ones to get to the body," Pete anxiously volunteered. Jon could see how revved up Pete was to tell his story, so he sat back and let him go. "Barb's screams got us out there."

"Kids, go into the house! Right now! You're done!" said Bobby Benson. His little girl was trying to burn her marshmallows, and his older son was running in and out of the circle aimlessly. Both kids heard the tone of their Dad's voice and complied without protest, which everyone admired. He must beat hell out of them once in a while, Jon thought.

"What about the body?" Fred leaned in and asked as soon as the kids were out of earshot. He had the tanned good looks and reddish blonde hair that you'd somehow expect from a golf pro (which he was, sort of), which everyone in the circle thought must be the best job in the world. Unless there was a job like Supervisor of Strippers, or something similar to that.

"Well… I didn't actually see the body," Pete said sheepishly.

"You didn't? The kids said you were puking all over the place! What the hell!" Fred could be, and usually was, wonderfully direct, in a way that came off as alternately charming or insulting, depending upon the circumstance. He wasn't helping Pete now. The men all laughed and poor Pete turned a shade of red that could be detected even in the last gasps of dusk.

"I saw the corpse, after Barb did, of course," Jon said, coming to Pete's rescue. He was also trying to give a tip of the hat to Barb, but Bruce just glared.

Jon saw that all eyes, and all ears, were turned and tuned in on him. As he looked into the intent faces around him, he thought briefly of Boy Scout Camp so many years ago, with everyone on the edge of their seats, waiting for the ghost story to begin.

"What did it look like? Come on!" Fred demanded.

"Well. There were no eyes in the skull," Jon began. His voice was casual; factual, but the effect on everyone was predictably dramatic. Jon realized he was enjoying this, in some kind of sick way, so he took his time. He took a long pull from his Bud Light.

"No eyes? What do you mean, no eyes? Is that what Barb said too?" Fred demanded, and all eyes turned to Bruce. Bruce nodded, but said nothing, choosing to take his own drink from his Michelob Ultra instead.

"I know there were no eyes because I'll never forget what I saw," Jon said. All the eyes shifted back toward him. "I saw a fly crawl into one of the eye-holes, and back out again," he said, exaggerating slightly. "The skin was leathery. Grey. The guy had been dead for a long time, I'd guess. And he smelled horrible….the smell of death, guys."

Jon was enjoying himself.

Pete felt his stomach clinch and quickly looked down at the pavement by his feet. He tried to think about baseball. The rest of the men sat in silence as they leaned forward, trying to absorb what they had just heard, and not wanting to miss a word of what might be coming next. It was almost completely dark now, and that added to the suspense.

"It scared the hell out of me, I'll be honest," Jon added. His mind was searching for any details that might further fascinate his listeners, but he was drawing a blank. Just like his "book project."

"The kids said they handcuffed you, and then they let you go. What the hell was that all about?" Fred demanded.

Jon took another drink before answering. Fred wasn't so damn funny when he was asking *you* the question. "I brought a knife out when I heard Barb scream. A big 'ol butcher knife, guys. I was ready to kill whoever was attacking Barb." he said, looking over at Bruce. Bruce nodded to him. A thanks? Maybe. A good sign anyway, Jon decided. "One cop thought I was a murderer, I guess," Jon concluded, trying to give this part of the story some finality. He didn't want to have to tell them about the blood, and how he got hurt, for obvious reasons.

"What about that fat cop this afternoon? Kids said he blew his siren up to your house, and took you in? What about that?" the insatiable Fred demanded.

"He just made me go over everything again. Same with Barb. He wanted us to tell him what I'm telling you guys, again." He looked over at Bruce again, but he was studying the pavement in front of him, seemingly lost in thought.

There was silence for a minute or so. Fred seemed to be out of questions, and no one else could think of what to say next. It was starting to cool off remarkably quickly, and though it was still humid, being around a fire didn't seem half as insane an idea as it had earlier. By silent consensus, the men moved their chairs up a little closer. It was easier to see faces that way, even if they didn't need the warmth.

"It bothers me a hell of a lot guys," Pete said in breaking the silence a few moments later. "This is a safe neighborhood, in a safe town." He was leaning forward with his elbows on his knees and both meaty hands cupped around his beer, almost completely covering it. He was looking into the fire as he spoke. "Why in God's Holy Name would somebody choose Devonshire Court in Highland, Illinois to dump a dead body?"

"Street, isn't it? Isn't it Devonshire Street?" Fred asked.

"Jesus Christ Fred!" Pete shot back, "What God Damned difference does that make, jag off?"

Everyone chuckled, and Pete felt a little bit of respect come back his way. Even Fred thought it was funny. It was hard to insult Fred.

"Jon, or Pete, or hell…Bruce? Did the police tell anybody, or give you any clue as to who this poor sucker was? This dead guy?" Jerry Closter asked.

Jon looked over at him and saw the worried frown he wore, and felt sorry for him. Sometimes it's scarier to hear about something bad than it is to actually experience it. Here he was, after a whole day to think about it and, perhaps, rationalize it away, but these guys, getting the gruesome details for the first time, were scared out of their wits. He found himself wanting to reassure Jerry, and the rest of his neighbors. "Guys, the dead guy…no way he was from around here," he said. "I saw that body, and it was…"

Jon's next word was lost to a huge, sharp cracking sound that startled them all. There was a stunned two second delay, and then the circle became a chaos of tipped over lawn chairs and men jumping to their feet in alarm, pointing and shouting. The sound had come from, unmistakably, the field behind the cul-de-sac, from just behind Jon Parker's house.

Someone yelled "That was a shotgun!" and someone else said it sounded like a tree splitting. Someone else, who turned out to be Bruce, just yelled, thunderously, for quiet. His voice, one they hadn't heard yet that night, was loud and authoritative enough to get the job done.

"That was too loud," Bruce said. "Had to be a gun. Pete, go in and call the police. Jerry and Jon you come with me. Bobby, you stay here and see if you see anything." Bruce ordered. He was about to finish off his magnificent display of calm and command by yelling "Let's GO!" when Fred interrupted.

"What about me?" he asked.

"Christ Fred! Stay here with…" he couldn't think of the name, "Just stay here! NOW LET'S GO!"

Bruce charged through the street to the west side of Jon's house with Jon right behind him and the badly overweight Jerry bringing up the rear. It took less than 10 seconds for the first two to get around the house and make the sharp left turn that got them to the pitch black back yard. Jerry crashed into a garbage can on the side of Jon's house at the same time the other two stopped, and Bruce and Jon could hear him swearing as they stood looking out into the blackness, breathing hard, and without a real clue as to what to do next.

They stood looking out, and seeing nothing. "Maybe I should turn on the deck lights…or go get a flashlight. What do ya think?" Jon asked.

"A flashlight would be good," Bruce whispered. He was still out of breath, and he was trying to listen.

Jon dashed up the slight hill and toward the deck and his back door. Jerry finally got there, right after Jon left. He couldn't see at all, and ran right into Bruce, who was staggered, but didn't fall.

"Oh Jesus, I'm sorry!" Jerry puffed. He strained his eyes to try to see anything at all in the dark. "Where's Jon?" he asked with alarm.

Before Bruce could answer they heard a loud "God damn it to hell!" coming from up on the deck. "Fucker's locked! Gotta go around front!"

"Oh Jesus!" Jerry yelled, grabbing theatrically at his heart, even though there was no one who could see. "The son-of-a bitch almost gave me a heart attack!"

"SSSHHHH!" Bruce whispered fiercely. "Be quiet, man!"

Jerry tried, but he was still trying to catch his breath, and it sounded almost as if he was snoring when he exhaled.

"Jesus! You sound like you're calling a god damned moose or something! Shut the hell up!" Bruce whispered violently.

Suddenly, they were bathed in a blinding light. They both flinched and brought their hands up to their eyes instinctively'

"Mary, Mother of God!" Jerry screamed, "What's that?" He closed his eyes tight and reached for his heart with both hands again.

"SHUT OFF THAT LIGHT!" Bruce yelled. "NOW!"

They heard the glass door to Jon's deck slide open. "What?" he asked.

"SHUT THE LIGHTS OFF!" Bruce screamed again.

Jon looked down at his friend from the deck, and saw that he was literally purple with rage. "O.K, O.K….Jesus. Keep your shirt on," and he went to turn off the lights.

Within another minute they were all standing together in the dark again, listening. They could only hear the bugs and frogs of the night, and the distant sound of a siren headed their way.

"What about the flashlights?" Bruce whispered to Jon. He was still insisting on silence as the best way to get a clue about this.

"Couldn't find one," Jon whispered back.

"Do either of you smell gun smoke?" Jerry whispered, a little too heavily. Bruce could smell the onions on his breath.

"No…do you?" Jon whispered back.

"No," Jerry said in his normal voice.

"SSSHHHH!" whispered Bruce.

They stood in silence, hearing nothing but the siren getting closer, and some loud but inaudible conversation coming from the street behind them.

Finally Bruce let out a long sigh, and said without whispering "Well, we better go around front. We've got to try to explain this to the cops."

At that, they turned to walk back toward the street and their fire.

"Maybe it was a sonic boom," Jerry said. Neither of the other two responded, because, for a change, what Jerry said had a ring of sense to it.

"Listen!" Jon said suddenly. He grabbed Bruce's arm tightly for emphasis. "Listen!" he repeated urgently.

They all stopped, and listened, without taking a breath, as intently as they could.

Do you hear that?" Jon cried.

And within a handful of seconds, all three of them did. It was very faint at first, and coming from the pasture, or maybe beyond that, up in the trees far away. At first it sounded like the whinnying of a horse, but it was deeper, and more disturbing than that. Then it stopped for at least a full ten seconds, which seemed like forever to the men frozen like statues and straining to hear. Then it was back again, closer this time, with a clearer, more brittle sound. It stopped, and they could hear, ever faintly at first, but then more definitively, a thrashing sound coming from the distant trees. Then the eerie, grating sound again, even closer.

"That's laughing," Jon said quietly. "Someone is out there laughing…"

Chapter 7

Only Christmas Eve could have competed with the number of lights turned on; the amount of voltage being consumed; the sum of natural resources willingly being wasted on that starless night in July on Devonshire Court. Or, perhaps, Street. If an aerial photograph of the peaceful hamlet of Highland had been taken at say, 3:00 A.M. that night (or technically, morning) it would have shown only the pale yellow glow of an occasional streetlight covering 99.9% of the sleepy little town, with the dramatic exception of one little cul-de-sac on the southeast side. There, every front and back porch light, and almost every living room and dining room light was burning brightly, as well as a fair number of bedroom lights, along with a finished basement light or two. And the children's night lights? It goes without saying.

Unfortunately though, for solid proof and the sake of posterity, no aerial photograph is known to have been taken that night, so we can surmise only that perhaps some lonely, tired airline pilot or passenger who was headed for home may have, by chance, looked momentarily down while passing over, and were the only witnesses to that night's lighting of Devonshire.

It was a night when outside pets were surprised and delighted to be taken in, doors everywhere were locked and tested; and a night when there was a general scrambling for new batteries to replace the old after frantic testing of long forgotten flashlights. In at least two houses, weapons were carefully loaded, and were now at the ready. Many times that long night worried faces could be seen peering furtively around their living room curtains, keenly watching for any suspicious movement in the street, or in the remaining mysterious dark patches between houses. The tension seemed to be felt even by Highland's stray cats and dogs, who, as survivors by their own mysterious instincts, scrupulously avoided the little cul-de-sac that night.

The cause of all of this frantic preparation, paranoia and illumination was from the neighborhood meeting; the meeting after the meeting, you might say. The police left soon after receiving the report of the gun-shot, sonic boom or tree falling - whatever it was, and the horse neighing, animal in distress, or human laughter - whatever that was. There simply wasn't much to investigate. The two officers (neither of whom had been there that morning, though well aware of the goings on) took an obligatory walk to Jon's back yard, and shined powerful flashlights into the empty pasture and woods for a while, giving the scene a ghostly glow, but they saw and heard nothing. It didn't take long for them to see that there was nothing for them to do but to reassure the alarmed residents that they would be on patrol, and to "call us if anything else happens."

It was after they left that the real meeting started, again around the now dying fire in Pete's grate. Representatives from the other houses, Ralph and Barb Carmine, Rory Frey, and Dick and Ginger Korte all came out to question the original fire-sitters, all of whom were, understandably, spooked. The new-comers heard theories on the original booming sound (only Ralph and Barb had heard it from inside their house), and three different versions of the "laughter." Bruce described it as like "a horse or some other large animal being tortured," Jerry said it sounded like a "witch or something," and Jon, being an English teacher and more literarily inclined, said that, to him, it sounded like "laughter from something purely evil, even demonic; a dark message from Hades."

When all the descriptions were in (including Jon's reprise of the dead body's looks for the benefit of the newcomers) there was a series of theories put forth, along with some overtly wild speculation, from almost everyone, all attempting to make sense of what had happened, or to tie the horrific events of the day together.

"After what happened this morning, we can't take this shit lightly," Bobby warned indelicately. "We've got us a nut out there, guys" he added, pointing dramatically to the pasture and woods.

"What makes the most sense, is that some gangsters happened to dump the body here, and now we got some twisted kid out there in the woods trying to scare hell out of us," Jerry Closter said sensibly.

"Jerry, how could you hear that laugh and think it was a kid?" Jon asked, which frightened everyone even more.

"I thought you guys said it sounded like something in pain? Didn't somebody say that?" Ginger Korte asked. Ginger was little, wiry and always cold, and was now shivering even though the temperature was still in the 80's, even though she had a long-sleeved robe on, along with a shawl around her shoulders

"I said that, but I can't be sure…I mean I said it, but I'm not sure about the pain part…" Bruce tried to explain.

"We're all crazy if we're sayin' this isn't all tied together. Anybody besides me gotta gun?" Pete asked excitedly.

"They'll be no guns!" Ginger said.

"Who died and made you Queen?" her husband Dick sneered.

"This is for the police to take care of. They're on the case," Ralph interjected.

"Like shit they are," answered the always fired up Fred.

It went on like this for almost an hour, the group arguing,

postulating and eventually awkwardly bonding with a loose consensus to "stick together and help each other out." One by one, they drifted home, as there were children to be put into bed, late news to catch, ball games to watch, and bedtime snacks to savor. Truth be told though, they had all been made insecure by the things that had happened. In everyone's mind there was a new thread of doubt about safety, and their control over the everyday events in their lives, and for some, a new, real feeling of fear. The evening was far from routine in each of their households.

Dick Korte didn't watch the news for more than a few minutes. As soon as he saw that the Highland dead body story wasn't in the headlines, he knew there was nothing new. He turned off the set, grabbed a flashlight just in case, and went out to smoke, quietly, on his back patio.

Pete Vanderberg went to his basement to get his pistol. He brought it upstairs and loaded while sitting at his kitchen table, despite the whining protests of his distraught wife Margie.

When Bruce Ellsworth came back into the house, Barb asked him immediately to hold her, and then go to bed with her. Thinking sex was in the offing, he quickly ran through the shower, but she was sound asleep by the time he got out. He got dressed, checked the locks on the doors and windows, and then sat in his living room, watching Sports Center with the volume turned so low that he could barely hear it.

Cathy Closter insisted on locking their two small children in their bedrooms, providing both of them a walkie-talkie to call her if they needed her in the night. Jerry told her this was silly, but didn't try to overrule her. He couldn't settle down, and was still pacing the house long after the kids were asleep.

Bobby and Mary Benson's kids were older and generally had more freedom on summer nights (even though he had chased them inside that night with all the dead body talk going on). Tonight though, Bobby told them to go to bed as soon as he got inside, and he uncharacteristically asked his wife to come and talk with him about "all this stuff that's going on."

Rory Frey lived down at the far end, or more properly the beginning, of the cul-de-sac, right across from Fred and Carol Knots, so he walked home with Fred after the meeting broke up. Since Fred was a real "witness" to the night's events, he did all of the talking. Fred liked to do the talking. By the time they parted to go in and talk to their wives, Rory had committed himself to purchasing a gun as soon as possible to get some immediate protection for his family. He was unaware of the three day waiting period in Illinois.

Jon Parker, who arguably had the most to worry about, given his house's geographical proximity to the body, as well as the mysterious noise and laughter, was at least relatively calm. He found himself tending to buy into big Jerry's theory that some kid, or group of kids was out there making noise to scare everyone. At least he hoped so. When everyone went home, Jon came inside, and instead of drinking (out of beer, hated the hard stuff) he made a pot of coffee. Between his long afternoon nap and all the excitement, he knew he'd be up half the night. Later, after a failed attempt to find something good on television, he found comfort in sipping that coffee while sitting out on his deck in the dark, and listening, well into the night.

Well past midnight, most of the adults in the well lit neighborhood were still awake, wrestling with their own doubts and fears. In fact, there were only two exceptions:

Barb Ellsworth, whose horrible discovery had started this longest of days, was sleeping as soundly as she ever had in her life.

Fred Knotts was sleeping just as soundly as he always did, but this night, not in his bed. He could be found snoring heavily in his easy chair, with his loaded gun on his lap.

All the rest wrestled with the demons of the night.

Chapter 8

There is, always, in the sunshine of a new day, new hope.

For the residents of Devonshire Court, even though there were tired yawns everywhere, there seemed to be plenty of reason to smile that sunny Thursday, July 16th morning. The smell of coffee brewing and bacon frying, the warm, reassuring voices of normalcy coming from their radios and televisions, and even the simple, everyday tasks of shaving, brushing teeth, and applying make-up all seemed wondrously life confirming, now that the sunrise had chased the scurrying demons of the night away.

Neighbors smiled and waved to each other as they went out for the morning paper, and when they left for work that morning there was generally no real thought of the night before. No one wanted to think about it. They were, instead, intent on enjoying fully the warm embrace of normalcy.

Jonathon Parker slept in until well after the neighborhood had emptied. He had finally fallen asleep in his chair in the wee hours of the morning, and after a fitful 45 minute half-sleep he woke up stiff from sitting for so long in a confining position. He staggered off in exhaustion to his bed then, not caring if the Devil himself came for a visit.

Only the Ellsworth house retained a sense of abnormality that glorious morning. Barb had finally woken as her husband was finishing shaving. She sprang out of bed, even though a bit disoriented, and frantically called for her husband.

"Bruce! Bruce? Where are you?"

Bruce stepped out of the bathroom that adjoined their bedroom with some of the shaving cream still on his face. "Hey, hey…I'm right here honey." He could only take one step toward her before she reached him, throwing herself into his arms. He felt her soft breasts against him and remembered his bad luck the night before. "Easy now. Easy honey," he soothed. She was hugging him as tightly as she could.

"Don't go to work today!" she begged. Her voice suggested to him that she wasn't very far from tears. He'd seen this before, although it had been a while now. She tended to get emotional when life was off its even keel, good or bad. And yesterday had been very bad.

"There there, honey. Easy now…" he said soothingly, as close to her ear as he could get. He knew better than to directly argue the point. There would be instant hysterics then. He held her, patted her, and looked at the two of them in the bathroom mirror, which he could see from where they were standing. "What a beautiful couple!" he thought. He looked at her lovely petite figure in his favorite nightie, her golden hair, his own handsome face with that sexy dimpled chin. Still the Homecoming King and Queen. "SSHHH…there there now…" he whispered. He was again aware of her breasts heaving against him.

Maybe he could take a day, or part of one. "What the hell," he thought, as he guided his willing Homecoming Queen over to the bed.

Jon was sure about one thing. He was sick of answering the God damned doorbell.

"I am so sick of answering the God damned doorbell!" he said as he walked sleepily down the hall toward his front door after being rudely awoken again from a sound sleep. "I'm coming! I'm coming!" he yelled when it rang again before he could get there.

He was expecting it to be that Detective Foster again, or maybe even a neighbor, so he was surprised when he opened it to see an unshaven Darrin Crandle standing there smiling at him.

"Don't tell me you were still asleep! It's 10:30 in the morning, man!" he exclaimed.

Jon yawned and opened the door wider to let him in. He was glad to see him, even though he'd been rudely awakened. "I guess you could say I worked the late-shift last night," he answered as he stretched his sore muscles.

"That's what I hear. Had another little incident, did ya?"

"You could say that, yea. You want some coffee or something? You already drank all my beer."

"Sure," Darrin answered. "if you don't mind. And by the way, boy, don't you ever wear a shirt?"

"And don't you own a razor, pretty boy? And don't you ever go to work?" Jon fired back.

Jon made coffee while he filled Darrin in on the goings on from the previous night. Darrin listened intently, and didn't ask any questions until Jon was finished.

"..and that's the whole story," Jon said in finishing. "Not much to it. Some kid spooked the whole neighborhood, is my guess. Hell, I stayed up half the night out there listening." He nodded toward the deck while pouring the just brewed coffee. "There was nothing more. Kid probably had to be home at curfew."

Darrin looked out the glass door and out to the pasture and woods for a long minute, then scratched his stubble and turned back toward Jon, "Who'd you say owned that land again?"

Jon brought the steaming cups over to the kitchen table and handed Darrin one before sitting down and answering. "Stuff's hot, be careful. I've been meaning to get a new coffee maker. This one burns me once a week, at least. And I said I couldn't remember, remember? The real estate gal told me years ago, but I've forgotten."

Darrin took a sip of his coffee and jerked his head back. "Damnit!" he yelled, wiping his scalded mouth with his free hand, "Shit, that's hot!"

"Told ya. For a cop you don't listen too well," Jon chuckled.

"Well…damn." Darrin said, continuing to rub his lips. "It's not funny."

Jon leaned over and blew into his own cup. He knew Darrin wanted more information, but he didn't know what else to tell him. The whole thing seemed silly in the light of day. Except for the dead body, of course.

"You say you've been back there? In those woods?" Darrin asked. He was looking out the glass door again.

Jon looked out too. "Yea, sort of," he answered after a moment. "I kind of skirted around the woods. They're pretty thick. I wanted to see where it all ended. It was a couple of years ago."

Darrin turned to Jon. He was grinning widely again. Jon couldn't help being jealous of his movie star looks. He imagined women were no problem for this guy. Not like they were for him.

"Let's you and me take a walk back in there. Maybe we'll find a clue as to who was scaring you guys. You and me! What do ya think?"

Darrin had an infectious enthusiasm that was hard to resist, but going out and getting poison ivy on a hot July day didn't sound like a whole lot of fun to Jon. "Now? Today?" he asked. "Don't you have to go to work later?"

"Hell, no! It's my 2nd day off, I told ya! Thursday is my Sunday, man," he said, grinning like a mischievous little boy. He stood up and pushed his chair back. Let's go have a look. I'll teach you how to spot clues, man!"

Unbelievably (to him), Jon's doorbell rang again. This time

he was glad though, because it might be Detective Foster or some other on-duty cop that would throw cold water on the hike Darrin was proposing.

"Damnit," Jon mock protested as he got up to answer the door. "It better not be that detective again, or I'll know you guys are working together."

"Foster can kiss my ass," Darrin said. His smile now gone, he sat back down.

It was Jon's neighbor and friend Bruce at the door, and he also had a big smile on his face. "Hey Jonny!" he said jovially. "Got a few minutes to talk?"

"Doesn't anybody have a job to go to around here?" Jon asked incredulously. "Sure... come on in." They exchanged a warm handshake, and Jon was relieved that his friend had apparently lost the edginess that he'd had the night before. "There's somebody in here I want you to meet."

Jon asked Bruce how Barb was doing on their way to the kitchen, and he just smiled and said "Just fine, now..." in a way that made his meaning unmistakable. Jon pursued it no further.

Jon introduced Darrin as the first cop on the scene, "... who hasn't worked since," and Bruce as his neighbor friend "... who doesn't work either," and the two shook hands. To Jon, the two of them looked like they could have been brothers; both tall dark and handsome types, with Darrin being the younger, skinnier version of Bruce. His ever present inferiority complex as he watched the guys shake reinforced to him that his shorter, heavier profile just didn't compare. But maybe his blue eyes held a trump though, he thought.

Jon got a cup of coffee for Bruce, and the three of them hunched around the small kitchen table meant for no more than two. It wasn't long before Darrin asked Bruce for his version of the events of the night before. Bruce was, naturally, still unsure of Darrin, and he looked at Jon, who gave a silent "this guy's OK" nod before he answered.

"It was a pretty screwed up night," he began. "I think, well I know that everyone was upset to begin with, so it didn't take much to get us going. I guess Jon probably told you who was out there and all, discussing the, uh, dead body. The sound we heard, the more I think about it...I don't think it was a gunshot. I really don't. It was more like a branch cracking, and falling off a tree. It was real loud, though, so it could have been a sonic boom, I guess. But we didn't hear a jet or anything, so I don't know..."

"What about the laughing then, or whatever it was? What did it sound like to you?" Darrin asked, and more directly than he had Jon.

"I've been thinking about that too," Bruce said as he leaned back on Jon's wobbly kitchen chair. "Last night we were scared shitless, at the time, you know. It could be that we exaggerated how...scary it was."

"But what did it sound like to you?" Darrin pressed.

"Like...like somebody who was changing his voice... on purpose. Making it more scary on purpose, ya know? It was unreal, in a way."

"A male voice?"

Bruce gave Jon a "what do you think?" look.

"I don't know that you could say, really," Jon answered for them both. "I think he's got a point there though, on the unrealness of it. You know how people try to talk like Grover on 'Sesame Street'?"

"You're telling me it sounded like Grover?" Darrin said smiling.

"No. no, it was like someone tried to change their voice like that. Bruce?"

Bruce just nodded his head. After he did, Darrin took a sip of his now-cooled coffee, then got up and walked over toward the deck. "We were just about to take a walk up there to look around," he said with his back to the two others. "You want to go with us Bruce?"

Jon and Bruce looked at each other then answered simultaneously, with Jon saying "No, we weren't!" and Bruce saying "That's a great idea!"

Darrin turned and looked at the two of them sitting at the table. "Good! We leave in five minutes. Put on some long pants, boys, unless you're fond of chiggers and poison ivy."

Chapter 9

Detective Gus Foster entered the Highland Police Department, as any neutral observer would have undoubtedly said, "…like he owned the place." He went right up to the front desk and demanded to know where the chief was. The hapless officer manning the desk (who, as it happens, was the Mayor's son-in-law) quickly pointed to the Chief of Police's office, even though he hadn't asked for identification, like he was supposed to, and even though the Chief wasn't in. Detective Foster was very intimidating.

"Uh, sir…he's not in there, at the moment," the nervous policemen said just as Foster had reached the door.

Foster whirled around, hand still on the doorknob. "Then why the hell did you send me over here?" he demanded.

"I…I just pointed, sir," the officer stammered. "He's…he's usually there…in his office, I mean."

"But he's not there now."

"N-n-n-no, sir."

Foster took his hand off the knob, and turned his enormous girth fully around toward the stuttering officer. "Would you mind, then, telling me…just where the hell he is?"

"D-d-don't know," he said. Foster's eyes looked black to him. His wrinkled forehead looked very angry.

"Can you page him? Now!"

The officer tried to move so quickly that his phone-pager

flew out of his hand and skittered across the floor. It stopped within inches of Foster's left foot.

Foster looked down at the pager, then very slowly and deliberately up to the flustered desk officer. Then, very calmly, he asked "What's your name officer?"

The officer's first few efforts to answer were all spittle, but he finally got out "B-b-b-Bradley, sir…"

"What's the trouble here Lance?" said Highland Chief of Police Rodney Thomas. It took him only a second after entering the front door to see that his man at the desk was troubled. He'd seen him flushed and upset like this before. Many times. "Oh, it's you," he added when he followed Lance's eyes to Detective Foster. "What can I do for you, Gus?" Reading the situation quickly, realizing that Foster was about to unload on Lance, he didn't wait for an answer. He pointed to his office instead and began walking quickly in that direction. "Step into my office, Detective Foster," he said.

Foster looked at Chief Thomas, then back at Lance, as if deciding just what to say, but, for once, kept his silence. He waited for Thomas to go by, then turned and followed him into his office.

"Why in the hell would you put a kid who can't talk in charge of the desk?" Foster asked as soon as they were inside Thomas' cramped quaters.

"It's a long story, believe me," Thomas responded as he sat down behind his desk. "What can I do for ya, Gus?" He was anxious to get through this. His day had already been hectic, he was worried half to death, and talking to Gus wasn't going to make it any better.

"Heard you had another call out to the crime scene last night, so I thought I'd stop by to see if there was anything up. Why the hell else would I be bugging you Rodney? And do you know anything that I should know from the medical examiners yet?"

Thomas glared at him. He didn't like Gus Foster personally,

and frankly didn't like working with him either, but he was used to him-mostly from long past days. He was a big shot with a big reputation and big city experience, and he let everybody know about it. Foster spent most of his time in places like East St. Louis, Belleville, even St.Louis itself when he was moonlighting a bit, always on big murder cases. Places like peaceful little Highland, where most of the time a domestic dispute was the big news of the year, bored him to tears. Or at least he acted like it did. But Chief Thomas needed all the help he could get right now, and an expert like Foster had to be tolerated.

"First of all, the call was a false alarm from a bunch of beer drinkers out there. " Thomas said tersely. "And secondly, it's been just over 24 hours Gus. This guy…there wasn't much left of this guy. It's going to take a while to identify him," Thomas said. He saw Lance look into the window of his door right behind Foster. He decided to ignore him. Damn kid couldn't figure out anything electronic. He just brought messages to him in person. "I don't even know if this is our case yet. Could be FBI, I don't know," he added.

"Shit. I hope so. It had to come from across the river, even Chicago, maybe." Gus reached into his pocket for his chew, but kept his hand on it. He'd wait until he was back in his car. "Fingerprints?" he asked. "Surely they've had time to try to match something…What have you got on that?"

"Still waiting. Get this: the first report yesterday afternoon? They said there weren't any!"

"No fingerprints? Were his hands gone? Mutilated?" Gus was actually interested in this bit of news.

"No. He's got hands," Chief Thomas answered. Lance was at the window again, waving. "Must have been amateur hour up there. I told them to get prints, dental records, all that shit, and get it to us ASAP. You'll know when I know, but like you said, this don't look local." Lance was still waving for his attention.

"Look Gus, I gotta go," Thomas said as he slid his chair back and stood up to move Foster along.

But Foster didn't move. Not right away. He was staring at the spot where Chief Thomas had been sitting, eyebrows knitted in concentration. "No fingerprints," he said more to himself than Thomas. "These guys… might be very good." He looked up at Thomas. "No fingerprints, they told you?"

"Damnit!" Jon yelled out. He looked down at the bloodied palm of his hand that had just pushed what turned out to be a thorned vine out of his way. "Damnit to hell!" he added for emphasis.

The other two turned back to look at the lagger. They had crossed the pasture, first going up, then mostly downhill through the thick green grass, and then sharply up before getting to the edge of the woods. Jon, who had put on jeans, a long-sleeved sweatshirt and thigh high wading boots to try to avoid the perils of poison oak or ivy, had lagged behind from the beginning, and now five feet into the mysterious forest he had managed to wound one of the few unprotected parts of his body.

"Either of you guys carrying a bandage?" he asked.

Both shook their heads no. "Let me see what you got there," Darrin said as he walked back toward Jon. Bruce and he were only ten feet further into the woods, struggling through heavy undergrowth and fallen branches below huge oak and maple trees, looking for any signs that kids, or anybody else, had been in the area recently. They were trying to get through the initial rough stuff and reach a stand of pines that Darrin had spotted from Jon's deck. He thought that there may be clearer ground for walking under the pines; ground that the sounds from the night before may have come from.

"It's just a scratch, sissy. You'll survive," Darrin said. He was anxious to continue.

Jon looked up from his wound to Darrin and then to

Bruce. "Yea, well this is nuts," he said. "All we're going to do is get sweaty and scratched up. And these damned boots are impossible."

Darrin sighed impatiently. "Look, I just want to get to those pine trees. It can't be that far. If anybody was out here last night, that's where they would have operated from, and we'll be able to tell, believe me." He could see only resentment and frustration in Jon's face, so he ended his plea by turning toward Bruce. "What do you think?" he asked.

"I think that now that we're out here, we might as well finish it," Bruce said. He punctuated his statement with a quick slap at a mosquito on his arm. No problem in the pasture, they seemed to be everywhere in the shadier, slightly cooler woods.

"You two go on," Jon said as he turned to head back. "I shouldn't have worn these damned boots."

Bruce was about to ask him what difference the boots made, but decided against it. His friend needed an excuse to turn back, he figured, so he let him have it.

Darrin and Bruce watched him walk clumsily out of the woods and into the sunny pasture, then turned and trudged on.

After hearing all the advantages and disadvantages explained to him by his neighbor and the salesman, Rory Frey picked one of the revolvers over the assortment of semi-automatics arrayed in front of him. His friend Fred, who had met him there over the lunch hour to help him out, approved by smiling broadly when Rory firmly made his choice. "You did good, Rory boy," he said, patting him on the back.

Rory tried not to act surprised at the paperwork that had to be filled out, along with the three-day waiting period. He just nodded through it all, and handed over his credit card at the appropriate time.

Out in the parking lot, before parting to head back to work, they shook hands. "Thanks Fred," Rory said gratefully, "I really appreciate it, man."

"No problem little buddy," Fred said with his big golf-pro smile. "Now all we got to do is teach you how to shoot the damn thing! You'll do fine, kid. You'll see."

"I feel safer already," Rory said. And he did.

Jon had already laboriously crossed the pasture, and was in the act of putting his leg up to climb over the fence that divided his land and the unknown farmer's, when he heard the yell. It was a short, clear shout; as though someone had gotten hurt, or had been badly frightened by something.. And it came from behind him, toward the woods.

He put his leg down, turned around, and held still to listen. He heard nothing else, and as the seconds rolled by, his always fertile imagination began working. Had one of the guys gotten hurt? Did they find something that scared the crap out of them? Had one of them run across a snake...or maybe another body... or a person hiding back there? Did they need help?

After waiting and listening for a minute, but hearing nothing but the bees of summer and a persistent cardinal's call, he decided he'd better go back up the pasture again to make sure everything was all right. He tried to trot, or at least walk double-time, but his boots weren't cooperating, and he cussed them under his breath. He got down the hill fairly easily, considering his boot handicap, but was almost completely out of breath by the time he made the first uphill grade. He stopped there, breathing hard and sweating profusely, and listening while looking at the woods ahead. Suddenly, he saw the tops of the trees begin to stir crazily, and seconds later the strong breeze that caused it got to him. It came straight from the south where the woods were, but the air felt remarkably cool, at least for summer. Jon looked up instinctively to see if a storm was coming, but there was only the blazing sun, and not one cloud on the horizon. And then, just as suddenly as it had come, it was gone, and he was standing there at the top of the rise on a breathlessly hot summer day again. He had to wonder if he had imagined the whole thing.

Then he heard the crackling of sticks, and small branches. He couldn't see anything yet, but he knew they were coming back out. He cupped his hands around his mouth and yelled "Bruce! Darrin! You guys all right?"

There was no immediate answer, but he could hear more crackling. Finally, he saw movement, and it was Darrin who yelled out, "Fine! We'll be right there!"

Jon stood where he was, and waited. A minute or so later they were at the pasture's edge and walking toward him. Jon could see that there was nothing physically wrong with either of them. He was relieved about that, but now even more curious about the yell. When they got within easy hearing distance, he said "What the hell happened in there? I heard one of you sissies all the way across the pasture." He could see Darrin's broad smile at what he'd said, but Bruce just kept looking at the ground in front of him. When they reached Jon, Bruce walked right by him. He didn't even look up. He just kept walking toward the house.

Darrin stopped and stood by Jon, and they both looked at Bruce trudge away. When he was out of earshot, Darrin leaned toward Jon and said in a low, mock-conspiratorial voice, "Your friend Bruce just saw a ghost."

Chapter 10

Bruce walked into his house, right past the smiling wife who was holding her arms out to him, and straight to the liquor cabinet. He grabbed the first bottle he saw (which happened to be bourbon), grabbed a glass, and poured himself at least a double shot. He drank it down while still standing by the cabinet, then took a deep breath, looked at the label on the bottle for a second, then turned and sat down at the dining room table, with the bottle and glass still in his hands. He poured himself another drink, then looked up at his totally befuddled wife. "Hi, honey," he said.

Barb was still standing where she had expected to greet him, arms now down at her sides, but with her mouth opened in a silent 0 of shock. When she recovered a bit of composure, her first instinct was to look at the clock. "It's not even noon!" she said.

Bruce turned to look at the clock, which was directly behind and above him, for himself. "It's five minutes till," he said casually. "Close enough."

Barb saw that despite his outwardly cool demeanor, his hand was shaking when he raised the glass again. Something was very wrong. Bruce never drank before noon. In fact, except for the occasional beer with the boys (which he inevitably didn't handle very well), he rarely drank at all. That was one of the things Barb loved about him; that he wasn't like her father in that way. Barb had grown up watching her Dad wait for noon to start drinking. It was one of the few, odd rules that he followed religiously.

"Bruce, honey, what's the matter?" she asked, as she at last broke her frozen posture to walk over to him in concern.

Bruce took another drink. He looked at his beautiful wife, whose lips were beginning to tremble with emotion. He really didn't want to cause a scene. Not after their wonderful morning. Not after all that she'd been through.

"Nothing's wrong, honey," he lied. "It's just the stress of what happened yesterday, I think. I'm putting the bottle away right now."

And he did, but not before swallowing first what he'd already poured. Barb came over and hugged him then, and he hugged her back. They held their embrace for a long while, and only broke it when Bruce asked "Honey, what would you think about us moving?"

"It's what he said he felt, actually, more than what he said he saw," Darrin explained. "He really didn't tell me much."

They were once again sitting at Jon's tiny table, this time drinking cold water and reveling in the air-conditioning after their hike. Jon could see that Darrin was dubious, at best, about what had really happened to Bruce in the woods. At first, he didn't even want to tell Jon about it, waving away Jon's questions dismissively, and insisting instead that they go in and get something cold to drink. Now, with one glass of water down and another one in front of him, he was finally explaining to Jon what had happened.

"We're under the pine trees, looking around for any sign that someone had been out there last night, or any time recently, right? We're not finding a thing, so I tell him the kind of thing we should be looking for, and we kind of split up. Next thing I know, he yells like he just got electrified or something. Scared the shit out of me. I go running over to him to make sure he's all right, and I find him turning in a circle under one of the trees, pale as a ghost, like he's being attacked by wolves that are circling all around him. Invisible wolves though, because nothing was there."

Darrin shook his head and took a long drink of water. It was obvious to Jon that whatever had happened to Bruce didn't impress Darrin much. He was acting as though it was a bother to even tell the story. To Jon though, it was fascinating, and he couldn't wait to get over to Bruce's house to grill him on it.

"Well, what else happened, man? What did he say about a ghost?" Jon asked in irritation.

"He didn't say anything about a ghost. Those were my words," Darrin said. Then he put his glass down and leaned over the table conspiratorially again, with a big grin on his face. "He said that someone put a hand on his shoulder, and turned him around. *So I figured it must have been a ghost!*" he said dramatically, with eyes widened in mock horror.

For the first time since he'd met him, Jon was beginning to wonder if he really liked Darrin all that much. Here he was, sitting at his kitchen table, uninvited once again, and seeming to take juvenile delight in a good friend's apparently traumatic experience. He seemed more like the high school bully than anything else. At least at the moment.

"Look Darrin," Jon began angrily, "Bruce is a stand-up guy. He's a good friend. He's got as much common sense as anybody I know. Hell… that deal last night? He was the only one who kept his head. He's the one who took charge, man." Darrin's grin was gone now. The harsh tone of Jon's words had at least gotten his attention. "All I'm saying is, if he says something happened to him out there, we should at least listen to him. He's not a bullshitter." Jon had almost added "…like you" to the end of his sentence, but thought better of it.

The two sat through a long awkward silence. Darrin was surprised at Jon's outburst, and Jon was already feeling both pride and regret about it. Both waited for the other to speak first. It felt like high school all right. Maybe junior high.

Finally, Jon got up to go fill his water glass, and from the sink he asked "Did he say he *saw* anything?"

"Not really," Darrin answered soberly, "but maybe I didn't give him much of a chance. I thought he was goofing around... trying to scare me, ya know? Look, I'm sorry. I thought maybe you two were in on it, trying to spook a cop. I don't know Bruce, and I barely know you. Sorry."

"Ah, don't worry about it," Jon said, waving his free hand through the air in a dismissive gesture indicating he was past all that. "The point is, you guys didn't find anything to indicate that anybody had been out there. Right?"

"Right. Nothing."

"Then I think we try to get Bruce back here, away from that clinging bitch of his, and listen to his story...whether it makes sense, or not."

Pam Frey, Ginger Korte and Cathy Closter all met at "Marx Brothers" at noon that day for lunch. They were at least casual friends from the neighborhood cook-outs and gatherings, they all worked uptown, and with all the excitement from the previous day and night, it seemed like a natural, even comforting thing to do.

They took a table in the bar room side of the restaurant, which was crowded as usual at noon on workdays. Before they could order and have their talk though, there was quite a bit of give-and-take between the waitresses, and several of the patrons at the bar and other tables, all of whom they knew.

"Any more dead bodies out there this morning?" a smiling Jim Kuntsler yelled out from his table, which caused Lana Kuntsler to slap his hand and give him a pretend dirty look.

"I heard the police were out there again last night, you

poor things. Nothing more bad happened, did it?" asked their frowningly sympathetic waitress Barbara Keevan.

"They identify the body yet, do you know?" asked lawyer and former Highland High School basketball legend Jim Michelson.

Funeral Director Bill Bellicheck just did the same joke he always did when anybody so much as sneezed; he soberly walked over to the girls' table and handed them each one of his business cards, and everyone laughed, as usual.

It was a good ten minutes of friendly, concerned banter before the three, who truthfully rather enjoyed their new-found celebrity, could begin normal conversation. It was the aggressive Pam Frey who kicked things off with a bang.

"Rory is buying a gun today, do you believe it?" she whispered fiercely to the others. Pam was loud, gregarious and funny. She was also tough and strong, with an almost masculine upper torso from working for years at Bragge Furniture (her Father's store) doing a lot of heavy lifting. In fact, when most people saw Pam and the smallish Rory together, it was easy to conclude that she was the one wearing the pants.

"You're kidding!" Cathy Closter said. "Don't let him talk Jerry into getting one. He'd shoot himself in the ass in one flat minute!" There was much laughter at this. Cathy was a smiling, friendly bank teller that everyone knew and trusted. She and Jerry were life-long Highlanders, who were the warm, plump, gregarious couple that everyone is comfortable around, and that you can find in every community, if you're lucky.

They all three giggled when Ginger Korte added "Oh, Dick would too. Absolutely!" Ginger was on her lunch break from the Super Valu down the street, where she was a cashier. Of the three, Ginger had had the least amount of sleep the night before, and terrible nightmares when she finally did drift off. She had been very afraid about what she had heard, and wanted to be in a more serious conversation now. So when the chuckling died down, she tried. "Did you guys hear anything else last night; anything unusual?"

The other two looked at each other. Cathy shook her head no, then Pam looked back at Ginger and said "No, did you?"

Ginger suddenly felt chilly and reached for the sweater on the back of her chair. Though a petite redhead of only 105 pounds, which many were envious of, the little redhead was having trouble keeping warm once again, and she worked in the super cooled Super Valu all day, which didn't help. "I just wondered," she said as she put her sweater on. "I thought I heard something at about 3:00 in the morning, after Rory had gone to sleep…but I was probably imagining it."

"What did you think you heard?" Pam asked. Pam had awoken about that time too, but she wasn't aware that anything had woken her.

"It was like, uh…oh this is embarrassing… like a woman screaming. Something like that."

Pam studied Ginger's worried face for a moment, then said "Probably just a cat. They're all over town. Probably just some damn cat looking for a little action."

And the girls laughed again at that.

"I know it sounds nuts, but it happened. It was like…it was a hand…it grabbed me by the shoulder and turned me around." Bruce said. He, Jon and Darrin were standing out in Bruce's front yard in the hot sun, so that Barb wouldn't hear what he was saying.

"Have you been drinking?" Darrin asked. He had been trained to detect such things, and the bourbon was easy to smell.

"Sure have. Is that illegal officer?" Bruce said, looking directly at Darrin. It was easy to see that there was now some tension between them.

"I didn't mean.." Darrin began

"I had a couple of drinks as soon as I got back. You would've too. Scared hell out of Barb though. I shouldn't have."

Jon had been watching his friend closely, watching how sincere he was, and he was truthfully beginning to feel a vague sense of real alarm. Either his friend had had the hallucination of all hallucinations, or something really, really strange was taking place. Now, he had questions to ask. "Did you see anything Bruce? Anything at all?"

Bruce shook his head, like he didn't want to think about it, or discuss it. "I can't be sure, but, for just a second, I thought I saw the fingers of the hand on my shoulder, as it was pulling me back. I know it sounds crazy, but…"

"Exactly what did it look like?" Darrin asked, his police training kicking in again.

Bruce shook his head again. He was blushing in discomfort at the course of this conversation, and with embarrassment. "White…bony, I guess. It was just a flash. Jesus Christ this is crazy, guys…"

"Did either of you feel, and I know this sounds crazy too, but, did either of you feel a cool breeze, that didn't last very long, all of the sudden when you were in there?" Jon asked. He looked at Darrin's face first. He shook his head no, and had that cynical grimace on his face again; as though he was about at the point where he had had enough of this.

"Yea, I did," Bruce said. "Twice. Once when the hand thing happened, and again when we were walking out of there. Why?"

Jon didn't answer. He was standing there, still in his ridiculous anti-poison ivy boots, beginning to feel sick from the sun, and from the new knot of fear, or something close to it, in his stomach.

"Tell you what guys, I've got a proposal," Darrin said. He sounded rational and in charge again. "Tonight's my last night off for a week. "I'll by the beer, it's my turn," he said looking at

Jon with a smile. "Something weird's going on. Why don't we stake it out, from Jon's deck? We'll down some cold ones, sit out there, and see what happens. What do ya say?"

"I don't know," Bruce said. "Barb's still a mess, and I got to work early tomorrow…"

"Bring her over too!" Darrin said enthusiastically. Now it was Jon who glared. "Tell her the long arm of the law will be there! Nothing bad will happen."

"I don't know…" Bruce said. "Right now, I don't want to look at those woods in the daytime, much less at night. I think that…"

"Sounds good to me," Jon cut in, "especially the beer part." What he didn't say out loud, of course, was that having the law there was even better.

Chapter 11

Toward the end of the lunch hour at "Marx Brothers," as the girls were finishing their sandwiches, and most of the place was emptying out, Detective Foster walked in. Though few knew his name, just about everyone in town knew that he was the fat, loud homicide detective that was in town to help investigate the murder, if that's what it was. Word still traveled fast around Highland, even if it was becoming a lot bigger place than it used to be.

Detective Foster strode right up to the bar, slapped his palm on it, and said "Hey!" several times until one of the waitresses, busy clearing off tables, stopped to respond to him.

"Can I help you?"

"I'll have a beer and a cheeseburger!" the big man yelled out as he spun his barstool around to see just who was asking. The waitress nodded and left the room with her arms full of dishes. Foster's eyes landed on the ladies finishing their lunches. All three had been looking at him, but two quickly looked away to avoid his eyes. One of them, though, just glared right back at him.

"What have you found out about the body?" asked Pam Frey, as both of her friends blushed and studied their plates.

Foster was both taken aback and pleased with the woman's boldness. It was unusual, in his experience, for a woman, or most men for that matter, to be so direct. Besides that, of the three, she was the best looking. He liked "tough" sexy.

"Why, you know I can't discuss that with you, young lady," he said as he turned fully toward her and smiled.

"Sure you can," Pam shot right back, "we live there."

Foster sensed an opening, in more ways than one, and slid off his stool to walk over to their table. "Is that so young lady?" he asked.

"Oh God!"Cathy whispered into her plate.

"Is that so," he repeated as he walked up to the edge of the table, right next to Pam. Ginger could see his massive stomach out of the corner of her eye.

"Yea, that's so," Pam said, a little less aggressively. The huge man's proximity made even her a little nervous.

"And just who might you be?" he asked.

Pam introduced herself, and then her friends. Then she gave a quick description of where they lived on Devonshire. She was hoping his food and beer would arrive so that he would go away, but it didn't, and to the dismay of all three, he grabbed a chair from a nearby table and pulled it up right next to Pam.

"Tell ya what, Pam," he said as he sat down close enough to her that she could smell his breath, "you level with me, and I'll tell you something about the case that you don't know. How's that sound, honey?"

"I've gotta go. See you guys," Ginger said suddenly. She stood up quickly, grabbed her purse, and started to walk out. Then she remembered she hadn't paid, so she reached into her purse and grabbed the first bill she could find, a ten, which was too much, but she threw it on the table and scurried away anyway.

"That gal must be late for a fire!" Foster laughed. He was wishing the other one would leave too, and briefly glared at Cathy to see if he could perhaps drive her away, but she was studying her plate, and wasn't budging.

"My name is not 'honey'. Don't call me that," Pam said evenly. She stared straight ahead, and didn't look at him.

"Sure Pam. Just teasin' a little. No harm meant." It seemed

to Pam like he was getting even closer. "Tell me what happened in your neighborhood last night?"

"Nothing happened, really. The guys thought they heard noises, is all," Cathy answered. She was still looking down. She wanted desperately to leave, but she was trying to rescue Pam from this sloth.

"What kind of noises?" he asked, still looking at Pam.

"A big booming sound, they said. Like a gun, or a tree falling down. The police came. They didn't find anything." Cathy answered. She looked up at him, and he finally broke his stare away from Pam long enough to look Cathy in the eyes.

"Is that all?" he asked.

"The guys thought they heard someone after that…out in the woods," Cathy said. His eyes frightened her, but they were mesmerizing. "The police thought it was probably some kid trying to scare us. That's all."

Foster looked back at Pam. He smiled. "Anything to add to that, sweetie?"

Pam jumped to her feet at that, almost catching Foster in the mouth with her elbow as she did. She also found her tongue. "That's enough!" she said. "Come on Cathy. Let's go."

"But you haven't heard what I got for you, Pam!" he shouted.

They each put money onto the ten that Ginger had left, and hurried out the door. Detective Foster just laughed, and had his beer and sandwich brought to their table. Ginger had left most of her fries.

Pete Vanderberg had spent another seemingly endless day at work, and practically raced out of the Wicks' Factory when the 4:00 whistle sounded. In normal times, Pete was in no hurry to get home. In fact, stopping by the bar at the Cypress for a couple of cold beers before going home to Margie was his usual habit. Now though, things were different.

Yesterday, he sincerely felt, had changed his life. The long work day hours had given him plenty of time to think about it. The mystery of the dead body, getting to hold Barb Ellsworth (he had dreamed about that many times), a gunshot in the dark, and the mysterious sounds coming from the trees had shaken him, but also energized him in way he didn't think was possible anymore. His neighborhood was in some kind of war, he had concluded, and he was ready for it.

He had even gotten to sleep with his gun.

When he got home after the five minute ride from work though, things were, at least at first, depressingly normal. Marge wasn't home yet (she usually worked until 5:00), no one was hanging out in their yards for him to talk to, and in fact, the whole cul-de-sac seemed to be slumbering away to the hum of air-conditioners on that hot and humid summer afternoon. Pete left his car in the driveway, thinking that Margie had probably left Bobo, their Labrador, in the garage instead of leaving him in his cage out back, because of the heat. She babied the hell out of that dog, in Pete's opinion, and he didn't feel like having him slobber all over him when he opened the garage door.

After looking over at Jon's, then Barb's, and then down the street again, and seeing no sign of life, Pete unlocked his front door, went to the fridge and grabbed a beer, and then sat down in front of the TV to see if he could catch any news on the identity of the dead body.

Chief Thomas was having trouble believing what he was hearing. The Chief Medical Examiner for Madison County, the Coroner's Office along with the State's Attorneys' Office and at least several other offices were on the conference call with him, and what he was hearing didn't make sense.

"This is Chief Thomas from Highland," he finally interrupted, "are you telling me that this victim had no fingerprints... and no blood? It was drained of blood?"

"That's about it. That's what we're saying Chief," someone answered.

"What about DNA? Surely you got that?" he asked, but someone else had asked another question first, then there were a cacophony of voices, and his follow-up was lost in the ensuing chaos. He held the phone away from his ear, and leaned back in his chair. Then he looked up to see Lance gesturing for his attention through the window of his office door, once again.

Jon had, at last, a relatively peaceful afternoon, that ended with him thinking and writing notes down while sitting on his deck out back. After Darrin finally left, he took a shower, changed into jean shorts and a t-shirt, and tried to watch the Cubs game on TV. He only lasted to the fifth inning though, and realized he didn't even know the score when he turned it off. There was just too much on his mind; too much to think about.

So after making and returning a few overdue phone calls, he found himself in his favorite spot, this time on the corner of his deck, in the shade and out of the hot sun. He was happy that afternoon, because he finally had something to write about. His whole misadventure over the past day and a half had finally lighted the flame that he had been waiting for. At least he was hopeful now. The whole picture was far from clear, but he now had at least a blurry outline in his head. He spent several hours preparing for what he imagined would be the novel that he knew was inside of him. He was making lists; of everything that had happened, and then, in another column, he was writing down possible suppositions as to cause. In a third column, he wrote words that best described his feelings as a witness.

The truth of it all was stranger than fiction could ever be; so he would use the germ of these events to eventually form a great creation of art. The more he wrote down about what had happened, and perhaps why, the more ideas he got for his book to be. At least that was the plan.

Despite feeling the interminable heat of the afternoon, a pleasant breeze wafted over him occasionally from the south, and all around him it was peaceful and quiet. He imagined himself as John Keats, sitting out in the splendor of nature, gathering material for a sonnet about a nightingale, that would change the world.

Margie got home at 4:45, and as always, Pete half dreaded her arrival, or at least the monotonous routine it would invoke. She would try to say something cheerful, he would try to be at least somewhat polite with his answer, but even if it worked, it would all be phony. It was something to be gotten over with, every day.

Pete and Margie had fallen out of real love and into apathetic tolerance of each other long ago. Each cared about the other, but true affection was a rare visitor. They pursued completely separate interests, and stayed together without question for the sake of family and their standing in the church. There was nothing particularly unhappy about it, and in that way was not untypical, truth be told.

Pete heard the garage door opening, heard her enter the house and put the keys on the table, heard her go out the back door, then come back in again, and then purposefully and heavily walk into the room he was sitting in.

"Where's Bobo?" she asked accusingly.

Pete looked up at her heavily pancaked face. To Pete, everything Margie did was too much. Too much lipstick, too many layers of weird clothes, and too much make-up. If she watered the flowers, she drowned them. She ate too much. And she was too attached to the damn dog. The fact that Margie had been battling clinical depression through most of the years of their marriage did not enter into Pete's thinking. That was her doctoring.

"How should I know where Bobo is? Didn't you put him in the garage this morning?"

"No! I left him out in the cage like you always want me to!" Pete could see by her flushing color that she was getting very upset, very quickly. This too was not untypical. Reluctantly, he got to his feet. "Where's Bobo, Pete?" she screamed as she practically ran out of the room.

She sounded like Marge Simpson when she got excited, Pete thought. Kind of looked like her too. Just like Homer's wife.

Chapter 12

Rory Frey met Fred Knotts at the "Sharpshooters' Firing Range" at a few minutes after 6:00. Fred was a little late because his last golf lesson of the day had gone a little over. Despite this, Fred found his newest pupil and neighbor smiling from ear to ear with anticipation when he saw Fred pull his convertible up into the Sharpshooters' parking lot.

"I can't thank you enough for taking the time to do this, Fred," Rory said as he shook Fred's hand in greeting.

"No problem, little buddy!" Fred said gregariously. "Need some target practice myself."

Fred had called Rory where he worked, at Ace Hardware, just a few hours before to ask him if he'd like his first handgun lesson, and Rory had readily agreed. Even with the excitement of purchasing his own first gun earlier in the day, Rory had been feeling a little depressed, even a little emasculated all afternoon. First, there was the stupid three day waiting period for a criminal background check before he could have his gun (which made him feel like some kind of criminal, instead of an American man trying to protect his home and family), and then there had been the deeply disturbing phone call from Pam, telling him that she had been harassed - and even pursued - by some sick cop.

Learning how to handle and fire a gun was just what he needed. Fred was a lifesaver.

A few minutes later they were on the range. It had an

instantaneously magical effect on Rory. He felt almost immediately that this was the place he was meant to be. Everything looked bright and wonderful to him: the targets, the bullets, the ear-cover thingies, and especially the gun itself. "This is what men do," he thought unashamedly.

As Fred began his lengthy and imperious instruction on gun safety, Rory found it difficult to concentrate on what his expert was saying. He looked down at his hands and realized he was actually shaking with excitement. In truth, he had never fired a gun before, even though he'd mumbled to Fred that he'd hunted as a kid.

Jon was rudely shaken out of his writing reverie by, of all things, his doorbell ringing. This time the surprise of the loud chime only caused a wildly erratic, but ultimately harmless scribble mark on his yellow legal pad, instead of the intended letter 'e'.

"At least I didn't fall out of my God-damned chair," Jon mumbled, as he irritably but dutifully went inside to answer it. He looked at the time on his way through the kitchen. It was almost 6:00. He hoped this wasn't Darrin Crandle already. "This guy could get to be a pain in the ass," he thought.

It was Pete Vanderberg. "Sorry to bother you at dinner time, buddy," he said, "but have you seen Bobo?"

Jon had been concentrating for so long, and had been in such a different world than he found himself in now, that he could only look at Pete in wonder. He had no idea what he was talking about.

"Bobo?..My dog, Bobo?" Pete said when he saw Jon's puzzled look.

"Jeez, I'm sorry Pete," Jon said sheepishly, "it's just that I…I've been working on something else, and I…no, I haven't seen Bobo. Did he get out of his pen or something?"

"Yea, but I don't see how. The door's still locked, and the fence is way too high for him to jump over, and…"

Jon had quit listening. Having broken out of his stupor, he now was feeling two basic needs: he badly needed to urinate, and he realized that he was famished. "My phone's ringing, Pete. Hope you find the dog. Gotta run." And he closed the door and dashed for the bathroom.

Pete was left surprised and disappointed. It hadn't taken him long to realize that the missing Bobo had given him an opportunity. He could circle the cul-de-sac knocking on doors to ask if anyone had seen his dog, and try to get another Devonshire get together going for that night at the same time. It also got him away from the hysterical Margie at the same time. But Jon hadn't given him time to bring up a neighbors' get together. He thought momentarily about ringing the doorbell again, but then decided he'd get back to Jon later. He had other things on his mind.

The Ellsworth house was next. Maybe Barb would answer the door in a tight t-shirt or something.

Rory was late for dinner, and Pam was starting to worry about it. She had called his cell phone three times in the last half hour but he hadn't answered. In the Frey home, that was unheard of. Dinner was ready, and Rory had never been late for a meal without telling her in advance. He knew better than that. So after telling their 12 year-old son Robert (don't call him Bob… ever) to go ahead and start eating, she thought she'd walk across the street to see if Carol Knotts was at home. It was a long shot, but if Fred and Rory had met together earlier to buy some silly gun, maybe they were together now.

She stepped out the front door into the heat of the early evening just as Pete was giving up on getting an answer from the Korte doorbell next door. He saw Pam starting on her jaunt across the street and hailed her down by yelling out "Hey, Pam, have you seen my dog?"

She turned to see Pete waving as he walked quickly her way. The shout had startled her, and with her nerves already on edge from her afternoon encounter with the fat detective, along with Rory's overt rudeness regarding dinner, her eyes now flashed with anger. Besides, unfortunately, the only words she had clearly understood were "Pam" and "dog."

"What the hell do you want, Pete!" she demanded.

Pete's walk slowed perceptibly at the tone of her voice. An angry Pam Frey was not someone he, or anybody else, usually wanted to encounter.

"Hey…hey," he stuttered as he pulled to a halt. "What's wrong Pammy? I'm just looking for my dog is all. Bobo. Bobo ran away on us."

Pam felt a bit sorry now that she began to understand, but not much. "Look Pete, I don't have time now. I've got bigger problems." She turned and started walking double time toward Carol's. "Hope you find the damn thing!" she yelled without looking back.

Pete watched her go, and thought it best not to bring up the neighborhood meeting thing right then.

It was almost 8:00, about 40 minutes before dark, when Darrin arrived. He brought a friend with him.

"You remember this guy, don't you?" Darrin asked with his charming smile.

It was Dick Blackwell, the policemen who had (temporarily) handcuffed Jon just the morning before, although it now seemed like a lot longer ago. The slightly built cop was standing partially behind Darrin, his nervous black eyes jumping back and forth, while holding a case of beer that he seemed to be struggling with.

Jon gave Darrin a long look. He was trying to appear pissed off, but Darrin's casual "to-hell with it all" manner, and his ridiculous grin, was hard for anyone to resist.

"Hell, man, these cases are heavy! Open the door and get the hell out of the way," Darrin demanded good-naturedly.

Jon stepped back and let them in. There was no use fighting it.

Darrin had a case and a 12-pack of Bud Light, and Dick had a case of regular Budweiser. It was far more than his refrigerator could hold, so Jon was kept busy filling two coolers with beer and ice over the next 15 minutes. During that time, Dick apologized, sheepishly, to Jon for handcuffing him and held out his hand to shake, but Jon was too busy and didn't see the gesture. He did say "Don't worry about it," over his shoulder though. Dick withdrew his hand and opened a can of beer.

"I ran into Dick here and told him about all the weird things that have happened since the body was found," Darrin said as he leaned against the counter and watched Jon work. Dick had sauntered out to the deck to have his first look at the pasture and woods. "He wasn't doing anything tonight, so I asked him to come along. I knew you wouldn't mind. He's a good man. Another brain we can use to figure all this out."

Jon didn't answer, but a part of him wondered while he was working if he was just being used by these guys. They were both young cops who would love nothing better than to solve a case before the big shots could. "'I knew you wouldn't mind'" he'd said. The guy had a lot of balls, even if he was a kick to have around.

"Oh, I almost forgot to tell you," Darrin said. "Do you know a guy named, uh… Reggie Frey?"

"No," Jon said shortly as he put the last of the ice in one of the coolers.

"Well, hell, he lives on your street. Right down at the end, I think."

Still in a squatting position, Jon pivoted around and looked at Darin, who was looking at messages on his phone. "You mean Rory Frey?"

"Yea, maybe that's it. Dumb ass shot himself in the foot out at Sharpshooters' a few hours ago. Must be a real winner, huh?"

Jon stood up. "You gotta be shittin' me. Is he gonna be all right?"

Darrin looked up from his phone. "I said his foot. Sure, he'll be all right. Nobody dies from shooting their own foot, for Chrissakes."

Jon looked out onto his deck, where Dick was standing, staring out at the pasture. "He doesn't seem like the gun type to me. He's a good guy, Rory. Wife's a bitch, but Rory's OK."

Darrin went back to his messages. "Yea, well... now he's an OK guy with a shot up foot," he said.

Pete felt like climbing the walls. After a rotten dinner (Margie was too distraught about Bobo to do anything more than to warm up a can of chicken noodle soup) he was caught in the no-man's land between the evening meal and dusk. Normally his nap and news time, it quickly became a prison sentence of high anxiety.

Margie was pacing all over the place, occasionally crying, or suddenly lurching out the front or back door to give a shrill and embarrassing cry for Bobo. It made his spine crawl.

His own efforts at organizing a neighborhood get-together, using the search for Bobo as his excuse, had failed miserably, with everyone either not home, involved in other plans, or just plain, if politely, uninterested. It was hard for Pete to understand. Only Bob Benson next door had said he'd come out, and he had acted like he was doing Pete a favor. "OK, but I gotta check with Mary first," the pussy had said.

So Pete watched the clock, and the slowly setting sun, and

he started drinking beer. He paced around restlessly nearly as much as Margie; who thought that the only good (if surprising) thing about their crises was that Pete was as worried about Bobo as she was.

At a little after 8:00, Pete couldn't take it anymore. He finished the beer he was currently working on, secretively tucked his revolver into his pants, and told Margie that he was going out to look for Bobo.

It was actually Fred who shot Rory in the foot, but only the two of them would ever know about that.

"Remember, this gun is your friend, but never forget… he can be a dangerous friend,' were the grave, ironic last words Fred spoke as he held out the weapon toward Rory. It was a solemn transfer of power that never took place.

One second later there was the boom, both men jumping back in utter surprise, the gun skittering across the floor, and then Rory's first scream of pain.

"Holy shit! You shot your God-damned foot off!" were Fred's first words when he'd recovered from the shock of it.

Fred never panicked. He prided himself on that. He told stories about that. And now, faced with a sudden crisis of major proportions, he summoned all his training from the golf course, all of his legendary coolness, and went into action. As Rory thrashed around and cried out on the ground beside him, he composed, and then carried through with cool detachment, a plan that he carried out on the spot.

First the 911 call: "Yea. This is Fred Knotts. Gotta guy out here at Sharpshooter's that shot himself in the foot…No, not life-threatening, but send an ambulance."

Then he picked up the gun, and unloaded it.

Then he made sure he got Rory's fingerprints on the thing as he got down on his knees and talked into Rory's ear. "You're gonna be fine, little buddy. You shot your foot, but they'll fix you right up. You should have listened! You shot your foot."

And finally, after the paramedics had arrived and were in the process of treating Rory, he called Pam Frey.

Pam, of course, was across the street at Fred's house, talking to Carol and having a glass of wine, so it was young Robert who answered, with a mouth full of his dinner.

"Hewo?"

"Who is this?"

"Wabert Fwey."

"Robert? Is your Mom there Robert?"

"No sir." (He had swallowed)

"Well, go find her. Tell her that Fred called. Tell her that your Dad shot himself. Tell her we're headed to the hospital. Can you do that?'

"Yesh shir," Robert said through a mouth full of mashed potatoes and gravy.

Chapter 13

The three men had just gotten comfortable on Jon's deck, their chairs all facing out toward the pasture, with the beer coolers carefully placed between them, when the doorbell rang.

Jon cursed, started to get up, and then abruptly sat back down. "Screw it!" he said. "I'm not answering it this time. Whoever it is can just go away."

Darrin and Dick, who were seated on either side of Jon, both looked over at him. It was getting close to dusk. Faces would soon get harder to see.

"You sure?" Darrin asked. "I'd be glad to get it for you."

"Me too…if ya want," Dick said.

"Naw…if it's Bruce, he'll know to come around the side of the house to the back. If it's anybody else, I don't give a shit."

That settled, they sat there uncomfortably through two more rings before it stopped.

"Probably Pete, from next door," Jon said a few minutes later. "He lives next door on the other side. He's looking for his lost dog, or something."

"Isn't he the other one I took a statement from?" Dick asked.

"Yea. He's probably too dumb to figure out we're back here. He's just trying to get away from his wife."

"He smelled like vomit," Dick volunteered. Neither of the others offered to comment on this.

It was turning into a beautiful evening. The temperature

had dropped to at least tolerable, the pasture and woods were a gorgeous deepening reddish purple under the last dying rays of the sun, and the slight breeze from the south blew a damp, pleasant odor of forest and grass into their faces. It was a perfect night for sitting outside, and there were long stretches of very little conversation (and what talk there was, was general, convivial talk of sports and women) until it was completely dark.

When it got to the point where the stars were the only light, Jon went in and turned on a lamp so that they wouldn't be completely in the black. It cast a very faint glow onto the deck that didn't interfere with their view, but, more importantly, showed them clearly where the beer coolers were located.

It was when Jon came back out to return to his chair that Darrin shared some information with him and Dick. "Did a little research this afternoon," he began, "and a little poking around. The guy that owns the land we were on today is named David Meredith. Does that ring a bell?"

"Can't say it does," Jon said as he reached into the cooler between the two to get another cold one. He knew he'd better slow down soon.

"You mean the Meredith's own that too?" Dick asked. Jon thought that it was kind of strange to hear Blackwell's voice. He'd been mostly silent even during the previous small talk.

"Yea, they do. Or at least this David guy does. What do you know about them, Dick?" Darrin asked.

"They own half the damned county, is all," Dick answered. "They're the biggest, richest farmers you'll ever meet. David's the only son. He had an older brother that got killed in a farm accident years ago. David inherited most everything, I think. His old man, the one that built it all up, he died years ago. His name was Chester, I think, or something old-fashioned like that."

"See!" Darrin said triumphantly to Jon. "Pays to have a townie on the investigation, don't it!" Imagining Darrin's self-satisfied smile, Jon just nodded, which of course Darrin couldn't see.

"Every field you drive by, especially out to the south of town and even into Clinton and St. Clair Counties, the Merediths either farm, or lease." Dick added. He was pleased with his contribution, and decided he deserved another beer.

"Well then, let me ask you boys a question," Darrin began. "If they own so much God-damned land, and they're so rich and efficient and everything, why the hell don't they farm the acres we're looking at right now?"

The other two sipped their beers and thought about this for a minute. "Here it is," Jon thought, "it's finally dark, and we're sitting around the fire getting paranoid again. Drunk and paranoid."

"Maybe they use it for hunting?" Dick asked. He felt like maybe he was on a roll, but Jon stopped his momentum.

"There's never been any hunters back there. Not even during deer season. I would know. I've never even seen mushroom hunters out there in the Spring."

They all sipped beer and thought about this for a moment, then Darrin said "That's pretty strange, you gotta admit," to drive home whatever point he was making.

There was, perhaps, silent agreement that it was strange, but no one said so. "Well, I'm glad they don't do anything with it," Jon said after a few moments. "The view here is why I bought the place," he said, for about the thousandth time. He then reached for another beer, realizing he'd pretty much quaffed his last one. "Gotta slow down," he told himself. "Gonna be a long night…'

"Something else I heard today," Darrin said. "They can't get any fingerprints from that body you found. And it looks like it was drained of blood, too. It's what my source told me."

"What? What does that mean?" Jon asked. Darrin had his full attention now, and he was turned and looking at his shadowy face.

Darrin took a long pull from his beer, then crushed it in his hand in what Jon imagined was his attempt at dramatic effect. "It means they'll have a hell of a time finding out who the guy was," he said, and then belched, loud and long enough to temporarily silence the crickets, tree frogs and cicada from singing in the summer night. It was an amazing performance that left all three of them laughing.

"So much for our stakeout," Jon said. Then Dick burped, or attempted to, but it came out as a little "ugh," and they all cracked up again.

Jon wanted to know more though, and was about to ask a follow-up question when all three of them were startled by a sudden, blinding light coming from their right side of the deck. Jon and Dick instinctively pulled their heads away to the left, and Darrin jumped to his feet, but was forced to shield his eyes.

"You guys back there? Hey! It's Pete!"

All three sighed with relief. Jon, still looking to his left, saw that Darrin had drawn a gun; from where he couldn't imagine. "Put that damned thing away!" he yelled, which had the immediate effect of having Pete's flashlight go off, leaving them all almost totally blind.

Jon stumbled over one of the coolers trying to get to his deck light, but kept his balance enough not to hurt himself. When he got it turned on, the first thing he saw was Pete's face looking through the slats of the deck railing with a ridiculous grin on his face. He also saw, a few seconds later, that Darrin's gun had been put back from wherever it had come from.

"What in the hell are you doing, Pete?" was all Jon could think of to say.

"I'm out scouting around, I guess. What are you guys doing?"

No one answered. They were all still jittery from being surprised.

"Hey Jon, mind if I join you guys?" Pete asked, in almost a

plea. It was obvious that the guy was desperate for some kind of company.

"Sure," Jon answered, "come on up."

With Pete there, the atmosphere changed. It was obvious that the guy had been drinking a lot longer than they had. He was in the mood to talk, and he was too loud, and occasionally slurred his words. He wanted to tell anyone who would listen about his dog Bobo and how his wife was driving him crazy. Jon left the light on for a few minutes, and eventually got Pete quiet enough to explain who the other two guys were, and why they were *quietly* sitting there with the lights off.

Once Pete understood, he was thrilled. This was what he had been hoping for. The thrill of adventure! A stakeout! With cops!

He urged Jon to turn the deck lights back off, and said "Yous guys can trust me to help yas. I'm in!" and then belched loud enough to wake the dead.

Jon shared looks of disgust with the other two, got up to shut off the lights, and plopped down in his chair to wait out what now seemed to be a very unpromising night.

Fred felt naked without his gun. Unable to sleep, he stood smoking on his front porch, looking down toward the other end of Devonshire to see if there were any signs of life…or any threats to it. All was quiet. "Maybe too quiet," he thought.

He'd had a rough night. Pam had come charging into the Emergency Waiting Room at St. Joseph's with fire in her eyes. It had taken both him and one of the nurses to physically restrain her and explain that it was only Rory's foot that was shot. When she turned her rage on Fred for not making that clear to Robert, it actually scared him. She had looked to him like a maniac, who was capable of anything.

"I can't help it if the boy didn't tell you the whole story!" Fred had reasoned. "He shot his own foot, Pam!"

Soon enough, she switched her anger back to Rory, Robert, and the hospital staff. Still, it had been a long night, a night that was made worse by the police insisting on keeping the weapon for "tests."

As he put his cigarette out, he saw a faint glow at the end of the street, coming from behind Jon Parker's house. Was it coming from his deck? Was someone out there? Fred stood motionless and watched. A chill run down his spine. He waited.

The light went off. He waited, and listened. Nothing.

Five minutes went by before he decided to go back in. He locked the front door, but still felt naked.

It was a heavy thumping sound; like someone, or some thing, some very heavy thing, had landed hard, right in front of them, after falling from a seven story building.

Jon leaped to his feet. Darrin was up a second later. They stared out at the pasture, but could see nothing, and looked toward each other's shadowy faces. Dick and Pete kept right on sleeping.

"What the hell was that?" Jon whispered fiercely, even though he was having trouble catching his breath. The suddenness, and apparent violence with whatever had happened left him shaking. The two of them stood as still as possible, listening, and trying to see.

"Just a minute…" Darrin whispered, and he reached down to a bag by his chair that Jon had noticed earlier, but ignored (…is that where the gun came from?). He rustled around in it, found what he was looking for, then stood, and turned on the brightest flashlight Jon had ever seen. Suddenly, the tall grass of the pasture in front of them, at least a narrow part of it, was as well-lit as daytime.

"Jesus Christ!" Jon said, not bothering to whisper anymore. "What the hell else do you have in that bag?" The light made him feel giddy, and secure, all at once. It was like magic.

"What's going on?" Dick yelled. He had gone from a sound sleep to full alert in a split second. He jumped up from his chair to stand by the others. The other two didn't answer, and the three of them studied everything the beam of light illuminated as Darrin moved it slowly back and forth, and up and down the field. There was no sound, except for Pete's strangled snoring. The sudden thumping sound seemed to have silenced even the natural sounds of the night.

"We heard something out there," Jon eventually whispered to Dick.

"I sort of figured that much," Dick whispered back. He didn't move his eyes from the light.

Darrin kept moving it, methodically, over every inch of ground he could. Once the powerful light caught the beginning of the woods, and Jon was tempted to ask him to cover the whole front line of trees, but thought better of it. The sound had come from much closer than the woods, and Darrin looked like he knew what he was doing.

"THERE! There was something there!" Dick yelled suddenly. Pete stirred, and the other two felt electrified. "Go back! Slowly…slowly…THERE! Hold it there!"

Jon strained his eyes on the spot as hard as he could, but could only see tall weeds and grass.

Dick started to move past Jon, but tripped and fell hard over something.

"Take Pete's flashlight!" Jon shouted as he worked his way back to the deck lights. When he got them on, Dick grabbed the flashlight out of Pete's lap and took off down the deck steps and across the short back yard.

"What…whatsa goin' on?" a confused Pete mumbled, shading his eyes from the light.

Dick made his way to the fence, and quickly climbed over it. Between the two flashlights, Jon could get some perspective, and he could see that the spot Darrin was highlighting was only 30 yards or so beyond the fence, so maybe 50 yards from where he was standing. It was close, whatever it was.

Darrin and Jon watched Dick's progress through the tall grass with excitement, and Pete watched with confusion. Jon felt the blood pounding in his temples. He still couldn't make out what Dick had seen,

"Do you see anything?" he asked Darrin.

"Not sure," Darrin said. He was staring intently.

Then Dick got there, and the two flashlights merged. Dick stood in the light, bending over, looking at something. He reached down to it, then stood up, then reached down again. This time he stood more quickly and turned partially away. "Oh, fuck me!…Oh shit!" they heard him cry as clearly as though he were still on the deck.

"What the hell is it?" Darrin yelled out more loudly than he needed to.

There was a long pause, and they saw Pete's flashlight moving away from Darrin's circle. He was coming back.

"It's a dead dog! Mutilated!" Dick yelled from out of the darkness. "Somebody, ouch!… Shit!…Somebody sick gouged the eyes out of a big, black dog."

Chapter 14

It was a full half-an-hour later, at 2:55 in the morning, when Pete finally got his key to work, stumbled into his house, walked weaving back to the bedroom, opened the door, and turned on the lights. Margie sat up with a short, breathless scream, and saw that it was her husband, holding on to the door and its handle for support.

"Where have you been!" she more exclaimed than asked.

Fred looked at his wife, still wearing her bright red lipstick and with curlers in her disarrayed hair like some fifties TV wife. He felt a sudden wave of nausea wash over him, though to be fair, it was totally unrelated to the way Margie looked at the moment. He knew he had to get to the bathroom. Fast.

"Booboo's dead. Found him…" and then he was out the door and running for the toilet.

When Margie fully comprehended what he had just tried to say, her scream was so loud that it literally woke up half of the neighborhood.

"Sounds like Pete got home," Darrin said coolly. He was sitting at the kitchen table with a cup of coffee that Jon had just brewed, knowing from experience not to sip it until it had time to cool. Jon had his cup on the counter, and was standing by it, too worked up to sit. Sharp-eyed Dick had gone home.

Jon smiled briefly at Darrin's comment, but Margie's scream seemed like some kind of metaphor for everything that had happened to the English teacher. He felt nauseas.

"The whole world will know what happened now that Pete witnessed this. You know that, don't you?" Jon asked.

"Yea, probably," Darrin conceded without looking up from his cup. His first instinct had been not to report it to the police. "I'm the police. Dick is too! We don't need to call in anybody. It's a dog, for Chrissakes," he'd said. Now he was second guessing himself. He just couldn't stand the thought of Foster and the other know-nothing bozos cutting in on this thing. But the mutilation… had been stunning.

"I just don't see how anybody could have gotten the dog there, right in front of us, without us hearing them," Jon said as he stared out the window at the black night. "And that sound… it was like the dog dropped from the sky, Darrin! How in the world…?"

"I've been thinking about that," Darrin said. He blew on his coffee as Jon turned back toward him to listen, wanting desperately for it all to make sense.

"Yea?" Jon prodded.

"Suppose…just suppose there's somebody out there, some crazy killer who's trying to mess with us." He blew on his coffee again, then took the first tentative sip.

"I think that goes without saying now, don't you?" Jon said sarcastically.

"Yea, OK. But just listen for a minute. He wants us to think he has supernatural powers, see? So that *we* won't think logically…so that he's harder to catch. Maybe that dog, Pete's dog, was in the pasture before we even sat down on your deck tonight. All he'd have to do, then, is make it *sound* like the dog landed out there. You know what I mean?" He took a long sip of coffee, now at a tolerable, perfect temperature, then looked up to see Jon's reaction.

Jon was getting more restless by the minute, and had begun

pacing back and forth, looking at his feet, trying to think clearly. "Wouldn't we have seen the dog before it got dark? Wouldn't we have seen it when we went traipsing out there today?"

"Not necessarily," Darrin answered. "We weren't looking for it. Tonight, after that sound, we were looking for it."

"I don't know...I don't know," Jon felt like he was losing control, of everything; of his sense of logic. "What about that noise? How could anybody do that?...And what about that hand on Bruce today? And the eyes...same on the dog as on that poor dead guy! What about all that?"

Darrin could see that his new friend was losing it a little. He reminded himself that Jon had been through a lot more than he had, and in his own back yard. He tried to answer calmly, without being argumentative. "Did you ever go snipe-hunting as a kid?" he asked.

Jon stopped pacing long enough to look at Darrin and say "What in the hell are you talking about?!"

"Easy...easy, just listen a minute. There are no snipes, at least I don't think so. But when I was a kid, this guy took us on a snipe-hunt. A whole gang of us." Darrin explained. Jon started pacing again. He had forgotten about his coffee. "Anyway, he gives us each a paper bag, and we go out right after dark. 'That's when the snipes come out,' he tells us. Anyway, pretty soon he starts saying stuff like, 'That's one over there!' and 'There's one, hurry up and git 'em,' and he's chugging rocks into the bushes when we're not looking. Pretty soon the whole group of us are running and diving all over the place, thinking we're catching snipes." He paused to drink his coffee.

"So you're saying we're on a snipe-hunt?" Jon asked incredulously. He sounded more angry than inquisitive.

"No, not exactly," Darrin said calmly. "I'm saying the power of the imagination is incredible. Maybe there's a logical explanation for everything that's happened, but we're not seeing it. I'm saying maybe we're *ready* to be tricked. Maybe he's got us *ready* to believe the impossible."

Jon listened, but he kept up his pacing, and was occasionally shaking his head no. "I don't know," he said, "I just don't know. This is a sick bastard, Darrin. Doesn't seem to me like he'd be playing games. And some of the stuff…seems impossible to do! We better call this in…"

"OK, OK…you're right. I'm just saying that maybe we should assume that there's an explanation here, that's all," Darrin said. Then he smiled at Jon and said, "After all, if that dog really fell out of the sky, we've got a hell of a lot more problems than we can solve anyway, right?"

Pete woke up shortly after dawn, when Margie opened his bathroom door and it hit his sprawled out feet. He'd been lying there, snoring heavily enough for his wife to hear down the hall, ever since throwing up a few hours before.

"Pete…Pete are you all right honey?" she asked from behind the door. The position of his feet and legs prevented her from opening it enough for her to get in.

Pete's eyes blinked open to a lazily spinning bathroom ceiling, and even attempting to focus caused a new wave of nausea to wash over him. He closed his eyes. The nausea receded, but his head was pounding unmercifully. He summoned all his strength, and said "Margie, call me in sick." Then the nausea came again.

Margie heard him. She also heard him scramble, and a few seconds later begin retching violently. She closed the door, and immediately turned and padded toward the kitchen to look up the number for Wicks' Organ Company. "Poor baby…poor baby" she said to herself over and over again as she walked. Margie knew that her husband was drunk; she'd seen it many times before. But this time, she had concluded that it was all because of their poor Bobo. Her husband had heroically stayed out all night to search for, and eventually, tragically, find their lost pet. Then he had gotten drunk in his grief.

Margie felt closer to Pete right then than she had in the last 30 years.

Ginger Korte woke up with the sun, as was her habit. She had had another rough night, and was more than glad to meet the dawn. She had woken almost every hour from either nightmares, or from imaging she had heard the screaming again, that wailing in the night that Pam and Cathy thought was probably a cat. It probably was a cat, she knew, but that had unnerved her completely.

Ginger didn't have to be at work until 8:30, and her husband Dick, not until 9:00, but that made her morning time all the more delicious. It was the best hour or two of the day for her. When she got downstairs, she let her poodle out into her fenced-in back yard, went out to her front yard to get her paper (it was going to be another beautiful, warm day, she noted) and then, as always, she put her bagel into the toaster, poured herself a hot cup of coffee, and sat down at the kitchen table to look at the headlines while waiting for the dog to scratch at the door, and her bagel to pop up toasted.

This morning, like the morning before, she was looking for something particular in the Belleville News-Democrat: any news at all about the body found on Devonshire. So instead of taking her usual time to pour over each story, she instead rapidly scanned the front pages, then the "Local News," then the front pages again. There was nothing. Other than yesterday's story about the discovery of the unidentified body, there had been nothing; not in the paper, not on the St. Louis TV stations, nothing. She thought that this was odd, yet she wasn't sure. They probably found dead bodies all the time, for all she knew.

Maybe it was only a real story when they found out who was dead.

Her bagel popped up before her dog asked in. This was unusual, but not unprecedented, and she thought nothing of it as she buttered her toast, put both slices on a paper plate, and took it over to the table to set next to her coffee. It was only when she heard Gizmo start barking that she went to the back door to get him in. She went quickly for fear that the noise would wake up Dick, or the neighbors.

When she slid open the glass door to let Gizmo in, he wasn't right there, as always, ready to hop the step and come in to be fed. Instead, he was over in the back corner of their yard, barking furiously at the apple tree there.

"Gizmo! "a puzzled Ginger scolded in what amounted to a furious whisper. When he paid no attention she immediately set out across the porch and over the dew soaked lawn, determined to grab him up, scold him, and above all, stop the barking.

But when she got there, he dodged her, and kept dodging her, to determinedly yelp at the tree. So she looked up at it.

Her first thought was that it was a bad case of bag-worm. It looked like a huge indistinguishable ball of fur from where she stood with the new sun shining just over the top of their fence and almost directly into her eyes. So she moved closer, and then walked right up to it.

It took a few seconds to process what she was looking at. It was a cat. A dead cat, hanging by the neck in her tree. A cat with no paws, and with only bloody spots where the eyes were supposed to be. Right there, in their fenced in back yard.

Ginger looked at it for a long time while the forgotten Gizmo circled, still barking his head off. Despite the growing sense of terror she felt inside, and her nervous nature, she was not a screamer. She stood there studying what she knew would be a permanent nightmare, the total loss of her inner security - in an outwardly calm way.

Eventually, she picked up Gizmo, who snapped at her for

the first time, then walked back across the yard and into the house, where she shut and locked the back door, and went upstairs to wake up her husband.

Chapter 15

Ginger's husband Dick called the police, who had just received a similar kind of call from off-duty Officer Crandle about an incident in the same neighborhood. So once again the residents of Devonshire found themselves starting the morning with police cars parked on their cul-de-sac. This time there were only two cars, and there were no alarming sirens or flashing lights (it was dogs and cats, after all, not a corpse in someone's front yard), but it was disturbing to all who glanced outside, nonetheless.

Soon, Officer Jim Melrose was in the Korte's back yard taking pictures of the hanging, mutilated cat, while the Highland Police Chief, himself, Rodney Thomas was standing in the pasture over a mutilated dog, with a very sleepy Jon Parker at his side.

"Jesus Christ," were Chief Thomas' first words. "Who in God's name would do such a thing?"

Jon didn't respond. He really couldn't. He was both emotionally and physically exhausted, and Chief Thomas' knocking on his door and ringing his doorbell repeatedly after only a half-an-hour of sleep hadn't helped.

"Melrose, bring that camera over here in the field behind the Parker residence when you're done," Thomas said into his radio. There was a short, garbled answer that Jon couldn't make out, but he was smart enough to figure out something else was going on.

"Did something else happen last night?" he asked.

"Just get over here Melrose," Thomas said back to his officer, with some irritation. Then he looked over at Jon. "Did you say something sir?"

"Did anything else happen last night...in the neighborhood?"

"You don't know? One of your neighbors found a cut-up cat hanging from a tree."

Jon looked at Chief Thomas for a long moment, then back down at the dog. There were dozens of flies all over its open mouth and missing eyes, making the wounds look, at times, completely black. Jon felt weak, and sick. He needed to lie down.

Within a few minutes after the police arrived every house in the cul-de-sac, excepting the Vanderberg, Korte and Parker residences (who were otherwise variously engaged), had at least one representative out in the street trying to figure out what was going on. Fred Knotts, Pam Frey, Ralph and Barb Carmine, Jerry Closter, and Bruce Ellsworth all gravitated toward where Bob Benson was standing in the street in front of his house, which was across the street and roughly equidistant between the two parked police cars (one being in front of the Korte's and one at the end of Jon Parker's driveway). It was the type of gathering Pete Vanderberg would have loved, had he not been puking his guts out at the time.

As each new group member arrived, they were quickly and anxiously quizzed as to whether they "knew anything." No one did, so the conversation turned to general rumor and wild speculation, until a policeman came out of the Korte's front door along with Dick Korte. There was absolute silence then, as all eyes watched the policeman, who was holding a camera. He said something to Dick, then walked from the Korte front door across the Closter and Ellsworth lawns and toward Jon Parker's back yard. When he had disappeared from view, all eyes turned toward Dick Korte, who was still standing on his front porch, also watching the policeman.

"What happened, Dick? Everybody all right?" Fred yelled out for the group, shattering the silence.

Dick looked over at his neighbors and friends, looked down briefly at his slippers and robe, as if trying to decide if he was dressed decently enough, and then began his walk across the street to join them.

Rory Frey watched Dick walk over from his living room window. He was on his new crutches, and wanted for all the world to be out there, finding out what had happened, sharing his fears and thoughts with the others; just being there. But even standing there at the window was against orders. Pam's orders. She was furious with him, and would be for a long time.

"Aren't chew 'sposed to be shitting down?" his son Robert called from behind him, with a mouth full of cereal.

"… All its legs were cut off at the end, and its eyes were cut out and bloody too," Dick told them directly, if a bit inartfully. "The cop said they did the same thing to a dog behind Jon's house."

"Oh-My-GOD!" Barb Carmine cried as she raised her hands to her mouth. Her voice, even more than Dick's cold facts, sent a chill of alarm through all of them.

"This is ridiculous! What the hell is going on here?" Ralph Carmine asked.

"Jesus. Shit!" Jerry added for emphasis.

"I'm getting my gun back," Fred declared.

There was general pandemonium and alarm as the pure, pernicious evil of it all began to sink in. Their neighborhood was clearly under siege. The dead body was not a random event. There was a real, virulent threat to them, their families, their pets…to the existence of them all. It seemed undeniable now.

After a few minutes of random ideas about arming the whole block, arranging a meeting with the Mayor, setting up a neighborhood watch, and even offering a reward for capture, Bruce came up with the idea that they should talk to the police, now, while they were here. He suggested that just a few should go, so that they wouldn't look like a mob. Fred and Jerry endorsed the idea, and the three of them left for Jon's back yard. The rest either stayed to wait for the results, or reluctantly went back home to get ready for work. As a group, despite the alarm, anger and confusion they felt, they were not quite ready to become vigilantes, yet.

A minute and a half later the three men were climbing over the fence (an especially difficult task for the hefty Jerry) to approach the threesome in the pasture. Officer Melrose was still taking pictures, Jon was standing a few yards away looking pale and distracted, and Chief Thomas was warily watching the approach of the three men.

"What the hell happened, Jon?" Bruce called out to his friend as he approached.

Jon hadn't seen the three coming, and jumped a bit with surprise before seeing who it was, and answering. "You don't want to know man. It's pretty bad," he said.

"I'm going to have to ask you men not to get too close to the scene here," warned Chief Thomas, who was holding up one hand in a stop sign motion for emphasis.

The three slowed, and then stopped about 10 yards away. Chief Thomas put his hand down.

You're telling us not to get close to a dead dog?" Fred asked. He wasn't feeling too good about police since they had taken his gun away the night before.

"Yes," Thomas said, looking directly at Fred. "That's exactly what I'm saying." Then he looked down at the dog again, then up to Officer Melrose. "I want this thing bagged and taken in. The cat too. Use gloves," he ordered.

Now it was Jim Melrose who grew pale. But he merely gave a long look at the fly-covered dog and said "Yes sir," before walking slowly away.

Chief Thomas then turned to the three men again. "Is there something I can help you gentlemen with?" he asked.

"Yea, there is, Chief," Bruce answered. He recognized Thomas from seeing his picture in the paper recently. He had won some kind of award. "We'd like to know, the whole neighborhood would like to know… what's going on here? And what you guys are going to do about it. Everyone's scared now."

Chief Thomas' cell phone was ringing. "Just a minute," he said to Bruce as he pulled it out and opened it. "Yea, what is it?" He listened intently, and began pacing back and forth between the dog and the four men. Jon had walked over to join the other three. "Slow down Lance," he said into his phone, "I can't understand you. Easy now…" Then he listened for a while again. "OK, OK, send him out. Tell him where we are and tell him to come out….Yes, you did the right thing, Lance." Then he hung up.

Thomas looked up at Bruce again and said, "One more minute," and talked into his radio. "Melrose, I want you to wait on bagging the animals. Detective Foster is headed out here, and I want him to see this first. You read me?"

There was a garbled response that seemed to satisfy the Chief, and he turned his attention back to the men. "We're going to do everything we can to protect the citizens of this neighborhood," he said. "And the pets," he added. "We'll put a man on your street tonight, and beyond that…well, we'll be working on that. A County Homicide Investigator is on his way out here right now."

"That fat guy who was here yesterday?" Jon asked.

Thomas decided to ignore that one. "We'll get to the bottom of this, guys," he continued, as reassuringly as possible.

"The body, and the animals…they were all, well, mutilated in the same way. It's the same killer, isn't it?" Bruce asked.

Chief Thomas didn't want to talk in detail about it, but tried to mollify them anyway. "Now we don't know that yet. Don't be jumping to conclusions, guys. We're going to run some tests. We could have a copycat thing going on here. But don't worry; we'll get to the bottom of it, like I said."

"But there was nothing in the papers, or on TV about how the eyes were missing on the body. How could there be a copycat?" Bruce persisted.

"Look fellas," a now clearly agitated Chief Thomas said, "I can't waste any more time right now. We've got an investigation to run." And with that, he started to walk away. He went about ten yards through the tall grass before turning to say, "And stay away from the dog, please!"

The four watched the Chief walk away without saying anything, and as soon as he was over the fence Bruce, Fred and Jerry went over to get a closer look at what was left of Bobo. Jon had no stomach for it, and told the others he was going inside. He said he had a call to make.

Chapter 16

Everyone on the cul-de-sac eventually went to work that morning, albeit with troubled minds, except for Jon, Barb Ellsworth and Pete, the original corpse discoverers.

Against his better judgment, because he knew she'd now find out soon enough anyway, Bruce had come in to the house that morning and told Barb everything that had happened, with the exception of his experience in the woods. Predictably, she went hysterical, begged him to stay home from work, and kept hugging him at awkward moments as he was getting shaved and dressed, saying things like, "Oh, honey, you're right. Let's move." When he left to go to his job, she locked the door behind him, then checked to see that all the windows were latched and curtains drawn. Then she alternately read, and watched television throughout the rest of the day; too upset to do any housework, and counting the hours before Bruce returned. There would be no jogging or tanning on that day.

Pete woke up for good at noon, having no idea about the morning chaos in his neighborhood, and had two aspirins and a beer for lunch to try to appease his giant headache. He then padded around the house aimlessly with the TV on (but turned to low volume), trying to regain his physical and mental sense of balance, and trying to remember, and put in correct sequence, the events of the night before. He was cognizant of one fact though, as upset as his mind was: it was beautifully peaceful without a barking dog or Margie around.

At about 1:00, he got dressed, grabbed a shovel from the garage, and went out to get his dog and bury it before Margie came home to see it. The sun was too bright, and brought his headache back, and despite his best efforts he couldn't find Bobo. He thought maybe he had misremembered the exact spot, and so wandered in the pasture for almost half an hour, but to no avail. He went up to Jon's house to check with him, but he wasn't home, or at least didn't answer the door. He eventually gave up, went back in the house, cracked open a cold one, and found a good nature show about wolves on the "Animal Channel." He had trouble concentrating on what was happening though. He wasn't all excited about what was happening in the neighborhood any more. He had yet to admit it to himself, but he didn't want another night to come.

Jon knew that going back to bed would be impossible that morning, and as tired as he was, he knew that he had to get away, somehow. Not only would the police be all over the place, but now the press would be there in spades, he was betting. It's one thing to have an unidentified corpse to report on, but mutilated animals? They'd go nuts with that one.

He did make a call when he went back into the house, to Darrin's apartment. Darrin was sleeping, and he left a message about the cat, and about a visit he was going to make that he knew Darrin would be interested in. He then looked up another number and address, wrote it down on a piece of paper that he put in his wallet, then showered, dressed hurriedly, grabbed his keys, wallet and cell phone, and ran out to open his garage door, only to find Chief Thomas' car blocking his driveway. He had hoped to escape before Detective Foster got there with his endless questions, but no such luck.

There was no one in his back yard or in the pasture, so he trudged over to the Korte's to find Chief Thomas. When no one answered the doorbell, he walked around back and opened the gate to their fenced in back yard. There, by the apple tree, were Chief Thomas and Detective Foster, watching Officer

Jim Melrose carefully cutting down a dead cat hanging from a tree.

"Ah, excuse me? I have an appointment, and I need you to move your car. Sorry," Jon said.

Thomas and Foster turned toward him. Melrose kept working. He looked to Jon like he was about to get sick.

"What sort of appointment?" Foster asked suspiciously as Thomas began walking his way, fumbling for his keys.

"Dentist," Jon lied.

"Who's your dentist?"

"Come on Gus," Thomas said. "The kid's a teacher down at the high school." He motioned for Jon to follow him. "Come on. I'll let you out. Sorry about that."

"I've got some questions for you later!" Foster shouted as they went out the gate. "When are you getting back?"

"Bla-bla-bla, bab bla," Jon answered, purposefully too low for Foster to hear. Chief Thomas chuckled.

Two minutes later, he was a free man, and it was, unexpectedly, exhilarating. Even the act of steering his Mustang convertible around the corner and out of the Devonshire cul-de-sac was like losing the weight of the world off his shoulders. At the first stop sign, he put down the top, and turned the air-conditioning up full blast. Then he just drove and drove; out into the country, looping back into town, then back out into the country the other way… everywhere and anywhere. It was all bright and wonderful to him, whether it was cows, fields of corn, buildings, or just people walking down the street. It was freedom, normalcy and relief. He relished every minute of it.

After an hour of driving wherever the hell he felt like, he stopped at the 8th Street Café, a block off the town square, for a combination of breakfast and lunch. He felt hungry enough to order the whole menu, but settled for a double batch of scrambled eggs, toast and sausage. He remembered that Darrin had complained that he couldn't get breakfast there late one morning, and wondered what he had been talking about. The menu clearly said breakfast all day. For being so smart, he sure was dumb sometimes.

While waiting for his food, he checked his cell phone, which he had purposefully left off while he was driving. His Mother had called twice (probably saw something on the news) and Darrin had called once. He decided he would call them back later. He didn't want to talk about his neighborhood problems right then, except…

He reached for his wallet and pulled the slip of paper he had written the number and address on. It was for David Meredith, the rich farmer that Darrin and Dick had told him about, the guy that owned the pasture, the woods, and half the county. The drive had been so great; he had temporarily forgotten what he intended to do

The waitress brought the food right then, and he put the number back in his wallet to commence with a more important task: feeding his face. He would have sworn to anybody who asked that it was the best meal he had ever had, but no one did. Not even the waitress.

It wasn't until half-an-hour later, while he was outside walking toward his car with a satisfied stomach and toothpick firmly in place, that he thought to pull out the number again. He looked around and saw that no one else was outside, so he pulled out his cell, stepped into the shade of the oak tree by his parked car, and dialed the number. He got Mrs. Meredith, who within a minute or so of pleasant conversation, gave Jon her husband's cell phone number.

David Meredith answered his cell on the first ring. He was the kind of guy who sounded busy when he said "Hello," so Jon went to work fast.

"Mr. Meredith, my name's Jon Parker. I'm an English teacher down at the high school and…"

"Which high school?"

"Highland High School, sir, and I…"

"My boy goes to Highland! His name is John, too. You know him? He was a freshman this year, gonna be a sophomore."

"No sir. I teach mostly juniors. I'm calling because…"

"You'll have him in a couple of years then. He'll be a junior the year after this one, God willing."

"Yes, sir. I'll look forward to that."

"He's a good kid. You'll see."

"Yes, sir. Anyway, I'm calling because I live on Devonshire, right next to your property, and you may have heard, that… that we've had some trouble down there the last couple of days, and…"

"Yea, I heard. They find out who the dead guy was yet?"

"No, not that I know of, yet. Anyway, I was wondering if I could meet with you and ask you about a few things. It wouldn't take very long, and I…"

"Well it weren't me that kilt him!" David Meredith said, and then proceeded to laugh his head off. It took a minute for Jon to get him to listen again.

"No sir…that's not why I…"

"Come on over to the office," Meredith said, still chuckling and pleased with himself. "I do better talkin' in person. Be glad to talk to a teacher who's gonna teach my son. You know where it is, on Broadway, uptown?"

"I think so sir. I'm almost there now, I'm just over at…"

"See ya then!" And he hung up.

"Dad never farmed it, and he told me never to farm it," David Meredith said frankly. He had his feet up on his desk in a way that indicated that it was his usual posture in his "office," which wasn't more than a spare room with a lot of boxes in it that he rented from the SuperValu. It was where he did his wheeling and dealing though, and a lot of money deals took place here.

"Why didn't he want you to farm it, or put cattle there, or something?" Jon asked.

"Why? Don't you like the view the way it is?" Meredith smiled. He had the weathered Mid-Western farmer forehead that furrowed when he did business and flattened when he smiled.

"Oh no, don't get me wrong. I love it! That's why I bought it. The woods, and the pasture…are you kidding?"

"I imagine it's a nice view," Meredith said.

"But, did he ever give you a reason for staying off of it? I mean, with all the land you guys own, what's different about that land?"

"Why do you want to know?" Meredith asked sternly, forehead furrowed. Then his face turned into his big smile again, and he swung his feet suddenly down to the floor. "You're fixin' to make me an offer on it, ain't ya!" he said happily. "Teacher gonna buy him some land! Good huntin' in them woods, ya know. Gotta be!"

"No, no, no," Jon said as he waved his hands to slow the wheeler-dealer down. "I'm a teacher, remember? Can't afford that. No. It's just that, besides the body being found…some other strange things have been happening out there. It's got us wondering, that's all."

Meredith put his booted feet back up on the desk. A puzzled look had replaced his smile. "What sort of strange things?" he asked.

So Jon told him, trying to give him the facts without sounding like he was out of his mind. He covered the noise, the laughing, and the dead dog, but left out the part about the hand that Bruce felt on his shoulder.

"Sounds like you got some nut that's trying to scare the shit outta ya. That's what it sounds like to me," Meredith said when Jon had finished. "You got ya a gun?" he asked seriously.

"No, but I'm thinking about it," Jon said. He was realizing

that this was going nowhere, and thought he'd give it one more try, and then find a way to leave.

"Shotgun! That's what you need," Meredith was saying. "Don't have to aim good if you got one of them."

Jon found himself hoping that Meredith's son's grammar was better than his Dad's. "But you never had your Dad give you a reason…for not farming there?"

Meredith sighed as though he was suddenly bored. He put his hands behind his head and leaned back even further in his chair, and looked up at the ceiling. "Dad didn't explain nothin' about things like that. Rules was rules. If I woulda asked him, and I don't think I ever did, he woulda just given me one of his looks, and then go about his business." Meredith tilted his head down enough to look Jon in the eye. "And you didn't want one of them looks," he said, and then he looked back up to study his ceiling. "I had a feeling though, even when I was little, that something….something bad musta happened up there. It wasn't just Dad, but the way Mom acted too. Just a feelin' I had."

Jon felt he was finally on to something, even though he had no idea what. When Meredith didn't say anymore, he took a chance on another question. "Is your Mom, uh, still alive, Dave?"

Meredith snapped his head down sharply. "Yea. What about it?" he demanded.

This guy was as mercurial as they come, Jon thought. It made him nervous.

"I…I just thought maybe she'd know about…whatever bad happened," Jon stammered.

Meredith seemed to relax again, but he sat up and put his feet on the floor, which Jon took as a clear sign that he was about through with this talk. "On some days, she might remember, I guess," he said breezily. "She's in the nursing home in town here now. Got the dementia thing…whatever you call it."

Jon wanted to keep talking, to keep probing, but Meredith stood up, and it was obviously time to go.

They shook hands, Meredith told Jon he hoped he got his boy in class, and Jon thanked him and turned to go. As he opened the door, though, he turned around again and took one more shot; "And you haven't touched that land since your Dad died?" he asked.

Meredith smiled again. "Well," he said sheepishly, "now that you mention it…we put a few rows of winter wheat in on the south side just a week or so ago. Nothing that'll bother your view on the north end, though. But whatever the hell you do, don't tell Dad!" And with that, David Meredith laughed so hard that he had to bend over and hold onto his knees to keep his balance.

Chapter 17

Gus Foster and Rodney Thomas were sitting at a table in the back of the bar side of the Cypress Restaurant, where it was relatively dark. Sharon had brought them menus, but it was too early to eat. Gus was drinking Budweiser, while Rodney, who was technically still on duty, was sipping a cup of hot, black coffee.

"Best prime rib in town, right here," Chief Thomas was telling Detective Foster. "Best prime rib anywhere, really. Every Friday and Saturday night. Sharon is incredible. She does the cooking."

Gus was barely listening. He was enjoying the air-conditioning and the beer, and was looking up at the television news, which he couldn't hear at all, but watched intently.

It had been a long day for both of them, and it was only 4:30 in the afternoon. The "Animal Murders", as one of the TV reporters had called them, were mystifying, and unfortunately for the police, headline grabbers. Once word leaked out as to what had happened, the Highland Police Department had been besieged with calls from not only the press, but from animal lovers everywhere. Things had been relatively peaceful at the scene, until about 3:00, and then all hell had broken loose. Reporters, TV trucks, people following the TV trucks in their cars; all seemed to arrive at the Devonshire cul-de-sac at one time. Someone said that it had even been mentioned on CNN, and that they were on the way, but no one was really sure. The good part was that by the time they arrived, there was only one man home willing to give an interview. The bad part was, they headed right for the police station after that.

"N-n-no interviews t-t-t-oday. N-n-n-none!" Lance had told them as the Chief and Detective Foster made their getaway out the back door.

The Cypress had been Rodney's idea, and it had worked. They were alone, except for Sharon and a few after-work customers at the bar. It had given the two men time to think, and to relax for a bit.

"I don't know Gus. I don't know. This one's beginning to scare me a little bit, I'll be honest."

Rodney was staring into his coffee, and Gus was still staring at the TV. Gus heard him this time though. "I've called for some extra help from the state guys already, and after the TV stations broadcast this stuff, we'll be up to our asses in volunteers. We'll be fine." Gus said. "Look!" he said suddenly.

The Chief turned to see the news film of Devonshire Street, looking absolutely deserted, right up there on the television. It then quickly cut to Pete Vanderberg talking on his front lawn, then the stuttering Lance Bradley. By the time Sharon went over to turn up the volume, the story was over.

Chief Thomas was glad. "Sweet Jesus. This is turning into a circus," he mumbled into his coffee.

"Oh yea, no doubt about it. What time did you say they start serving that prime rib, Rodney?" Detective Foster asked.

Pete had had no idea what was going on when his doorbell rang that afternoon. When he answered it and saw that it was a reporter who he saw on the evening news almost every night, he was absolutely stunned. When she asked him if he would be kind enough to answer a few questions about what was going on in his neighborhood, he could only nod numbly. Before he knew it, he was being filmed right there in his front yard. It didn't go well at first:

"What was your reaction when you discovered that not only a person, but pets were turning up dead in your neighborhood?"

"It was only Bobo, my poor dog, that got killed."

"You don't know about the cat?"

"I don't have a cat."

"CUT!"

After the reporter explained that a cat had also been found dead, and Pete had been given time to collect himself a bit, things went better. Pete finished the interview, becoming more expansive as he became more comfortable, and was glad to also give quotes to the local Newsleader, and the Belleville and St. Louis papers. He said things like "We're not going to put up with this in Highland, I can tell you that much!" and generally enjoyed a half- an-hour's worth of his 15 minutes of fame.

It was only when he went back inside, pumped up again and anxious for his neighbors to come home so that he could tell them, that he had a dreadful thought.

His co-workers, and bosses, at Wicks' Organ would see him on the news - on a day he called in sick.

There were two things Jon knew when he left David Meredith's office: he had to talk to Darrin, and he wasn't going home. Not anytime soon. His car was so hot from sitting out in the sun on Broadway that he started it from a standing position, put the top up and let the air-conditioner run for a while before he got in. He tried calling Darrin twice while standing in the street waiting, but got his answering machine both times. The second time he left a message urging Darrin to call him right away.

When it was tolerable enough to get in the car, he headed across town for the Dairy Queen, where he got a frozen Coke and sat in a booth by a window to sip it slowly and kill some time. He was getting very tired, but his mind was in overdrive.

His thoughts were going all over the place, and he really wanted Darrin to call to bounce some of the stuff he learned from Meredith off him. Darrin was the realist, and Jon was starting to think about some unreal things. "…something bad musta happened up there," Meredith had said. What? What could have been so bad that a sensible man; a good, practical businessman, would want to avoid it forever…and want his son to avoid it forever? What about that first son? The one that Blackwell said died in a farm accident? Could that be important?

His phone rang. He looked quickly, saw that it was Darrin, and answered it.

Ginger had been fine all morning, but started coming apart on her lunch break. She was alone then, at Yogi's having one of the delicious cheeseburgers that she loved so much. The trouble was, there was time to think.

It started when she was chewing on her first bite of cheeseburger, with the simple thought that she would be going home in three more hours. She started shaking then, and she didn't know why, and she couldn't control it. She tried to sip her Diet Pepsi, and spilled some on the table. The cat. She could still see that poor cat.

She couldn't catch her breath.

She left, without eating another bite.

Twenty minutes later she was working checking out groceries again, but she was crying softly. The customers could see it. The assistant manager saw it, and she was soon in the manager's office, trying to explain.

But she couldn't. She just cried.

And then she was sent to the last place she wanted to go. Home.

Darrin's apartment was a wreck. To Jon, who was neat by nature, it looked like the bachelor pad from hell, with clothes strewn literally everywhere, the furniture dirty and beyond shabby, and what passed for a kitchen table covered with uneaten parts of meals.

"Jesus, you're a pig!" he said in wonder after his first look around.

"Eat shit," Darrin answered as he picked the clothes off a chair that he was going to invite Jon to sit on. "I'm a busy man. Sit down and fill me in, asswipe."

Jon walked over to the chair Darrin had cleared and dusted it off elaborately with both hands so that Darrin would see.

"All right, all right, you made your point," Darrin said grinning. "Want a beer?"

"Sure… if it's not covered with dirt or something."

Jon had a Bud while Darrin sipped a Pepsi (this being a working night), and Jon told him about his visit with David Meredith, emphasizing Chester Meredith's mysterious order never to farm the land, David's feeling that "something bad" had happened up there, and the recent planting of the winter wheat on a south side portion of it.

When he had finished, Darrin seemed to be lost in thought for a few moments, but then snapped back with "That's all bullshit. Weird bullshit, but bullshit."

"You were the one who said get all the facts," Jon said defensively. "I'm just telling you what the man told me!"

Darrin got up and started pacing the room. "You're thinking there's somebody, or something in those woods, aren't you?" he asked, a bit derisively. "You and your friend Bruce are trying to convince yourselves that it's haunted, or something, aren't you?" He was grinning broadly, as though it was all ridiculous and laughable, but he was also pacing around, Jon noticed. He's a little more unsure of himself than he's acting, Jon surmised.

"I'm not saying I believe anything like that, but I'm trying to look at all the facts," Jon repeated. "We've got a dead body that they can't identify, right? Isn't that unusual, with DNA, and all that shit?"

"That stuff takes time…"

"We've got a dog killed the same way, it looks like. And a cat! You should have seen the cat! And the laughing, or whatever it was, and…damn it! Do you have an explanation for any of this stuff?"

Darrin stopped pacing and looked at his worked up friend. "Easy. Easy partner…I'm on your side, remember? I just think there's got to be something here that we're missing. I agree it's strange, but…"

"Where are you assigned tonight?" Jon said suddenly.

"I…I don't know," Darrin answered, a little taken aback by the change in tone. "Probably general patrol. I won't know until I get there."

"Can you request Devonshire? The Police Chief said he was going to assign a cop to our street tonight."

"I'll ask, but who knows?"

"God…that place will be nuts tonight," Jon said as he looked absently out Darrin's dirty kitchen window. "Pete…and Fred… oh Jesus, Fred." Then he suddenly looked up at Darrin, got to his feet, and said "Gotta go!"

"What? You haven't even opened your beer?"

"Going to see somebody at the nursing home. Talk to you later, Darrin."

And he was out the door.

Chapter 18

Between 4:30 and 5:00 on that scorching hot Friday afternoon, most of the worried residents of Devonshire Street began arriving home. Unlike other, normal days though, each new arrival had a growing number of witnesses. The instinct of everyone was to watch who came home, and then to walk over and talk with them. In appearance, if we once again imagine a soundless, overhead shot of the neighborhood, it would have not looked too different from the early part of Halloween night, with parents accompanying their children from house to house for candy and friendly conversation. But today instead of jackets and gloves, the residents willingly sweated through whatever work apparel they happened to have on, and instead of candy, they sought reassuring company in a time of worry.

It was Mary Benson's idea that a potluck should be organized. It was Friday night, she had said, and a perfect time for everyone to get together and have some fun. Pam Frey, Cathy Closter and Pete Vanderberg, who were standing in the street talking with Mary at the time, all hailed this as a wonderful idea, and quickly split up to tell everyone about, and to prepare for, a giant neighborhood cookout.

They decided, even in the 98 degree weather, to hold their party right there in the street in front of the Benson's house, rather than in the cool shade of someone's back yard. No one said it, but it felt somehow safer that way. 6:30 was the designated time, shorts and t-shirts the order of the day, and soon the neighborhood was bustling with people, tables, grills and lawn chairs all happily moving toward the cul-de-sac's end.

No matter how good they tried to make nursing homes smell, Jon could always detect the faint odor of urine. The sickening, sour smell hit him as soon as he walked through the front doors of Highland Towers. It reminded him instantly of the seemingly endless visits he made as a boy, tagging along with his Mom to see his grandmother in the years before she died. He remembered the smell, the crushing boredom, and, eventually, the sadness of it, vividly, as he approached the cross-looking woman at the front desk.

"Yes?" she said with a raised eyebrow that reminded him of some probably long dead old teacher he'd had in grade school.

"I'm here to see Mrs. Meredith, please." He didn't have a clue as to what her first name was.

She immediately referred to some list that she had in front of her, and said "Are you related to Mrs. Meredith?" without looking up.

"I'm her brother," Jon said.

The old bat's head snapped up so fast that it scared him.

"I mean nephew! Nephew. Did I say brother? That was silly of me, wasn't it?"

She looked at him, with that eyebrow arched even higher, for a long moment. It was like she was waiting for him to crack. "Name please?" she said finally.

"Jon Meredith," he lied.

At that, she seemed to give up, and told him to sign in, and where Mrs. Meredith could be found.

She was in her room, in a wheelchair, watching television with the volume turned so far up that it made Jon's head throb.

She looked as grey, frail and old to him as his grandmother used to, and as all the other residents probably did too.

He decided to be bold. What was there to lose? He walked right over to the TV, turned it way down, then grabbed a chair from the corner as though he'd done it a thousand times before, placed it in front of her wheelchair, and smiled at her confidently as he sat down. "Hi, Auntie! Do you remember me?"

The old woman looked totally confused and surprised. Her mouth opened, but she didn't say anything. She looked at him intently. Jon waited, and smiled, and wondered if he had just made a huge mistake.

Suddenly, her face changed into the beginning of, perhaps, a smile. "Of course I remember you!" she said in a croaking voice. "I would never forget my Billy!"

And so it went. Whoever Billy was, Lilly Melrose had a lot to tell him. Jon was soon overwhelmed with story after story from the past; and usually the far distant past. He could hardly get in a word edgewise for the first 20 minutes, other than an occasional "Yes ma'am," or a "Yes, I remember." The old woman seemed to think that Billy, despite the huge age difference between the two, had been with her through all of what she remembered. So Jon listened, and nodded, and listened, and told himself that even if he found out nothing of value, he was at least doing a service. The poor old thing acted like she'd never had a visitor before.

"Can you get me a glass of water Billy?" she said right in the middle of a story about her school days. Then she stopped talking and just looked at him.

"Sure! Sure! Coming right up!" Jon said, seeing his chance. He went over to her bedside, poured her a half a glass of ice-water, and took it over to her wheelchair. He waited until she was fully engaged in chugging it down before he spoke.

"Grandma?...I mean Auntie, tell me about the farm land that Chester would never farm. The land where something bad happened."

She finished off the last of the water, sighed heavily, and held the glass out to Jon. "More please Billy," she said as she wiped her mouth with her free hand. "Who's Chester?" she asked.

By 6:30, the neighborhood feast was in full swing. The smell of hamburgers, ribs and even steaks wafted through the air, and smiling men, women and children were filling their plates with an impossible variety of salads, beans and even homegrown vegetables. Lawn chairs and mini-tables were scattered from the front lawns of the Bensons and Vanderbergs to the middle of the street in front of those two residences. There were games of washers, horseshoes and cards, and an atmosphere of joy and camaraderie that no one had expected, but everyone wanted to hold onto. Even Ginger Korte and Barb Ellsworth had joined the upbeat gathering; the former after a long talk with Pam, the latter after a similar talk with Bruce. And yes, even the wounded Rory Frey had been given permission to come.

The sight of all this more than shocked Jon Parker as he whipped his Mustang into the Devonshire cul-de-sac, after having eaten a delicious supper at E.L. Flannagin's, in order to stay away from his neighborhood for as long as possible. He saw the crowd at the end of the street by his house, suspected something awful, and slammed on the brakes as hard as he could. The car skidded to a stop, eventually facing sideways, with an enormous screeching sound that so alarmed Fred Knotts that he dropped his full plate of food right onto his wife Carol's lap, and shocked everyone else enough to make them momentarily duck away in unison.

Jon sat in his car for a few seconds and looked at his neighbors. They all stared back at him like motionless mannequins, excepting Carol Knotts, who was jumping up and down and frantically fanning her lap. Jon saw the food, the tables, the games, and surmised the truth of the matter in just a few moments. So he turned off the engine, got out of his car, and yelled "Honey! I'm home!" to all his neighbors.

Only Fred laughed.

When Darrin pulled up in his police car, parking it in front of the Korte's in deference to the party, it was like pulling the curtain down on the happy gathering. It didn't cause the total silence that Jon's already legendary arrival had earlier, but it had a sobering effect on everyone. Most of them watched the car park, and then, instinctively, teamed that with a look up at the slowly disappearing sun. Uneasy, cold reality began to seep back in.

Darrin, for his part, could see this as he walked up, and used his smile and a cheery "Good evening, folks," to try to dissipate the new gloom as best he could. It worked partially, as a smiling Cathy Closter offered him a plate of food, and a few of the men he didn't know came over to introduce themselves. Though the mood was dampened, no one left the party for home. There wasn't even a thought of it.

Darrin politely declined all offers of food and drink, and eventually worked his way over to where Jon was sitting in his lawn chair next to Bruce and Barb (though men tended to sit and talk with men, and women did the same, Barb would not leave her husband's side).

"Find out anything on your trip?" he asked Jon.

Jon gave a quick glance toward Barb, then shook his head no. Darrin looked at Barb, saw her clinging to Bruce's arm, and understood.

"Are you going to be here all night, or what?" This rude sounding question came from Fred, who was standing right behind Darrin.

Before he could turn and answer there was an "OW!!! Jesus

Christ, watch where you're going. DAMNIT!" shouted from one of the tables, so everyone turned and looked. It was Rory Frey, whose wounded foot had just been stepped on by his son, Robert.

"Soowy. I didn't do it on poopus. Soowy," Robert said. He had a mouth full of hot dog at the time.

"I'm assigned to Devonshire for the whole night, sir," Darrin informed Fred. "Hopefully, you can all rest easy tonight."

"That's good," Fred said. "Why don't we tell the others? It'll make everybody feel better." Before Darrin could react, or Jon could say that he thought everyone already knew, Fred yelled out in a booming voice "Hey everybody! The cop's going to be here all night! We can all rest easier!" Then, for some reason known only to Fred, he turned in the direction of the pasture and woods, cupped his hands to his mouth and shouted, "DO YOU HEAR THAT OUT THERE! THE COPS ARE HERE ALL NIGHT!"

No one but Fred laughed. And then it was quiet, again.

Chapter 19

Ginger Korte couldn't sleep, which wasn't surprising. Her husband Dick had held her tight and reassured her over and over, until he fell asleep. He was snoring, like he always did when he had been drinking, and it was loud enough for her to hear at the kitchen table, where she was smoking a cigarette in the late night, even though she had quit smoking, again, two months before. The snoring didn't bother her. In fact, it was reassuring somehow. It was rhythmic, predictable, steady. She sat at the table, in the dark, with a confused Gizmo asleep at her feet, smoking, and trying to get up the nerve to look outside again. It was getting close to 2:00 in the morning.

She had looked out back once, and out front twice. There had been nothing out back, and just the policeman out front. But he had been sitting in his car the first time, and the second time the car was empty. This was a small thing, but it had unnerved her terribly. So she didn't look out back the second time or out front for the third. She was afraid to. She knew it was silly, but that's the way it was.

So she sat, and smoked, and waited. After a while, she told herself, she'd get up her nerve, and look out front again. If the policeman was out there, she would try to go back to bed. If he was not, she would stay up, and smoke. And listen. And worry.

There Comes a Moment...

Pam Frey couldn't sleep. Rory was sleeping like a baby, and Robert had been in bed before his parents even got home from the cookout. She had tried, but after an hour of tossing and turning she gave up, came downstairs and turned on the television. She had gone through the channels, trying to find something interesting, but now was giving up on that too. She switched off the remote, and looked up at the clock. Almost 2:00 A.M. At least she didn't have to work in the morning.

She went to the refrigerator, opened the door, and found nothing interesting. Then she heard the noise, very clearly. It was like something very large and very heavy, had fallen down somewhere outside, right as she closed the refrigerator door. She stood absolutely still, and listened. She heard only the ticking of the clock. As best as she could tell, the noise had come from the front of the house. At least she thought so. At least that's what it sounded like. Something big. Something very close to her house.

Very slowly, and quietly, she began walking in that direction.

Jon had been sleeping very soundly, but woke with a start. He saw his clock first thing, again. It said 1:58. He knew something had just happened, again, but he didn't have any idea what. He lay motionless, and listened. He actually prayed that there would not be a scream. There wasn't. There was nothing. He took a deep breath, and sat up. A flash of light whizzed by his backyard window. Then again.

He whipped off the sheet covering him, and fumbled for his sandals by the bed in the dark. He felt like his heart was in his throat. When he got them on he scrambled out of the bedroom, down the hall, through the kitchen and to the door leading out to his deck. He turned on the light, tried to pull the door open once, forgetting that he had locked it, and hurt his hand in the process. He cursed, unlocked it, pulled it open, and stepped out onto the deck.

It was Darrin. He was standing in the yard just off the deck, pointing his flashlight out toward the pasture.

"You jackass!" Jon yelled. "You scared the hell out of me!"

"Turn off the light, will ya?" Darrin said without bothering to look at Jon. "I heard something out there."

Jon followed the flashlight's beam out into the pasture. He saw only grass, waving in the slight, chilly breeze that had come up. But he dutifully reached in to shut off the light, closed the door, and walked across the deck toward Darrin. "What kind of noise, Mr. Policeman?" Jon asked. He enjoyed getting the chance to play the cynic for a change.

Darrin looked over at him. His face looked troubled. "I can't explain it, exactly," he said. "I guess it wasn't too different from the sound...the sound we heard when we found the dog."

He looked back out toward the pasture and woods, and Jon did too. The wind seemed to be picking up. Darrin flashed the light all the way to the woods, and ran it slowly along the tree line, but neither of them saw anything unusual. The branches of the trees were moving in the new wind, which looked eerie in the powerful light, but there was nothing unusual.

"Maybe it was..."

"SSSHHH!"

Darrin grabbed Jon's arm hard to shut him up, and kept it there. They both held their breath and listened.

There it was. It was the laughing sound again. An inhuman, gurgling, laughing sound, coming from out there, somewhere. It was clear, and sounded close, then further away. It started, then stopped abruptly, then started again, only this time it seemed, from a slightly different direction. Both men stood listening, and (they couldn't help it) terrified.

Then there seemed to be two voices. Then one again. Then it stopped. They stood frozen, listening, but heard only the wind, which was diminishing slowly again. They waited, but the laughing was gone.

"Oh Jesus," Jon said, and as soon as he said it, there was a piercing, terrifying woman's scream, coming from the street behind them. For a moment Jon and Darrin, already on sensory overload, just looked at each other. "I think it'd be better if you quit talking," Darrin said.

They turned in tandem and started running; around the east side of Jon's house, through the yard and onto Devonshire where, as soon as they were even with the Ellsworth house they saw something so surprising, so unexpected, that they slowed to a trot, and then stopped in the middle of the street.

There in front of them, like some sort of optical illusion, was Darrin's police car, covered in white.

"What in God's name?" Darrin exclaimed. "What the hell?" He drew his weapon and started walking, carefully, toward what had been his vehicle a few minutes before. "You better stay back," he told Jon.

When he got past the Closters and within 20 feet of his car he saw Pam Frey out of the corner of his eye, and quickly whirled and pointed his gun at her. She was standing in her yard with her hands up to her face, and he saw immediately that she wasn't a threat. She had been the screamer.

The front porch light at the Korte's came on, then the Carmine's across the street, giving an even more ghostly effect to the covered car. The light sleeping neighbors were getting up to see what had happened.

Darrin walked steadily right up to his car with his weapon at the ready. After a moment of indecision, he took his left hand off the gun and reached out to touch it. Then he pulled on it. "It's some kind of sheet!" He yelled out to Jon, and anyone else who might be listening. "Some joker covered it up with a sheet!" he shouted angrily as he began pulling it off the police car.

"They don't make sheets that big," was John's first thought, as he began, with any danger apparently past, walking over to have a look for himself.

"Did you see who did this?" Darrin shouted at Pam. He was mad enough to shoot somebody. She just shook her head no, with her hands still covering her mouth.

The Korte's front door opened, and Ginger stepped out. At the same time Ralph Carmine yelled "What's going on over there?" from his porch. Lights were coming on everywhere.

Darrin pulled, with some difficulty and with Jon's help, the rest of the heavy white cloth off of the car.

"It feels more like a blanket than a sheet," Jon said, but Darrin wasn't listening. His anger was boiling over. He had been set up.

"How about you?" he shouted at Ginger, whose porch was close enough that he could have used his normal voice. "Did you see anything? Did you see who did this?"

Ginger looked at him as though she was in a sleepwalking daze, and didn't respond immediately. Jon thought she looked tinier, and more helpless than ever.

"Lady, did you see anything?" Darrin repeated impatiently.

Ginger switched her gaze from Darrin, to the car, and then to Jon. "It …just wasn't there…and then it was…" she said softly; hypnotically. Then she looked at the white cloth that Darrin was holding. "Like a burial shroud…" she said.

Chapter 20

"So you come back from investigating the noise, and the police car is covered, with that…that thing," Chief Thomas said, pointing to the white cloth "evidence" from the night before. "Then what?"

"Well, I pulled the thing off, of course, and asked if anyone had seen who had pulled the prank," Darrin said.

"So you think someone was pulling a prank. Someone from the neighborhood, maybe?" Detective Foster asked.

"I really don't know. Maybe." Darrin answered.

The three of them were "debriefing" Darrin's night shift in the hot, stuffy Police Chief's office. It was 8:30 on another steaming July St, Louis morning. The door opened before anyone else could say anything. "C-c-coffee's r-r-ready. Anybody w-w-want some?" Lance Bradley asked with his head leaning around the door.

"Not now, Lance," Chief Thomas answered for them. "Maybe in a few minutes." Lance nodded and closed the door…

"Well, I c-c-c-c-could have used some!" Foster said, then laughed at his own joke.

Chief Thomas ignored him. He leaned back in his chair and ran his hand through his thinning black hair. He felt like he'd aged five years in the last few days. "You said there seemed to be one person who saw it happen…ah," he sat up abruptly and looked down at report in front of him, "ah, Ginger Korte. Yea, that's it. Tell us about her," he said as he looked up at Darrin.

Darrin looked resentfully over at Detective Foster first, irked by his remark about Lance, then back at his boss. "She was out of it. She was the woman who had the cat hung in her yard. You could tell that she was scared shitless, sir, if you'll pardon the expression."

"But what did she say?" Chief Thomas asked. His eyes were almost pleading.

Darrin sighed. "She said, 'it wasn't there, and then it was,' or something like that. She said it just appeared. She's a little nuts, I'm telling ya. I'm not even sure she really saw anything."

Chief Thomas leaned back in his chair again, yawned a nervous yawn, then looked over at Gus Foster. "So now we've got somebody playing games," he said dryly, "and we know there had to be at least two of them - one for the distraction, and one for the, uh, trick. And we don't know if they had anything at all to do with the… the other stuff."

"Tell me again about the noise you heard, that made you leave your car…to investigate, or whatever?" Foster asked. Darrin could hear unmistakable sarcasm in his words, but he tried to ignore it. Foster tried to get to everybody. He could play that way.

"There was a loud, thumping kind of noise, a lot like what we heard right before we found the dog the night before. It seemed to be coming from the south, toward the Parker house, and the field. I took my flashlight and walked back there, and that's when I, and Mr. Parker, heard the laughing."

"You both heard it?" Foster asked.

"Absolutely, sir."

"What kind of laughing…Male? Female?"

Darrin was getting frustrated, because he'd already reported all this, and because it was almost impossible to answer this question. "It was like, it could have been either male or female… it was loud, louder than it should have been from so far away, like they had a megaphone, or something," he said. "It got our attention, let's put it that way."

"It had to be a bunch of kids, puttin' one over on you," Chief Thomas said, more dismissively than he actually felt. "Tonight I want two people, two cars out there, whether we can afford it or not. One man stays with the cars at all times."

"And I've got a couple of good men coming from up north for the day," Foster said. "I'm going to have those poor bastards walk every inch of them woods, see if they can find anything. Hey...at least there were no bodies this morning, Rod," he added, seemingly (if oddly) defending Darrin. Then he stretched and yawned as if he had been the one up all night, and he was the one who needed to sleep.

"What about the body Chief? It's been days now. Do we have anything yet?" Darrin asked. He felt like he deserved to know something they knew, after all this.

The Chief exchanged looks with Foster, as though he was trying to decide if he should give away information or not. Foster shrugged his shoulders. "The body you found, it looks like it's been dead a long time, Darrin, like we first thought," the Chief said. "They're telling us it was...mummified, sort of, and somebody hacked it up right before they put it out there on Devonshire. That's why there was still a smell to it. It was disfigured just hours before they put it there, but it might have been dead for years...decades maybe. Not like that cat and dog."

"So we don't have a recent murder victim. That's the bottom line. It'll be public in a few days, when the pathologists and those other fuck-ups finally get through with it," Foster added.

Darrin was startled, but not deeply surprised by this news. In a sick kind of way, it fit. "So that body...it could have been dug up from somewhere. It was already dead?" he asked.

"Well, maybe, but there's the mummy part of it to consider," Foster answered. "It takes special chemicals to do that, they tell me. We're still waiting for a full explanation, right Rod?"

"That's right," Chief Thomas concurred. "And the press is

all over us because we have an animal mutilator. They don't give a damn about some old body anyway."

He leaned back in his chair and ran his hand through his hair again. There wasn't much more that he could think of to do, and it was killing him.

After a minute, he decided to let Officer Crandle go home, and to have a talk with Detective Foster about not calling him "Rod" in front of his men.

It was, for the most part, a normal Saturday morning if you lived on the Devonshire cul-de-sac. Lawns needed mowing, groceries needed to be bought, and yard sales spotted throughout the Cambridge Meadows subdivision needed to be inspected. The residents of Devonshire had things to do, on what was a day off for nearly everyone.

Only Fred Knotts (golf pro) and Pete Vanderberg (his boss had called and left a message for him to work Saturday after watching the 10:00 news) had to work that day.

Most of the rest spent the morning in normal, blissfully simple and even boring domestic pursuits.

Only Jon Parker and Ginger Korte slept well toward noon while the others dawdled; Ginger's sleep the troubled, intermittent slumber of the deeply disturbed, Jon's the unknowing, blissful blackness of the dead tired. They had been, one by her nature and the other by geography, the most affected by it all, and they each sought in their own way, and for their own reasons, sweet unconsciousness during the busiest… and safest, time of the day.

Those who were spending time outdoors, however, could not help but notice one big change from the typical summer Saturday morning routine: traffic. Sightseers, many on the pretext of searching for yard sales, found themselves driving down Devonshire with depressing regularity, to satisfy their curiosity, all morning. At first Jerry Closter would raise one hand off his lawn mower to wave at each car that circled in front of his house. At first Ralph Carmine would turn on the step ladder he was standing on to clean the gutters, and strain to see which neighbor had, perhaps, arrived home with groceries. At first Pam Frey would look up from her spading and smile congenially at each vehicle turning onto her street, assuming it to be a comrade from the wonderful picnic the night before.

But soon all three, along with anyone else who happened to be tinkering outside, gave up greeting the visual looters. They were, their street was, their neighborhood was, suddenly infamous. The press had seen to that. They were objects to be studied from the safety of an air-conditioned front seat; with pity, and wonder. This neighborhood, this street, was where animals got mutilated.

Bruce Ellsworth watched them by continually peeking out his living room curtains each time he heard an engine turn the corner and head their way. Each one that came down, slowed, pointed, and slowly wheeled away in a circle only irritated him more. He was, nominally, trying to finish the novel he was reading, sitting there on his living room couch. In truth though, he kept starting the same page over and over again.

He had at least gotten Barb to go outside. With his persuasion, she had finally judged things safe enough to sunbathe in the privacy of their back yard…as long as Bruce was home. But he was growing more irritable as the long morning dragged on. He needed the clock to get to noon. That's when the realtor was coming over.

Dick Korte had called the doctor's office, and had spoken to a nurse. He was worried about his wife, and thought that perhaps something could be prescribed.

"You live there where they killed those poor animals?" the nurse had asked (nothing about the dead guy). She informed Dick that he would have to bring Ginger in to see Dr. Haffash, that they couldn't just give a prescription over the phone, and that they closed at 12:30.

He told the nurse he would bring her in and was pacing around the house now, trying to decide if he really should. The poor thing had only been asleep, really asleep, for three hours. And she might refuse to go in anyway, the way she was acting.

It was the kind of quandary he hated, but at 11:30, he went up the stairs to wake her up.

It was right about that time that Fred Knotts got his gun back. He had to cancel two lessons at the club to get away to do it, but he did. After leaving the police station he drove while holding his pretty baby in his right hand. He also found himself wondering if it was today that Rory got his weapon. He thought about calling his friend to see if he wanted a ride to go pick it up, but knew that Pam was home, and might answer, so he decided not to. To hell with it, he thought. They'd all be armed soon enough. The bottom line was, he felt complete now. Safe, now.

It was before Fred could get back to the golf course to give the fidgety and dangerously wild Beatrice Landiss her weekly lesson, right at noon, that Jon's blissful sleep was ended, once again, by the ringing of his doorbell. It rang once, twice, then a third time before he could even get out of bed, and kept ringing until he got to the door and opened it.

"What do you do kid, sleep all day so you can stay up all night and report weird shit to the police?" Detective Foster asked. To Jon, he looked somehow even heavier standing there in the doorway than he'd been the day before.

"Good one," Jon answered while yawning, "What do you want, anyway?"

Detective Foster did a half turn to watch the latest tourist making the turn-around in front of Jon's house. "You ought to set up a lemonade stand out here, you know it kid?" he turned back to Jon. "You could make some real money today, boy."

Jon had no idea how to take this guy, and didn't feel like trying. "What do you want?" he repeated.

Foster smiled. "Little touchy today?" he asked. When Jon didn't answer and just stared at him glumly, he said "Well, two things, teacher. One, I need to talk to you about what happened last night, along with a few other things. Second, I've got two guys that are gonna join one of the locals that are going to set up in your back yard in a few minutes. They'll be searching the field and woods, and your yard will be where they'll organize, and it'll get walked on a little. You OK with that? Cause if you're not, we're gonna do it anyway."

"Great," Jon said as sarcastically as he could. He opened the door wider. "Come on in. Let's get this over with."

Chapter 21

"We're supposed to cover every damn inch of ground of this damned pasture, and the God-damned woods too, looking for God knows what! That's what the hell we're gonna do!" answered one of the ill-tempered "special investigators" who had been assigned to Detective Foster for the day.

Officer Jim Melrose, the local policeman assigned to help the two, had asked an innocent enough question: "What exactly are we supposed to do?" he'd inquired. Now he knew. He looked out at the pasture that he'd been in so recently to photograph and bag up a dead dog, and where now he would be walking and sweating in the hot sun all afternoon. He was starting to wonder just how much he was going to like working day shift. The first two days were putting a real damper on his initial enthusiasm for the move.

He was in full uniform, and hardly ready for the trek. The other two had had enough advance notice to at least dress for the outdoors.

"Take one of the canteens there and fill it up, 'the other investigator said. "You're going to need it."

Officer Melrose went over to the pile of various equipment they might need that was piled in Jon Parker's back yard. He picked up a canteen that looked like it came from World War I, and dutifully went over to the garden hose to fill it up. He felt the mid-day sun burn the back of his neck while he bent over his task.

"This was going to be one hell of a damned afternoon," he called out to the other two.

Neither of them so much as smiled.

After patiently answering Foster's questions, which seemed designed to check out the story Darrin must have already told him, Jon showed his inquisitor the door, and went to get ready to get the hell out of there. There was no way he was going to stay around offering iced-tea all afternoon to whoever happened to be around, especially if it was Foster.

So after cleaning up and putting on jeans and a nicer shirt than usual (after all, he didn't know where he was going to end up), he sped his Mustang out of the cul-de-sac and into the normal world, without telling the Detective he was leaving.

It was going on 1:00, which was still the middle of the night for Darrin, but he decided to give him a ring anyway. To Jon's surprise, he answered; sleepily.

"Yea?"

"You're up!"

"Yea. What time is it?"

"You can't even find a clock in that mess of a place you've got, can you? It's almost 1:00. Feel like gettin' a cheeseburger?"

There was a pause, then "Yea, sure. Where?"

"How about 'Yogi's,' on the square. Ever been there?"

"Nope."

"Great burgers."

"Give me 15 minutes," Darrin said.

Margie Vanderberg didn't know the true story about what exactly had happened to her Bobo until early that Saturday afternoon. Though she had talked to nearly every adult in the neighborhood at the cook-out the night before, the subject of the mysterious dead body and the mutilated pets, by mutual, unspoken agreement, had never come up. Pete had told her that the dog was found dead, that's all, and she really hadn't wanted to know any more.

But now, by chance, as she was taking a bag of Bobo's things out to the curb for the garbage men to pick up (she already couldn't stand to look at them), she looked up and saw Cathy Closter standing in her yard across the street. Cathy was looking at the car in the Ellsworth's driveway, which had "Frey Real Estate" written on the side. The obvious implication of this made her want to share the news with someone, and when she saw Margie, with the ever present curlers in her hair, putting the bag out to the curb, she immediately walked over to share the gossip.

"The Ellsworth's have a realtor at their house! Do you believe it?" Cathy said before she had even fully crossed the street.

Margie looked up in confusion, first as to who was talking, second as to whether they were talking to her, and third, trying to remember who the Ellsworths were. Margie usually went by first names only.

"Do you think all these…killings, have them wanting to move?" Cathy asked her dumbstruck friend as she walked up beside her. "What are you throwing away, honey?" she asked, even though she could plainly see Bobo's dog toys in the open bag.

"Oh, nothing," Margie said, recovering a bit. Then she looked at the sympathetic face Cathy was giving her, and it made her feel like crying again. "It's just that I'm going to miss that dog so much!" she blubbered.

Cathy, who was an excellent sympathizer, held out her arms to hold Margie, which had the effect of making Margie start to sob openly, and very loudly. "Poor Bobo!" she wailed when she could catch her breath.

Cathy had not expected such an emotional and vociferous reaction from Margie, and rapidly became concerned about who might be looking, or hearing all this. So she began talking, and cooing, and talking some more to try to calm her down as quickly as possible. "There, there…shush now honey…Bobo's in a good place, a better place…ssshhhh…"

Eventually, it had an effect, and Margie began to gather herself, and eventually, Cathy felt confident enough to slowly end their embrace. She took a step back, pulled some Kleenex out of her pocket, and offered them to the make-up streaked Margie.

"I'm sorry," Margie cried, again, way too loud. "I'm sorry, Cathy!"

Cathy felt that Margie's own voice was upsetting her again, so she began talking rapidly to her in a low calming voice. It was here that the mistake was made by the well-meaning neighbor. "There, there Margie. They'll get the person that did this. Bobo's in heaven, honey! I know… I know they'll find out."

Find out?" Margie cried out.

Cathy was taken aback a bit by the question, and answered directly, "Why, who killed your dog honey. They'll find the person that mutilated those poor animals!"

Margie looked at Cathy for only a second or two. Then her eyes rolled back into her head, and she fainted, dropping like a rock and hitting her head on the curb before Cathy could reach her.

Once again, there would be a 911 call from Devonshire.

"So what do ya think?"

"I think," Darrin said with his mouth full, "that we've got a gang of psychos, probably…" he paused to swallow "like those… what do the kids call 'em? Goths, who are into sacrifice, and dead things. Some weird shit like that." He took another bite.

"I meant the cheeseburger, dumbass. What do you think of the cheeseburger?" Jon said.

"Oh!...Good!...Sowwy!"

In the minutes before the food had arrived, Darrin had filled Jon in about the dead body not being a recent dead body (which they both half knew already, though he trusted Jon to keep it to himself for a few days), and Jon told him about his interview with Foster, which irritated Darrin. He also told him about the search of the woods they were doing, which Darrin already knew about. Then they discussed Ginger's supposed eyewitness account of how the police car had gotten covered, which they were both skeptical about. Talk had stopped when the food arrived, which they attacked as voraciously as dogs on a meat-wagon. In a matter of minutes, only scraps were left, and the conversation began anew.

"I still think there's something more too all this...and don't accuse me of believing in ghosts or something. There's got to be a, a reason, I guess I'm saying," Jon said, then punctuated his sentence with a hearty, healthy belch.

"Jesus!" Darrin exclaimed, looking around the almost empty restaurant, "Do you want everybody to think we're pigs?"

Jon just shrugged his shoulders.

"What do you mean, 'there's gotta be a reason?'" Darrin asked

"I mean, for example, the whole Meredith thing. What the son said, and all. And I think the old lady knows something too, but she's crazy...out of her mind. She didn't remember her husband's name, man."

"Maybe you didn't ask her the right question?" Darrin said as he dabbed his last Yogi fry into the ketchup.

"What do you mean?"

"Well, you remember what Dick told us? One thing he said,

was that David Meredith had an older brother that got killed, in a farm accident, I think. Remember?"

"Yea."

"Well, maybe, and I don't mean to be cruel about this, but maybe that would jog the old woman's memory, something traumatic like that. Ask her how her son died." He leaned back in the booth, savoring the last fry, and looking Jon directly in the eye as he chewed.

"You're sick," Jon said.

Darrin leaned over the table. "Maybe, but people with Alzheimer's, sometimes they remember the past in detail, even if they can't remember what they ate five minutes ago. When are those cheeseburgers going to get here, anyway?"

"Very funny, asshole," Jon said after chuckling.

But Darrin had given him something else to think about. It was just possible that he had a point.

"The curlers saved her. She has a nasty concussion, but she's going to be all right," the doctor said.

Cathy fell to her knees, closed her eyes, and folded her hands in the attitude of prayer. "Oh thank you Lord..." she began, shortly after crossing herself.

Pete ignored her and looked instead at the doctor. "How long is she going to be down? Should I plan on ordering out Chinese or something for us tonight?"

Dr. Mangles sighed. "Well, Mr. Vanderberg, you may want to order for yourself. I'd like for your wife to stay overnight for observation, just to keep an eye on her," he said.

"Hail Mary, full of Grace..." Cathy was chanting.

"Is she throwing up and stuff?" Pete asked.

"Some. Nausea is a natural symptom of concussion."

"You better keep her then. Just to be sure, like you said." Pete said solemnly.

We'll let you in to see her in just a few minutes," Dr. Mangles said as he turned away to head back to his patient.

"God bless you!" Cathy called after him.

The Dr. raised his hand to symbolically accept the blessing without looking back. A few steps from the door though, he stopped short, turned and looked back toward Pete. "By the way…who is Booboo?" he asked.

Chapter 22

It started to rain hard after the two Special Investigators and Officer Melrose had hacked their way into about the one quarter mark of the woods they were supposed to investigate every inch of. To Jim Melrose, who was soaked with sweat and nearing exhaustion after the two hours they had already put in, the rain was like manna from heaven, and he turned his face up to feel the cool drops that were beginning to work their down from the leafy treetops.

For the two Investigators though, it was close to, if not *the*, final straw.

"Do you believe this shit?" the one called Bob hissed. "No way it was supposed to rain today! No way!"

"Well, it sure as looks like that's what we got," the one Melrose had heard called 'Bud' said.

The three of them had stopped there by silent acclamation, waiting to see if the cloudburst would pass quickly, but as the minutes passed by the storm seemed to only intensify, with lightning and thunder becoming more frequent, and alarming.

"We could get killed out here," Bob said. "Lightnin' loves to strike trees."

The other two said nothing. The rain seemed to pick up even more. They stood, and waited.

"What would you two think of callin' it a day," Bob said

a minute later. "We ain't going to find anything. No harm in sayin' we covered it all."

Bud was in full agreement, as he always was with Bob, but he waited for Melrose, the outsider, to speak first. He and Bob both knew it was Melrose who could screw everything up.

"I think we should finish the job," Jim Melrose said a few seconds later. "That's what they sent us out here to do, damnit." Jim was, easily, in the worst shape of the three. He was by far the most miserable. He was rapidly turning from overheated, to teeth-chattering cold as he gradually became soaked in the driving rain. But there was stubborn male pride at work here. The two of them had been openly dismissive of him all day. He had been made to feel very much what he in fact was, the lesser trained, local yokel. This was his chance to be the real man. Screw them.

Bob and Bud looked at one another as Officer Melrose looked nobly off into the distance. Bob winked at Bud before he spoke.

"You're right," he said, "but there's a way we can get done faster. You're all for that, aren't you?" He looked directly at Melrose.

"Well...sure," Jim answered.

"Good. Let's split up. We'll cover a lot more ground, much faster that way. You go that way, Melrose" Bob said, pointing to the southeast, "Bud will go straight, and I'll head this way." He pointed to the southwest. "When we get to the edge of the woods, we each head back on our own. Probably circling around to the pasture would be faster. Everybody agree?"

The other two nodded.

"Let's get this over with then," Bob said, and he started walking. The other two followed suit in the direction each was assigned.

It was less than five minutes later when Bob and Bud met back up to head in. They joked about the gullible local cop who was now wandering alone in the woods, the whole walk back.

Bruce stood looking out at the rain, feeling restless as hell. Barb was asleep (it seemed like sleeping and sunning were all she wanted to do lately), the storm had washed out the Cardinals game and knocked out the TV cable, he was finished messing with his boring book, and the realty lady had been a disappointment that afternoon ("I'm afraid all the bad publicity is going to make this a hard sell..."). He felt like a prisoner, especially with Barb's increasingly cloying behavior.

"You'll be here when I wake up, right honey? Or if I have a bad dream?" she had asked. Good God.

So when Bruce saw Jon's garage door open and then the Mustang pull up and into it a few seconds later, it was a no-brainer. He was going over to talk with his old buddy.

He left a note for Barb, grabbed an umbrella out of the closet and a six-pack out of the refrigerator, and a few minutes later he and Jon were sitting at Jon's kitchen table, each with a cold one in front of him.

"Ya ever feel like you've just got to get away?" Bruce asked.

"You bet. I've spent the last two days trying to get away from this place. You don't realize how depressing it is until you do. I almost wish school would start."

A large clap of thunder caused both of them to jump and then look out the back door. It was a useless thing to do though. It was raining so hard that you could barely see the deck.

"I don't remember rain being in the forecast," Bruce said.

"Yea, I heard there was a chance. Not like this though," Jon said.

Bruce suddenly felt like talking about what he had scrupulously avoided talking about. There was something about the rain that made him feel comfortable; secure. "Dick told me this morning that Ginger saw that cover thing drop over the police car," he said. "She said it came out of nowhere."

Jon turned to look at his friend, who was still looking out the glass door, even though there was nothing but water to see. "She said it like she was in a daze, Bruce. Like she was in shock. Why would she be standing there looking out at that time of the morning? And out of nowhere? Darrin and I don't believe her. She's messed up from the cat thing."

"So you don't believe her, because what she said she saw is impossible to see?" Bruce asked. Now he was looking at Jon. "So does that make me 'messed up' too?"

Jon didn't answer, but shook his head slowly.

"Let me tell you something, man," Bruce said with his face was reddening, "the second that thing in the woods touched me, it changed everything. What I saw, it changed everything, even if it was only for a second. My house is for sale, Jon. What happened to me was real... as real as that body Barb and you found. You and your cop buddy can think anything you want, but there's something out there, Jon. I damn-well know there is."

Bruce stopped, leaned back in his chair, and took a big swig of his beer, just as another huge clap of thunder roared, as though Mother Nature was adding an exclamation point to his testimony.

Jon said nothing. Bruce slammed his empty can down on the table in mock anger and said, "So what do you think of that, old buddy!"

"I think we should keep talking," Jon said as he stood up. "And I think you need another beer."

"So you didn't find a thing. No evidence that anybody had been out there at all. Not even a matchstick. Is that what you're telling me?" Detective Foster asked.

"Well, we found an empty bag of Fritos in the pasture," Special Investigator Bob said. His partner Bud snickered.

"What about my man. Why isn't Officer Melrose here reporting with you?" Chief Thomas asked.

Bud looked at Bob, trying to suppress a grin, but Bob looked soberly and straight ahead, at the Police Chief.

"Well sir, when the storm came, we changed tactics a bit," he said.

"Changed tactics?" interrupted Foster.

"Yes, sir. We split up to cover more ground, faster. It was just as effective, sir. Anyway, when we got back, your man hadn't shown up yet. We waited for a while, but then we thought we better report to you guys. I'm sure he's home in a warm shower by now."

Thomas and Foster looked at each other, but said nothing. Foster turned to his investigators and told them what they knew already. "Never leave a man in the field, boys. You know better than that." The two nodded earnestly.

"I want to thank you gentlemen for your help," Chief Thomas said as he stood to signal the short meeting's end. He was disappointed, but hadn't really expected much. He was also anxious to wrap things up and get home. It was his wife's birthday. "Your efforts are much appreciated. Thank you too, Gus." Then he offered a handshake to all, then turned around and abruptly left the office.

Detective Foster quickly dismissed his special investigators, who started laughing about something as soon as they got out of the room, then he hustled quickly to catch up with Chief Thomas.

"Hey, let's you and I go get another piece of that prime rib tonight, Rod. I've been thinking about it all day," he said.

"Not tonight Gus. Got a special birthday tonight. Maybe next weekend, if you're still here."

Foster slowed, and let Thomas proceed alone toward the door to the parking lot. "OK then," he said. "By the way, are you gonna check on your man in the field, or do you want me to?"

Thomas turned around, but kept walking backwards.

"Check on him? You mean Melrose? Sure, I'll give him a call on the drive home. Surely he's got his radio with him. Don't worry about it." And he was out the door and off.

Detective Foster would be feasting on his prime rib alone.

"...And what about the laughing, or...demonic, whatever sounds? You've heard that twice now. Are you gonna tell me that was normal, human laughter?" Bruce asked.

Jon and he had decided to argue about it all, in a friendly way...and with plenty of beer. The rules were: you got to ask a question, but then you had to shut up while the other guy answered. His answer ended it -you couldn't argue back. Then the roles reversed, for the next question. They had been at it for half an hour already, and they were getting a little drunk. Especially Bruce.

"Of course it was human laughter, what else could it be, a goblin?" Jon answered. "In fact, I think Darrin figured out why it sounded so weird. Whoever this is, is maybe using a megaphone of some kind. There are a hundred ways to distort, and magnify a voice. He's trying to scare the shit out of us, so he's going to go the extra mile, man."

Bruce shook his head and smiled.

"And here's your question," Jon continued. He took a long sip of beer first, trying to build up the drama, but Bruce only giggled at him. "Suppose...suppose you're right," Jon said, a little more soberly than the game called for, "Suppose what's happening is...all connected. And suppose it's not some twisted kids, or a psychopath, or a group of psychopaths. My question to you is: what is it? And why?"

Bruce looked down at his hands on the table, then out back, where the rain had finally let up, and where the beginning of a rainbow was visible in the far southern sky. Then he looked at Jon and said "You're not the least bit religious, are you?"

"You're supposed to answer the question, butthead, not ask one," Jon smiled.

"OK, OK," Bruce said, raising his hand. "I'm getting there."

"Not very fast, you're not."

"Shut up. OK, here goes," he said. He looked outside again to gather his thoughts. "If you read the Bible…if you have faith in the teachings, you can't just disregard the parts you're not comfortable with, you know? I believe there is such a thing as pure evil. I don't know how exactly it gets made, or why it's here now, but it is. Evil is here, now. And it's bigger than us, Jon. It's bigger than…"

Bruce's cell phone rang. He had set it on the highest volume, in case Barb called, and it startled both of them when it rang. Jon pantomimed a heart attack as Bruce fumbled to answer it.

It was indeed, Barb, who was in much distress, as she had awakened to an empty house. Bruce tried to calm her down in soft, low tones, while Jon went out onto the deck to look at the purpled sky; one that held a new rainbow's promise of a better day.

Chapter 23

The Dr. had been worried enough about Ginger's dehydrated physical condition, along with her alarmingly incoherent mental state, that he had informed Dick that she needed a day or two of treatment at the hospital. Dick, then, had spent the afternoon watching his wife sleep while hooked up to an IV (at least she seemed at peace now), before driving home in the rainstorm as now the second temporarily wifeless husband on the cul-de-sac.

A restless hour after getting home, he looked out the front window to see that the rain had stopped. There was a breathtaking rainbow in the sky to the south, there was still a police car parked on the curb in front of Jon's house (it had been there all afternoon), and he saw that Pete was cooking something on his grill in his front drive across the street. Dick wanted somebody to talk to, and he was hungry, so he grabbed a package of hot dogs from the frig and took a walk over to see his neighbor.

Jerry Closter saw Dick walking across the street to Pete's, and that's how it started. Before 20 minutes had gone by, half the adults in the neighborhood were gathered around Pete's grill, and the ingredients for a second straight neighborhood cookout were at hand. Unimaginable just a few days before, they all needed it now.

And all wanted to know about Margie's condition, which they'd all either seen or heard about. And all were surprised to hear the news of Ginger's hospitalization. When Jerry Closter realized that there were two poor men that had no one to cook for them, he enthusiastically said "We've got plenty left over from last night! Let's just set up a few tables and bring some food out," and they were off.

When a decidedly wobbly Bruce came out of Jon's front door into the delightfully cool, storm cleared weather (it was all the way down to 82 degrees!) and saw the growing gathering at Pete's, he stopped and yelled back into Jon's "Hey! Everybody's getting together again! Come on out!" Then he closed the door and trudged over to his house, knowing that it would be nearly impossible to convince Barb to join the others. He also knew that he was coming out, no matter what. His talk with Jon, along with the alcohol, had fired him up, and he wanted more of it.

Soon, every house but the Freys was represented by at least one member of the family at what someone called "Great Picnic II." The need to be together, in a neighborhood that, like most neighborhoods these days, *might* get wholly together once or twice a year at best, was now overwhelming.

This time, the adults wanted to talk; about everything. Kids were told to go play, or to go back to their video games in the house. Coolers and lawn chairs formed a circle in front of what were soon several grills, and the food became secondary to the need for therapeutic conversation and positive reinforcement.

At the beginning it was all reassurance and optimism, with no one bold enough to object to the consensus of opinion: the police car the night before had been covered by teen-aged pranksters trying to exploit the situation (Dick remained silent about what his wife saw), nothing else had happened last night (Jon said nothing about the haunting laughter), the body found a few days before had been dug up from an old grave, and there was no murder at all ("Were the cops leaking that already?" Jon wondered), and the police must have found some evidence in the woods, because one of their cars was still here.

It was Bruce, already more than half-drunk from the beers at Jon's, and the ones he was knocking back now, and who was still angry with his whiny, house-bound wife, who changed the mood. And he did it abruptly.

"You're all kidding yourselves," he drawled out loudly enough to get everyone's attention. "There's something out there…that isn't human."

Jon winced, and several of the others looked away in embarrassed silence.

"My housessss is for sale. Did jew guys know that?" he slurred, "That thing touched me out there…it grabbed me and, turned me the fuck around!"

Bruce made a violent turning motion to demonstrate. It was more than his lawn chair could take, and he and his beer were sent diving into the street as though they were thrown there. Jon and Jerry were the first to get there to help him up. He had scraped his left arm up pretty badly.

"Leaf me alone! Leaf me the hell alone!" Bruce protested at first, but the two men were able to show him his hurt arm, which he didn't know about, and slowly walk him across the street and over to his house, where Barb, after she finally unlocked the door, took him for nursing.

The mood of the neighbors that Jon and Jerry rejoined a minute later had soured.

"What did he mean that he was grabbed and turned around in the woods?" Dick demanded of Jon. "When did that happen?"

Jon shrugged his shoulders and tried to put a puzzled look on his face, thinking it was best not to feed this particular beast.

"They're selling their house? Really?" Mary Benson asked.

"Yes. I saw the realtor there today, before Margie got hurt," Cathy confirmed.

"Did you tell them about the way my dog died? How he just seemed to fall out of the sky?" Pete asked Jon.

"You were asleep Pete. How would you know?" Jon answered dismissively.

"What does he mean...fell out of the sky?" Dick asked.

And on it went. Bruce's drunken but alarming declaration seemed to have taken the cap off a bottle of paranoia, and over the course of the following hour everyone indulged, to a greater or lesser extent. A cloudy, cooler night was slowly descending, and that didn't help either. Now it *felt* like Halloween. Sweaters were fetched, Pete started a fire in his portable grate for folks to gather around, and by the time their police guards for the night arrived, there was a haunted feel to the evening.

Darrin and Dick Blackwell had been assigned to Devonshire for the night, and as the additional officer pulled his car up and parked, it unnerved the crowd. "What are they expecting to happen now?" was the simple, unstated question that hung in the air. As they had the night before, all were silent as the policemen got out of their cars.

Darrin walked, puzzled, not up to the crowd, but to the third police car that was parked in front of Darrin's house. He bent down to look inside, then stood and tried to spot Jon amongst the lawn chairs. "Is Officer Melrose still here?" he asked as a general question, as he couldn't make out who was around the fire.

"Who's Officer Melrose?" Jon shouted. Pete laughed.

"He's one of the guys that's been in your yard all day. And he was here with the Chief yesterday. Is he still here?"

"Beats me," Jon said, remembering the officer's face now. "He's not around here. We thought he left with the other guys."

Darrin went back to his car, sat inside, and started making calls. The neighbors could see him, but couldn't hear what he was saying. Officer Blackwell walked up to where Darrin was sitting and put one hand on the roof of the car and bent over to listen.

"You don't suppose..." Cathy said, and then stopped. No

one knew for sure what she meant, and no one said anything. But they all watched the silent, confusing scene playing out in front of them.

After several minutes, Darrin got out of the car. He talked with Dick Blackwell for a minute, then Dick headed back to his car, as though he was going to retrieve something, which he was. Darrin walked over to the crowd of neighbors.

"Did anyone here see the officers leave this afternoon?" he asked them.

There was a general shaking of heads. "There was a bad storm at the time," offered Jerry. "Sometime in there one of the cars left, but I didn't see when."

"Me neither," someone else in the group said.

Darrin was fully aware of the nervousness of this group of people. And he knew that they had every right to be. He tried to downplay things as he spoke.

"Folks, they probably did all leave together. It's just unusual that the car's still here. Probably wouldn't start in the rain. It's about the oldest car we've got, I think. My partner's going to look around a bit though, just to make sure, OK? I'll be right here with you folks. Nothing to worry about."

Then he turned and left abruptly to go talk to his partner, who was already waiting across the street.

"Maybe you should raise our taxes so you can get better police cars!" Fred shouted out. He had joined the gathering late, and had been uncharacteristically quiet. No one laughed, of course, but Fred.

Jon got up and followed Darrin. He caught up with him right as he got to Dick. "What's the story, man?" he asked.

Darrin turned quickly, surprised that Jon was there. "Probably nothing," he said, looking back at the fire. "I just don't want to cause a panic."

"Panic about what?"

"Jim hasn't been home. I talked to his wife. That part's not unusual. He didn't check in at the station, or call, at least that they could find, and that is unusual. Knowing Melrose, he's probably out getting drunk with the other guys, but…"

"I'm going to go have a look around out there," Dick said, holding up his flashlight.

"Want some help?" Jon asked. He couldn't believe he'd just spontaneously volunteered to do what he now feared the most in this world: be in those woods after dark.

"You better stay here. Calm down the folks. Get a game going or something." Darrin said.

"Game? Game? How about hide-and-go-seek in the woods! Would that work?" Jon asked.

"Go back over there, butthead," Darrin said, but he was smiling. Then he turned to talk to Officer Blackwell.

Jon did as he was told and walked back toward his neighbors and the comfort of the fire and his lawn chair, glad to be relieved of duty.

Chapter 24

The gathering around Pete's fire went on for several more hours. Again, no one seemed to want to go home. Jon threw out a challenge to everyone to describe their most embarrassing moment, to try to lighten the mood, and it worked. Some of the stories were hilarious, and that combined with the wine and beer being hoisted, made for an enjoyable time for a while.

Darrin kept an eye out for Officer Blackwell's return, as did Jon, who was considerably more nervous about it all than the neighbors. Darrin, after all, had only black coffee to drink, and Jon…Jon had seen too much, and was now always ready for the other shoe to drop. Finally, around 11:00 Dick came back with flashlight waving, and Jon slipped out of the circle to see what he had to report.

"Nothing," he said, "and I looked everywhere. Jeez, it's spooky as hell back there." He looked spooked. "Did you hear anything more?" he asked Darrin.

"Yea, a couple of things," Darrin answered. "I finally got through to the Chief, and he says the two investigators came back without Melrose. He's been trying to call him since then, but he doesn't answer."

"You're kidding!" Dick exclaimed.

"Nope. He said they split up in the storm and covered separate sections of the woods."

"You mean he could really still be out there?"

"That's not what his wife thinks. I talked to her again too.

She's convinced he's out getting drunk somewhere. She says he won't answer his cell phone, but he never does when he's drinking. I guess this is common practice for old Melrose." Darrin said.

Dick looked back over his shoulder at the pasture and woods he had just come from. "Well, this doesn't make sense," he said. "I yelled for him. Made a fool of myself, got mud and stickers up the ass…he would have heard me, guys," he said, turning back to look at Darrin and then Jon. "Those woods aren't all *that* deep. Even if he had fallen and broken an ankle out there, he would have heard me."

The three of them stood there, each trying to think of another possibility, if Melrose wasn't indeed drunk.

"What's the Chief gonna do?" Dick asked.

"Well, I could tell he was worried, but he doesn't think it makes sense, with Jim's drinking history, to do an all-out search until tomorrow. He says if he's lost, he ain't gonna freeze, and the likelihood is he'll show up drunk. He was going to try to get ahold of Detective Foster to track down his two boneheads, to see if Jim's with them someplace after all."

Dick again looked back toward the woods. "I guess there's nothing left to do but wait," he said.

Jon was as worried as they were, but he was also thinking about how much he had misjudged Dick. He had seemed so shy, sensitive, even wimpy at first. Now, he was the one with the guts to go into the pasture and woods by himself. He'd done it twice, and at night!

"Jon, you think you got something over there without alcohol in it, to quench a guy's thirst?" Dick asked.

The party, or gathering, or therapy session, for the Devonshire neighborhood started breaking up a while later. Though it was Sunday morning coming and a chance for most to sleep in, it was getting comparatively cold, and no one was used to it. Cathy Closter and Mary Benson had Sunday school classes to teach in the morning. Dick Korte and Pete Vanderberg had to get up and go to the hospital for their wives. Fred Knotts had early tee times for a club tournament to help organize, and Jon Parker was just exhausted. With so many looking for some early sleep, along with the fact that this was the second night in a row of partying (and worrying half the night) that they weren't used to, the momentum swung toward going to bed.

Jon folded up his lawn chair, grabbed his mini-cooler and walked over to Darrin's police car to tell his friends good night. The car was running, and they were both inside trying to warm up while eating sandwiches. Darrin rolled the window down when Jon approached.

"You leaving us out here to fight the Beast by ourselves?" Darrin asked.

"You know it," Jon said. "Try to remember not to wake me up with your damn flashlight this time, O.K.?"

"I'll try. I think it's too cold for pranksters tonight, anyway."

"Maybe you'll find Melrose asleep on your deck," Dick said. "Wouldn't that be something?"

"Yea, that'd be great. I'll throw out a blanket, just in case. Good night guys," Jon said as the other two laughed.

Pete was awake just before dawn. He had had a restless night, much more so than he had anticipated having. It wasn't because of worry that something else might happen (sleeping with his gun pretty much took care of that), and it wasn't that he'd had too much to drink. In fact, he'd actually drunk moderately for a change, especially for a Saturday night. He hated to admit it, even to himself, but it was because Margie was gone, of all things.

He had anticipated a sense of freedom. No one to nag at him. No one there saying stupid things that he would be bound to correct. A bachelor again. Freedom. Real freedom.

But it hadn't worked out that way. It had been so many years since they'd been apart, even though being together was more torment than anything else, that he couldn't get used to it. He found it eerily quiet, even upsetting, when he finally turned off the TV to go to bed. "I guess you'd even miss an old broom, if it was with you for over 30 years," he thought to himself when he turned out the lights.

He was shaved, dressed and was ready to go by 7:00 A.M., and was opening the garage door to head to the hospital by 7:15, even though visiting hours didn't start until 8:00. He saw the last police car leaving the cul-de-sac just as he turned out of his driveway to head up the street. It was going to be a cooler, beautiful day, and he was fired up for reasons he couldn't name.

He stopped at Walmart to pick up something for her, eventually settling on a bunch of artificial roses. "What I really should do is get her a puppy," he said to the girl at the checkout.

"We don't sell pets, sir," she said.

Pete didn't really care, though. He just wanted to see his Margie now, and nothing else mattered.

Jon opened his eyes after the best night of sleep he could ever remember to see that it was already 9:03 in the morning. He rolled over onto his back, stretched his arms over his head, and actually laughed out loud. He felt like a million dollars.

He swung his feet over the side of the bed, stretched again, then got up and went to his closet. He put on a pair of ratty old bedroom slippers and a robe before heading to the bathroom. A man of leisure on a Sunday morning, he told himself.

A minute later he was throwing water on his stubbled face, and he studied himself in the mirror before drying off. "Handsome as hell," he said out loud. His wound from falling out of bed a few days before was healing nicely, and though he could have used a shave and a haircut, he was generally pleased with the rugged, blonde, blue-eyed hunk of a man he was looking at.

After putting on some coffee, he went out front to get the Sunday paper in his driveway. As soon as he stepped outside he saw two things that made him even happier. First, it seemed to be the most beautiful day in the history of days, and second... there were no police cars parked on the street. Not even Melrose's car. Nothing. "They must have found that skunk in a bar somewhere after all," Jon thought. It was a beautiful sight. Normalcy, at last.

The cool air, low humidity and bright sunshine made him feel exuberant. He stood holding his paper for a while, and just breathed it in. "Day on the deck," he thought. He'd read the paper there, eat his meals out there, and most of all, write out there. He was inspired now, and there was a lot to catch up on.

He went in and poured himself a cup of too-hot coffee, tucked his paper under his arm, and went out onto the deck. It was bathed in the morning sun, too early for the Maple tree's shade to cover any part of the deck or his table, but that was perfect. It would be too cool in the shade.

He shooed away some flies that were on the table, put his coffee and paper down there, and saw that his potted hibiscus plant on the far end of his deck had blown over in yesterday's storm. The smell hit him with the first steps he took toward the plant. It was a dead animal smell. Just the last Spring, a big opossum had crawled under his deck and died, and it took Jon two days of enduring that smell before he found the cause. What he smelled now was much the same.

"Damn," he said aloud, but then noticed that a few steps later that the smell had gone away completely. He got to the plant, set it back up, and still smelled nothing. Maybe whatever it was hadn't been dead very long, he thought. He looked over the edge of the deck and into the yard, up and down, to make sure no animal was lying there. He didn't see anything. He took a deep breath, and didn't smell anything but the sweet scent of the dewy, grassy pasture. Satisfied, he went back to sit at the table and read his paper.

He had to shoo the flies away again, and he caught another whiff of the dead as he sat down. He decided to ignore it, and maybe find out what the cause was later. He opened up his paper, kicked out of his slippers and put his feet up under the table and onto the chair across from him.

Both feet hit something wet and rubbery as soon as he put them up. It felt like a soaked, half-deflated basketball. Immediately, flies seemed to be everywhere. He swatted at them with his paper, pulled his now wet feet back under him, and bent down to look under the table and up at what his feet had hit on the chair across from him...

At first, it made no sense to him, but eventually, after a long, long moment, he gradually came to realize; gradually comprehended what he was looking at through the shade under the table. It was an eyeless, open mouthed, bloodied head, and it was covered with flies.

It was the severed head of Officer Jim Melrose.

Chapter 25

Darrin didn't even attempt to return to Devonshire, or even to try to contact Jon until early that Sunday evening.

He had gotten Jon's message as he was getting ready to go to bed, somewhere close to 10:00 in the morning. He listened to it, twice, put the phone down and looked at it in shock for a minute; then simply got dressed again and went down to the police station. He knew two things: the crime scene would be a nightmare, and that they would want his statement, no matter how unhelpful it was going to be.

The fact was that nothing had happened the night before. It had been a quiet, completely uneventful evening. He and Dick had even had trouble staying awake. Except for the early search of the woods, it had been a long, dreadfully boring night.

To his disappointment, it was Detective Foster who did the interviewing when he got to the station. Chief Thomas, along with four other Highland officers, plus a bevy of new state investigators (the stakes had just risen dramatically), were all at the scene. Foster had stayed back to make some calls, and to interview Officers Crandle and Blackwell. Darrin figured the big man who he was beginning to loathe was probably pretty good about getting out of the leg-work, so it figured he'd stay back.

They had to wait a while for his partner Dick Blackwell to arrive. He had been asleep. When he finally did walk in, Darrin could see the tension between the two immediately, and remembered why. Foster had humiliated Dick at the first crime scene. You could see the anger in Dick's eyes, and the surprise and aggressiveness in Foster's. "It's a good thing there's not much to talk about," Darrin thought.

But there was a surprise. After Dick described his search of the pasture and woods, and after they'd reported as extensively as they could on everything else they did for the rest of the uneventful, long night, Darrin finished his part of the narration by saying that when they left at dawn, Officer Melrose's abandoned car was the only one left on the street.

Foster looked up sharply at that. "You say his car is still there?" he asked.

Darrin and Dick looked at each other with confusion, then back at Foster. "Well…yea," Darrin answered. "Is something wrong?"

"I don't know," Foster said, quickly dialing his cell phone. "Probably nothing, but I thought Rod told me that…" he stopped and held up his hand. "Rod! This is Gus. Say, didn't you tell me that that officer's car wasn't there? Right. And you're sure one of your guys didn't…uh-huh…Well, your men who were on night shift say it was still there when they left this morning… That's right…OK, then."

Foster hung up the phone, leaned back in Chief Thomas' chair and looked at the two men. "We better talk about exactly when you guys took off," he said. "To the minute. That car ain't there anymore."

When Darrin pulled onto Devonshire Street at 5:30 that evening, it actually looked like the shocked, terrified, paranoid neighborhood that it now was. There seemed to be people in front of almost every house, gathered in sober clusters, staring at his car in silence as he drove up the street. You could almost feel the depression. Darrin wondered if this was what a warzone looked like.

There were still two police cars parked on the street; one in front of the Kortes, and one in front of the Bensons. No officers were visible. Darrin suspected they were out canvassing this block and others, trying to gather any particle of information that they could. There was a cop dead now. New ballgame.

He pulled his car right into Jon's driveway, and didn't bother ringing the doorbell. He knew where Jon would be, if he was home, so he walked around back. And there he was.

Jon was scrubbing his deck. Darrin watched him dip his sponge into a bucket of soapy water, scrub the spot in front of him on hands and knees as hard as he could, then stand, pick up the garden hose and squirt it off. Then he bent down to work on the same spot again.

"How are you holding up Jon?" Darrin asked as he walked up to and onto the deck, trying not to frighten him with his approach.

Jon stood up and turned around. Darrin saw that he was pale, and that his eyes were bloodshot. "How the fuck do you think I'm holding up?" he answered angrily. "This was the longest day of my life." Then he turned back around, dropped to his knees and began scrubbing again.

Darrin stood there and alternated between watching Jon, and looking out at the once again empty pasture and dark woods. He thought that it might be best not to say anything for a while. Jon kept scrubbing. Hard.

It was a delightfully cool afternoon, for July. Despite everything, the view from Jon's deck was really breathtakingly beautiful, Darrin thought. That is, it was beautiful if you had no idea what had happened. To all who were involved in what had happened in the last few days, it was only ominous now.

Darrin knew that there had been a massive search of those woods, again, that day. He knew that they'd found nothing; no real clue of any kind, and no sign of the rest of Jim Melrose's body. He also knew that everyone in the neighborhood had been questioned, as well as (by now) everyone one block and two blocks over. He knew that the press had been barred, partially successfully, from being on Devonshire. It had been a traumatic day for the town, the Police Department family, the residents of the cul-de-sac, and maybe most of all (excepting the widow), for Jon Parker. Darrin knew all of that, and was just thankful that he hadn't had to go through it. At the moment, he just felt guilty about it. Very guilty.

"What are you doing here, anyway? Your shift doesn't start for hours," Jon asked him suddenly. He was spraying off the deck again.

"I don't know, really," Darrin answered. "I feel bad, Jon. If we had known that anything like that…"

"There was nothing you could have done," Jon interrupted. He turned and looked at Darrin, and for a moment Darrin thought he was going to squirt him with the hose. He would have gladly taken it. As it was, the stress-filled look on Jon's face made him feel even worse. "This… maniac would have done this anyway." Jon looked to Darrin like he was about to break down. "It was right on my porch, Darrin!" Then he turned away, still spraying the deck, going over and over the same spots.

A bright red cardinal landed on the deck railing. He seemed to cock his head to look at the puddles Jon was making with the hose, as if considering a dive and a bath. Jon raised the nozzle to frighten him away.

"We're going to have somebody behind every God-damned tree tonight, that's what!" Detective Gus Foster bellowed. "I want 'em in front of every house, and behind every house, that's what!"

Detective Foster was trying to take charge, which is what he had been asked to do by the Illinois State Government that afternoon. The Illinois Attorney General had promised that he would have as many resources to handle the spectacular case as the State could manage (and afford). It would be coming his way, as soon as tomorrow, they had promised. The trouble was, Gus knew that, realistically, they would only help for a few days, at most. They couldn't afford any more than that.

And the trouble was, Gus' sterling reputation as a "loner" homicide investigator was not because of his management skills, and at the first meeting with a total of four agencies involved (including the Highland Police Department), it seemed more like chaos than anything else.

His vehement response had been to Chief Thomas himself, one of the few people in the room who Gus knew, and wasn't intimidated by.

"So you want blanket coverage of the neighborhood for the short term. Is that what you're saying?" asked State Police Commander Frame.

"Absolutely!" Gus shouted.

"What about forensics? Do we need more help there?" asked someone who looked important, but that he couldn't remember from the introductions a half-an-hour before.

"Absolutely!" Gus repeated at top volume.

The room grew silent for a long moment. Chief Thomas, who had inadvertently started all this by asking "OK Gus, what do we do?" to try to cut through the chaos, was the first to brave his old companion's temper.

"Detective Foster," he said, "who do you want to be in charge of manpower and scheduling?"

"YOU!" Gus shouted, pointing a finger at the Chief for emphasis.

"Uh…that would be highly unusual, given the agencies involved here, and the…"

"I said him!" Gus screamed, pointing at Chief Riggs again.

It was going to be a very long meeting.

Dick Korte had driven home knowing that he would be spending his second night in a row alone. Dr. Mangles had told him that, while Ginger had improved, he was still worried about her "...well, frankly...her psychological state." Ginger was basically listless and confused; and definitely didn't want to go home. This was the alarming part, to both Dick and to Dr. Mangles.

When he got home Sunday afternoon, once again, he would be looking for company. He felt confused too, especially by the police cars that he saw when he turned into Devonshire, and the number of his neighbors that were out watching, well, whatever there was to watch.

Pete Vanderberg had filled him in. Pete had brought Margie home triumphantly, but after only a few hours there had been a fight. Margie had insisted on having Bobo's blanket to hold as she napped in her efforts to overcome her concussion, and Pete had been appalled by the flea-bitten thing, and had refused. He had therefore spent most of the afternoon outside, picking up tidbits of information, and when a confused looking Dick pulled into his driveway, he rushed over to fill in his cookout brother from the night before. Dick was alarmed, and realized right then that he may never get Ginger home. He felt like he was losing control of his life.

Now, as early evening came on they were standing outside in Dick's driveway, where they knew they would attract other neighbors. It wasn't long before Fred, and a limping Rory Frey, walked over to join them.

"What the hell do you guys think about that shit," Fred said with his usual indelicacy, pointing to Jon Parker's house, which had a police car in the driveway.

"This is incredible," Dick offered. He couldn't find any other words.

"Are you guys armed?" Rory asked. With the help of a little

bit of luck, one lie, and a lot of stealth, Fred had helped him pick up his revolver a few hours before. Pam had taken Robert to visit her mother that afternoon.

"Well, no," Dick answered. The thought had never occurred to him.

"Hell yes!" Pete said proudly. He raised his golf shirt to show the gun tucked into his waist band.

"Jesus, Pete. You'll shoot your dick off!" Fred exclaimed. He had a newly developed sensitivity to the possibility of firearms accidents.

Pete ignored him. "Listen, we need a plan, guys," he said seriously.

"What sort of plan?" Rory asked anxiously. His face began to flush with excitement.

Pete looked solemnly away, toward Jon's house and the woods. "A protection plan," he said. "The police ain't protecting us. We gotta do it ourselves."

"What does that mean?" Dick asked.

"I'm ready," Fred said.

"I'm more than ready," Rory said.

In the awkward silence that followed, each man exchanged questioning glances with each of the other three, waiting for someone to take charge and propose a plan of action.

No one came up with anything.

"Rory! Get in here for supper!" Pam yelled from her front yard.

Rory limped away.

"I was thinking maybe you'd like to take a little road trip with me," Darrin said, breaking at least five minutes of silence between he and Jon.

Jon looked up from where he was standing. He had quit scrubbing, turned off the hose, and now was just staring numbly at the cleaned up crime scene that was part of his home. "What are you talking about?" he asked irritably.

"A road trip…to get you out of here for an hour or so."

"What kind of road trip?" Jon asked a little less hostilely.

"Something exciting," Darrin said. "Like say, the Dairy Queen…and, if you're up to it… the nursing home. What about that?"

Jon half grinned, despite himself. Then his face tuned hard as he looked over at Darrin with as mean a look as he could muster, as though he were getting ready to chew him a new one. It didn't work. Darrin just stood there grinning like an idiot.

"Shit. Let me get my shoes on," Jon said as he turned to go into his house.

Chapter 26

Police cars, both marked and unmarked, began descending upon the Devonshire neighborhood right at the time that Darrin and Jon were pulling out. Detective Foster, given the frustrating absence of anything at all substantive to go on in their investigation, had decided in his bullish way to do one thing right first: make absolutely sure that nothing more happened in the neighborhood that Sunday night. Bullish, but perhaps a show of strength that could make a difference, he thought.

The strategy was simple: put men absolutely everywhere. Well before dark, there were uniformed and plain-clothes police on the street of Devonshire, on the next street over, in the pasture behind Jon's house, and even on the other side of the woods, to the south, in some farmer's field in the middle of the country. The manpower commitment was unprecedented, but so was the publicity. News of the Devonshire mystery had already made it into newspapers as far away as the Chicago Tribune, and the St. Louis TV, radio and print media were on the verge of giving it saturation coverage.

The story was perfect for them: a nice, suburban neighborhood terrorized by a series of inexplicable human and animal murders. "They wouldn't give a shit if this was East St. Louis," Detective Foster had grumbled, and for once, he was undoubtedly right.

Therefore, he had to waste some of the seemingly excessive manpower he had on media control, by at least temporarily blockading and carefully screening traffic at Sunflower and Coventry; the only way to get to the Devonshire cul-de-sac. Only residents and the police themselves were allowed in and out that night. The press, and the merely curious, were all turned away. If it was a violation of their rights, so much the better, as far as Foster was concerned. "Saturation coverage meets saturation coverage," he had declared.

And oddly, this gung-ho "balls out" approach was a morale booster…especially for the grieving Highland Police Department.

Darrin and Jon passed the set up, a makeshift blockade to block incoming traffic

(Darrin waved at his fellow officers) just as it was being established and organized. They headed up Sunflower and toward town. As he had each time before that week, Jon felt an exhilarating rush wash over him now that he was getting away. For the first time, as they drove through the more peaceful neighborhoods, he began thinking about moving away.

"You were right about this," he said, "It's so damned good to be getting out of here. If your apartment wasn't such a pigsty, I'd consider staying over at your place tonight, I swear."

Darrin glanced over at Jon. The poor guy looked more relaxed already. He tried to imagine what it would be like to be in his spot. "Maybe you should get away, " he said. "Doesn't a charming guy like you have some babe he could shack up with?"

Jon was watching the houses pass by; the blissfully untroubled houses that held people who would be innocently slumbering away in the next couple of hours. It was hard to imagine. Just 8 or 9 hours ago, he had woken up in the greatest mood, after the greatest sleep, that he could remember. Now it was all gone.

"Not anymore," he finally answered Darrin, "I broke up

with a girl, another teacher, about six months ago. Actually… she broke up with me, to be honest about it."

"Still carrying a torch for her?" Darrin asked. He figured it was good to talk about anything else, even if it was women.

"I guess," Jon said distractedly. "Let's talk about something else."

But neither of them could think of anything, so they rode with their own thoughts until they got to the Dairy Queen.

It was crowded, as it always was on Sunday afternoon and evening in summer. People had had enough family time by then, the end of the weekend. Time to take the old lady and the little brats out for a treat. Ice cream was a natural way to cap things off before the work week began.

Darrin insisted on going in and getting a table, even though Jon didn't want to see anyone. "This is my dinner, man," he'd said. "I work tonight. I'm not going to drive around and try not to spill anything just so you can mope."

They got a table by a window (at Jon's insistence), and Darrin worked at two cheeseburgers and a shake. Jon sipped at his vanilla malt while glumly looking out the window.

After finishing his first cheeseburger, Darrin thought it was time to start talking. "Did you always want to be a teacher?" he asked with a mouth full of food.

Jon turned from the window to look at him. "What kind of bologna is that?" he asked. Then, before Darrin could answer: "Look, I appreciate you trying to raise my spirits, or change the subject, or whatever…but, excuse me, I'm thinking about other things right now, like a guy's head on my porch…minor stuff like that. Hope you don't mind." Then he resumed looking out the window.

Darrin took a big bite of cheeseburger, chewed it up slowly while looking at Jon, and waited until he had swallowed this time to answer. "If it was me, I'd be furious," he said. "They'd have to hold me back. I'd be doing everything, anything I could to find this prick."

"Yea, you're a hero all right," Jon said absently. Then he looked at Darrin and said sharply "Isn't that your job? You aren't doing anything that I can see, except eating like a pig. Why aren't you out there catching this…prick!" The last word was loud enough for Jon to receive an immediate look of disapproval from what appeared to be a father of three at the next table. Jon almost told him to stuff it, but thought he'd better not.

"I am working on it," Darrin answered coolly, "but a man's got to eat." He stuffed the rest of the burger into his mouth. Jon had retreated to his window again, not able to think of any better way to answer Darrin's ridiculous contention. So when he finally got the big bite down, with the help of some milkshake, it was Darrin who continued.

"I didn't sleep more than a couple of hours today," he began. "I couldn't. I thought about everything that's happened. I went down to the station and read every report, from the beginning. Even my own. I made a list. A long one. I even wrote down all the stuff you said. Even the silly shit. I tried like hell to add it all up. And you know what?" he asked, and then gave Jon plenty of time to answer. Jon just stared out the window, so he answered himself: "It doesn't add up. Not at all. It was hard for me to admit it to myself."

Darrin stopped to noisily sip at the rest of his shake.

"So what are you getting at?" Jon asked. He slowly looked away from the window and toward Darrin, almost reluctantly.

"We got a dead guy with no fingerprints or blood, who looks like he was mummified. Been dead forever. We got a dog, and a burial shroud, symbolically, at least…falling right out of the sky. We've got sounds coming out of the woods that aren't human. We don't want to put it like that, but in our guts, we know it's not a human sound. We got the mutilated head of an innocent cop, but no body. Not a sign of it. We got no clues. No footprints. No fingerprints. Nothing. And oh, I don't know if you know this one: we got a missing police car. Somebody was watching us, Jon. As soon as Dick and I left this morning, somebody took Melrose's car. It disappeared."

Darrin stopped to noisily sip at his milkshake again. Jon watched him, intently now, and waited for him to go on. When he didn't right away, he prompted him with an "And…?"

"So we go back to the nursing home and talk to old lady Meredith, for starters," Darrin answered.

Jon's shoulders slumped. He had expected something more, for some reason. "What good will that do? She's nuts!" he said in exasperation.

"Maybe," Darrin answered nonchalantly, as he reached for his wallet, "but this whole thing is nuts. Seriously nuts. And I was thinking, this afternoon, that that's where you and I should start. It makes sense, if you think about it. We can't explain what's happening, so we need to open our minds to any possibility. We need to look under every rock. We have an illogical problem. Maybe there's an illogical solution."

This made Jon pause. Darrin had the makings of a brilliant detective some day, he thought, but he was too damned tired to help him right now. "I think I'm out," Jon said finally, "You go see her if you want."

Darrin was counting his money. "No. She knows you, even if it's by the wrong name. Don't they bring you the bill in this place?" he asked, looking around. Then he continued, focusing directly on Jon, "She knows you, and besides, what do you want to do? Go home?"

He had a point, Jon thought. He sighed deeply, and began sliding out of the booth. "You already paid when you ordered your food, dip shit," he said, "Let's go."

The meeting with Police Chief Thomas took place by logical happenstance. When the police started arriving and fanning out everywhere at about the same time a helicopter began hovering over Devonshire with NEWS-5 written on the sides, the residents naturally came outside, if they weren't out there already, to see the goings on. Chief Thomas was standing in the street where Devonshire met Coventry, trying to direct his men as they arrived as to where to go; yelling loud enough to be heard over the whirling blades above, so it was also natural for the concerned citizens to gravitate his way.

By the time the helicopter had taken its aerial film and flown away, every house but Jon's and the Ellsworth's had a representative down at the end of the block. They gathered in the Knots' front yard only a few feet away from where he stood, waiting for a chance to speak with their Police Chief.

For his part, Chief Thomas was pleased, rather than threatened, by the gathering crowd. It gave him the appearance of being on the job, and in charge, and he very much needed to feel something. It had been a long, guilt-ridden, numbing day; the worst he had ever experienced in all his years of police work. He wanted desperately to help someone, in some way.

When all the cars were in, Chief Thomas turned to them and said: "Folks, I want to explain to you what we're trying to do to protect you all, and then I'll be glad to answer any of your questions." No one spoke, and he could see clearly the anxiety; the fear, on all their faces. It made him feel even worse.

But, after clearing his throat, he continued.

"Tonight, we're going to be watching every inch of this neighborhood. I want you all to know that the city, the county and the state are all on the job. We'll make sure that nothing, I repeat nothing will go unseen here tonight. We're here to protect you from this…" he paused here when he saw the deeply worried face of Cathy Closter. He was going to say 'maniac,' or 'killer,' but thought he'd better not. "this…crime spree that we've got going on here. We're on the job. Now I'll be glad to answer your questions if I can. Remember, this is an ongoing investigation, so I may not be able to share everything I know."

But the truth was, he didn't know a hell of a lot.

"How long are you guys going to do this?" Fred asked. "I mean, if nothing happens, are you going to take your men off in a day or so? Will we have to protect ourselves then?" His eyes met Rory Frey when he asked the last question. Rory smiled.

"We are going to take one day, one decision at a time," the Chief said. "You may have noticed that we're even monitoring the traffic coming in and out of here," he pointed out proudly. "We're going to do everything we can, folks."

"Who makes that decision?" Pete asked. He didn't really have a good question, but wanted to ask one.

"Well, I'm in charge of the men here," Chief Thomas said proudly again. "The overall, uh, coordinator, is a great detective named Gus Foster…"

"Oh! My! God!" Pam interrupted with a shout. Chief Thomas gave her a look of surprise. "He's a pig!" she said to him, sure that that explained everything.

"Did you pick up any clues today? Do you have a suspect, or what do ya call it…Person of Interest?" Ralph Carmine asked.

This question honed in on the meat of the matter, and everyone looked at Chief Thomas. They looked to him like they were holding their collective breath. "Not at the present time," he said reluctantly, and his next words were drowned out by groans and swearing protests. He waited for it to subside, and then repeated what he had said. "Not at the present time, but we're working on it every minute of the day," he said with increasing volume.

There was much disgruntled head-shaking, and some started walking back to their tightly guarded homes.

"Who are you?" Lilly Meredith asked Jon and Darrin when they came in the door of her room at the nursing home. "Are you doctors? Can I go home now?"

Jon tried to act at ease by laughing reassuringly as he

grabbed a chair and put it right in front of her wheelchair, like he had the last time. Darrin stayed back by the door.

"I'm Billy! Don't you remember me?" Jon exclaimed as he smiled and sat down familiarly, like he did this all the time.

Lilly Meredith leaned forward and peered at him, first through her spectacles, then over them. "No," she said simply.

"Well, it's me," Jon said. "I've got some questions for you, Auntie!"

The grey-haired woman looked away, over at Darrin standing by the door. He smiled at her. "I need to go to bed," she said frankly.

"Sure Auntie. Just a few questions first though, OK?" Jon smiled.

"What questions?" she asked peevishly.

Jon looked over at Darrin, who just nodded. Jon was a little reluctant to go ahead. Her mood was the opposite of what it had been when he'd visited the first time. He couldn't shut her up, then. Now, she was apparently exhausted. He felt like he was picking on a helpless old woman.

He looked over at Darrin, who nodded firmly, with no smile on his face this time.

"Did you have a son that died?" he asked her suddenly. "Your first son? Do you remember Auntie?" Jon felt his upper lip begin to perspire. It was too hot in the room, and the question he'd just asked her was awful.

She looked at Jon for a long moment. It was very quiet in the room. "No," she said quietly. Then she looked back over at Darrin, for some reason.

Well, that's that, Jon thought with relief. He too was looking back at Darrin when she added "No, he didn't die," very softly.

Jon jerked his head back to look at her. She was still looking in Darrin's direction, but she didn't seem to be looking at him. Her eyes were vacant. She was seeing something else.

"What do you mean, he didn't die?" Jon asked quietly. He was trying hard not to upset her. When she didn't answer, he asked her in a different way. "What happened to him? What happened to your son?"

"He wasn't right," she said, almost wistfully, from someplace far away. "He wasn't right," she repeated, almost in a whisper. A spot of drool was working its way out of the right corner of her mouth and down her chin, but she didn't seem to notice.

Jon looked over at Darrin again, who waved at him fiercely to continue. Jon gave him the finger, but discreetly.

"What happened to him?" Jon repeated a moment later.

She took a deep breath, then seemed to come back from where ever she had been. She wiped her chin with her wrinkled hand and looked at Jon; her eyes large behind the powerful glasses; "He went away… little Chester went away. Chester took him away; long ago. A long time ago," she whispered softly.

Jon could see, unmistakably, that tears were forming in her eyes.

Chapter 27

Fred Knotts stood facing the giant American flag that covered fully 1/3rd of the south wall of his finished basement, with his back to his friends. He stood in a Patton-like posture…on purpose. "Gentlemen," he began, and then paused for effect, or perhaps he was desperately trying to think of what to say, "…the only thing we have to fear; is fear itself," he finally pronounced.

Sitting across the room at a card table, Rory Frey felt a thrilling jolt of exhilaration at these words, and his jaw literally dropped open in awe.

"That's Kennedy's words," said the considerably less impressed Pete Vanderberg, who sat waiting across from Rory.

Fred turned dramatically away from the flag, and toward his friends. It was a little too fast, and he stumbled a bit, but quickly recovered and pointed at the other two emphatically to compensate. "And great words they were!" he roared.

"What did you say?" a voice yelled from upstairs. It was Fred's daughter Melissa, who thought her father was perhaps calling her to bring down some beer.

"Nothing!" Fred yelled back irritably, "We're just talking down here!" His momentum at least temporarily in tatters, he walked over and sat with his friends at the card table. After collecting himself for a moment, he leaned conspiratorially over the table, and began talking in a low, but forceful voice: "Men, we have a problem here. We have a big problem. You heard the policeman out there. Within a few days, all this will die down, and we'll be left unprotected again. Mark my words."

"What do you think we should do?" an excited Rory asked.

"I'm getting to that," Fred scolded. He paused, put his hands on the table, and started again. "The first rule of warfare is this: 'know thine enemy.'" He looked at Pete, and then Rory straight in the eye, to let this sink in.

"What's that supposed to mean?" Pete asked after a moment.

Fred smiled patiently. "It means that we think through what we know about the enemy, that's what. We play *his* game."

"What kind of game is he playing?" Rory asked.

Fred took a deep breath, looked at his partners gravely, and said "He strikes at night. He comes through the woods to get at us. He's a maniac who doesn't care who or what he kills. Am I right?"

"Yea. So?" Pete asked. He shifted uncomfortably.

"When the cops leave, and they will leave, there will only us three armed men on Devonshire…at least as far as we know. I say we do the old 'bait and switch' on the bastard!" Fred said triumphantly.

Rory and Pete looked at each other, basically to see if the other one understood. Neither of them did, so they looked back at Fred and waited for him to go on.

"All three of us go out…we sneak out after the wives fall asleep. We go down to that damned field behind Jon's house. We'll have to let him know so he don't get all excited and call the cops. Anyways, after we get there it's simple: one of us sits out there in the pasture, in the wide open, where the killer can see him. The other two of us hide; one in the weeds, one up by the woods, maybe even in the woods. When the maniac shows up, it's all over."

Fred leaned back in his chair, folded his hands behind his

head and smiled, waiting for their reaction. Rory and Pete looked at each other, then back at Fred.

"We shoot 'em?" Rory asked in a shaking voice.

"Only if we have to," Fred answered coolly. "If he's not crazy, he'll give up when he sees three guns pointed at him. If not, we blow him away."

There was a long silence. Rory continued looking at Fred, trying to process all that he'd heard. Pete was looking down at his hands on the table. Fred just waited.

"I gotta admit," Pete said, at last breaking the silence, "I like it. That's a hell of a plan Fred."

"I can't believe you're this excited about it. She didn't know what she was talking about. She's out of it, Darrin," Jon said.

"No, no. We're on to something here!" Darrin said. He was driving Jon home, too fast, because he had to get back and get ready for work, and because he was pumped up about what the old widow had said. "Think about it! She said her first son didn't die. She said her husband took him away."

"So how does that help us, really?" Jon said. "She can't remember shit. She even used 'Chester' for her son's name and her husband's name."

"Hell, half the people out there name their sons after their fathers. Are you kiddin' me?"

Jon didn't answer. It was useless to, he thought, and they were getting close to Devonshire, and his house. He didn't want to go home.

"You know, they keep records on all that. Birth records, death records. I can look it all up tomorrow. I tell ya, we're gettin' somewhere man. I can feel it!" Darrin said.

He had to slow and wave to get through the barricade, and in another minute he had passed all the police cars and was making the circle in front of Jon's house to drop him off.

"It's starting to get dark earlier," Jon said glumly as he got out of the car. He leaned down to the window as an afterthought after he got out and closed the door. "Thanks Darrin," he said. "This helped."

"Maybe I'll see you tonight!" Darrin said brightly. "I don't know where I'll be assigned yet," he added.

When Jon made no immediate move to walk away from the car, it created an awkward moment. Jon was clearly reluctant to go inside; into his own house. He wanted nothing more, especially given what had happened that morning, than for all of this to go away. Darrin, on the other hand, was just as clearly anxious to leave, and he was as enthusiastic about the case as Jon was dour. Neither knew what more to say to the other.

"You know, our roles seem like they've reversed a little bit," Darrin eventually ventured from his seat behind the wheel. "Now I'm the one thinking the impossible, at least a little bit, and you're the rational one."

Jon didn't answer, but was still bent over and listening.

Darrin struggled for the right words. "Between the two of us…if we keep working on it…we'll solve this damned thing."

"Yea, maybe." Jon said. Then, without another word he stood, turned toward his house, and began trudging up to his front door.

The very moment he got in and closed the door, he heard a sharp knock on his back glass door. He froze, listening, and terrified. It wasn't a rational reaction, he would realize when he looked back on it later, but he was beyond being rational. His first thought was to of run back out front again, and try to catch Darrin, or somebody. But he waited instead. And waited some more. He could feel his heart beating through his chest. Then there it was; the sharp, insistent knocking again, definitely coming from the door that led out to the deck. He walked, with his mouth turning dry, through the living room and to the edge of his kitchen. Then slowly, reluctantly, he peeked his head around the corner and looked at the deck door.

It was a uniformed policeman with his hands cupped around his eyes, looking in.

"Hey, bud!" he yelled when he saw Jon's head, "Do you mind if I use your bathroom?"

To his extreme disappointment, Darrin was not assigned to Devonshire that night. Dick Blackwell was, and he had what he considered to be the worst assignment of them all. Instead of being camped in the field behind Jon's house, or patrolling the dark back yards like the Korte's where the mutilated cat had been found, he had been assigned to sit in his car, and occasionally walk around at the corner of Devonshire and Coventry, at the head of the cul-de-sac, just two blocks down from the guys at the barricade. There was no one to talk to, and not much to do under the bright streetlight where he had been posted.

He had hoped to be stationed somewhere near the woods, or at least within sight of them. The thought that he had searched the woods the night before and found nothing, when there was a murderer out there hacking a fellow officer to pieces, had kept him awake and upset most of the day. It had been haunting out there. It had deeply affected him, even before the news on Melrose. He wanted to be close, to maybe get a crack at whatever was out there. But it was not to be.

Instead, as the hours dragged by, he grew increasingly bored, and was growing more and more tired. By 2:00 in the morning, just half-way into his shift, he was getting out of his heated car and walking big circles up and back on Coventry, just to keep awake. His coffee thermos was already almost empty, and he was dreading the next almost 4 hours until the sun came up.

At precisely 2:15 he was sitting in his car when one of the police cars parked on Devonshire went into "panic alarm" mode. Its lights flashed off and on and its car horn blared intermittently, which sounded incredibly, piercingly loud in the quiet of the night.

"Stupid jag off!" Dick said aloud, figuring immediately that some cop hidden between the houses had fallen asleep on his car keys. As he quickly as he could, he opened his door and got out of his car to run down to see if he could stop it.

Before he could even get around to the front of his car, he heard, and then saw, the Knotts' garage door (the house he was closest to) start opening. He glanced that way, and saw that the neighbors next to the Knotts, the Carmines, had their garage door opening too. He turned at a grumbling sound coming from behind him, and saw that the Freys, and then the Korte's garage doors were opening. Then a second police car, this one parked in front of the Bensons, had its horn start blaring, and its lights begin flashing.

Dick stopped where he was, in the middle of the street, and watched it all in stunned amazement. Within a few more seconds, every police car, including his own, and at least a few of the cars in the now open garages, had their horns blaring away and their lights flashing on and off surreally in the night.

Policemen left their hiding places and came running from all directions. Bedroom, kitchen and living room lights turned on in every house. Panicked and confused people came to their windows and the braver ones came out onto their front porches.

And then it stopped, even more suddenly than it had started. All the cars stopped honking and flashing at once, then, about five seconds later, every garage door in the neighborhood rumbled and closed, all together. Everything was silent, again.

Chapter 28

"It was some kind of freakin' electrical anomaly, that's all," Gus Foster said right before biting into his second jelly doughnut of the morning. He was sitting with Chief Thomas in the break room, talking things over a little more than an hour before the general meeting was to take place with all the other "hotshots," as Gus had called them.

Chief Thomas eschewed the doughnuts (his wife had him trying another diet), but was on his third cup of coffee. "I don't know, Gus. The way they described it…Dick Blackwell saw the whole thing. He said it was the strangest thing he'd ever seen… And by the way, what the hell is an 'anomaly'?"

"Strange, but logical coincidence, sort of. Somebody may have played a trick, I'll grant you that, but more likely all the equipment we had out there somehow made everything go off." Gus put the last bite of doughnut in his mouth, and eyed the third one. "You gonna eat that?" he asked.

Thomas shook his head, and tried not to look as Detective Foster went after it. He had been trying to puzzle things out for hours now, since 4:30 in the morning, in fact, when he had awoken from a nightmare and called to see how the stakeout was going. When he heard what had happened, he got dressed and came in to his office, even though he knew there was nothing he could do. It was beginning to seem like it was always that way - nothing he could do. He had hoped Gus would have a better theory than he did.

"Where do we go from here, Gus? I mean, those people had to be terrified when all those horns went off. And we don't have a damned clue. What the hell are we gonna do?"

Gus was chewing, and was uncharacteristically polite enough to not talk with his mouth full. "We wait for the meeting with all the hotshots, and everybody's reports, and we come up with something, that's all, " he said after he'd swallowed. "Don't get too far ahead of yourself, Rodney. Maybe somebody saw somethin' out there. Who knows?"

"All I know is that I got a funeral for a cop coming up, and I don't even have his body for the widow. Damn it!" Chief Thomas pounded the table, and a big splash of his coffee spilled out of his cup and onto the table.

"Nobody got hurt last night, Rod. That's something. One day at a time, guy," Gus said with his mouth full.

The new morning's sunshine brought anything but optimism to the beleaguered residents of Devonshire. They were, collectively, well past that. Almost everyone had trouble getting back to sleep after the 2:15 incident, and some not at all. The shocking interruption of what they thought would finally be a good, safe night's sleep shattered; they found, each in their own way, the psychological aftereffects to be devastating. The assumption was, with everything else that had happened, that the same evil force was behind the incident, and that raised disturbing questions. How safe were they if, even with a massive police presence, someone could open and play with their electrically-controlled garage doors at will? How safe was anyone, when the police themselves could be messed around with in such a way? And most of all, they were asking that same question they had been asking for days now: who in God's name was doing this, and why?

There were sober family meetings at chilly breakfast tables

following flaming nightmares. There was talk everywhere of moving, or at least taking a trip somewhere. There were repeated warnings to children to keep all doors locked (and don't forget the windows too!). There were frantic searches for a place to send even the older ones away during the day, when parents with bags under their eyes were trying to work.

Adults went to their jobs that Monday morning with a strange mixture of apprehension, and relief. No one waved goodbye to anyone. No one commented on what a great weekend it had been to any neighbor, or even child or spouse.

It had become a neighborhood imprisoned.

Dick Korte made arrangements that day for Ginger to stay with her mother across town when she got out of the hospital. There was no way he was bringing her back to this.

Bob and Mary Benson were moving their vacation up from mid-August, to now. That Monday was their last day of work for a week, and they were planning to take off for somewhere, anywhere, before the sun went down.

Bruce Ellsworth had convinced his perpetually frightened wife in a middle of the night conversation to visit her mother and father in Wisconsin for a while. There were tears and much indecision at first, but she was leaving at noon that day for the long drive north.

Pete Vanderberg fretted about what to do with his still shaken Margie, who would be home alone while he worked, for at least a few days while she recovered from her concussion. Eventually there was an argument about teaching her how to use his gun, which ended with him leaving it, loaded, on the nightstand next to her side of the bed. At least it made Pete feel better when he left for Wicks.'

All in all it was a little cul-de-sac that was now in retreat; trying in the best way they knew how to react to a siege that was as indefinable as it was horrifying. They sought to send wives, children and pets out of the war zone. Various plans to flee, and in a few cases, to fight, percolated in the brains of the newly psychologically challenged- and now damaged residents. The Devonshire cul-de-sac would look like a very different place by that Monday night.

Jon slept until almost noon. He had finally fallen into a tortured sleep at midnight, but of course was awoken with a start, like everyone else at 2:15. Like many of the others, there had been no sleeping after that until daylight - even though the rest of the night had been uneventful. The advantage he had, and that he wouldn't have much longer, was that as a teacher in summer, he could sleep when he needed to. He was quickly learning to do just that. He'd slept soundly for almost six hours when the bright sun shining into his east bedroom window slowly, gently woke him up.

He went to the bathroom, and shaved and got dressed before going to the kitchen for coffee. With all the cops out there the night before, he thought he'd better not go walking around half-naked first. There was no sign of anyone though, when he made it out to the kitchen. The pasture and woods looked as empty as ever, and there were no heads on his deck (he had checked carefully). A look out front revealed only one police car, with no one in it. Probably left one guy back to patrol, he thought.

Satisfied that it was, at least for the time being, a normal, beautiful summer morning, he grabbed a cup of coffee and his cell phone, and headed out to the deck. He sat in his normal seat (but without putting his feet up) and checked his messages. There were two from his mother, one from Darrin, and one "Unknown Number." He knew he'd have to spend at least a half-an-hour reassuring Mom (even though he'd already done that twice the day before), so he called Darrin back first. He answered on the first ring.

"Hey buddy! You sleeping the day away again?" Darrin asked.

"There isn't much choice, the way you guys protect us."

"Yea, I heard about the horns and stuff... Weird, huh?"

"More than weird. It was unbelievable. Could one person have made that all happen, Darrin?"

"Hell if I know. They'll figure it out, I guess. Hey, do you mind if I hop over? I've got some information to share with you."

Jon didn't really feel like that yet, but he also appreciated it, in a way. Darrin was making a lot of effort. The guy should have been home asleep, but instead, he was knocking himself out. And at least this time, he had actually asked to come over. "Yea, sure. Come on by," he said, and hung up shortly thereafter.

He called his worried mother next, which was more about listening than talking. She was again trying to convince him to come home for a few days, something that he was halfway considering, if it wouldn't drive him crazy.

As she kept talking, he got up and went inside and walked to the front door to check for Darrin. He wasn't there yet, of course, but he went out and sat on his front steps anyway, because he didn't want the damn doorbell to ring, and he wanted to cut off Mom's call as soon as he saw Darrin turn into the cul-de-sac.

It was going to be a hot day. The refreshing cool front that the storm had brought in was losing its grip already, and Jon could feel himself start to perspire after only a minute of sitting out there in the sun, listening to his Mother rattle on. He was about to get up and go back inside when Darrin's Chevy Malibu ripped around the corner onto Devonshire.

"Mom, I'm sorry to interrupt you, but there's somebody at the door...No it's not a stranger Mom, it's a friend of mine...I will...I will...Talk to you later, Mom."

Darrin pulled into his driveway, got out of his car, and started walking toward Jon, but with his head turned toward the police car parked in front of the Ellsworths. His walk slowed, then stopped about ten feet from where Jon was standing in his yard at the top of the driveway

"Did you see who drove that car up?" Darrin asked. He was staring intently at the empty vehicle.

"No. It was there when I got up. Why?"

Darrin didn't answer, but after a moment started slowly walking toward the parked police car. He cut across Jon's lawn, into the street and right up to it, then bent over and cupped his hands to look inside. Then he quickly jerked away, as though something had pushed him back. Hard.

"What is it?" Jon yelled out. His stomach was starting to churn again.

Darrin didn't answer. He stood there, obviously stunned, looking to Jon like all the color had gone out of his face. Jon started to walk over. He didn't get very far.

"What is it, Darrin?" he asked as he walked.

"Stay back!" Darrin commanded, holding up his arm toward Jon without taking his eyes off the car. "Get my cell phone out of my car! Or use yours! Call 911! This is Melrose's car! He's in there, Jon. God damnit!" Darrin bent down and put his hands on his knees. "The rest of him's in there," he said, more quietly.

Chapter 29

Barb Ellsworth had already left for Wisconsin, and Margie Vanderberg would be sound asleep through the whole thing, and so, with everyone else at work or in secret *undisclosed locations*, only Jon, Darrin and young Robert Frey, who stood in his yard eating a sandwich while watching, were witnesses this time to the frantic, shrieking arrival of police cars and an ambulance.

The first officer to arrive, not knowing the gravity of the situation, hopped out of his car and said cheerily to Darrin: "We come hear more often than the nursing home!" with a big grin on his face. He would be suitably sobered within the next few seconds.

Once the whole situation was fully understood, enough vehicles arrived and parked haphazardly all over the street to create an impossible logjam, and several had to be moved to give the ambulance room to get close.

Jon stayed and watched until the passenger side door was unlocked and opened, but when he saw one of the trained professionals turn away and retch at the sight of what was in there, he decided to go back into his house. He'd seen enough of poor Jim Melrose already.

"I'm headed in," he told Darrin quietly.

Darrin turned and looked at him. "I'm sorry about this, Jon. It it's OK, I'll be over later. I need to bounce some things off you." He turned and looked at the beginning of the careful investigative operation around the car and body. It would be a while before they would take the remaining pieces of Jim Melrose away. "I'm going to have to work for a while first," he added, and walked back toward the scene.

"The guys who were at the blockade didn't see the car come in Chief. It had to be after they left," Police Captain John Twyman said. Twyman had been dispatched to question everyone he could find, cops and citizens alike, in most cases waking them up from a dead sleep after having worked all night around Devonshire.

Chief Thomas looked up with a pained expression from his desk chair, first at the man who was reporting to him, and then over at Detective Foster, who was sitting across from him. "So you're telling me that a police car, a stolen police car, drove onto Devonshire, in broad daylight, with a mutilated body in it, right after our blockade had been lifted?"

"Apparently, sir. There's no way it could have gotten in there without somebody seeing it…and seeing the driver, so it had to be after our guys left, and the residents were gone to work," Twyman concluded.

"Sit down Twyman. You're making me nervous," Gus said. Actually, he was just tired of looking up as this man, who had been standing at attention, for some reason, as he reported.

"And we've got no prints from the car?" the Chief asked the nervous, but now sitting Captain.

"Just from Melrose," Detective Foster answered for him as he grabbed a handful of jelly beans from the candy dish on Thomas' desk. "But the boys are still working on it."

And you questioned the people who were there…in, and around the neighborhood?" Chief Thomas asked Twyman.

"Yes, sir. There were only three around at the time. Officer Crandle, who discovered the car and the body…" he pulled a piece of paper out of his shirt pocket, "…a man named Jonathon Parker, and a boy named Robert Frey," he read, before looking back up at his Chief. "None of them saw anything; except of course Crandle, who like I said, discovered the body."

"What was Crandle doing there?"

"He said he was in the process of visiting his friend, Mr. Parker."

Chief Thomas leaned back in his chair, and soon was studying the ceiling with knitted brow and ever deepening worry lines. "I'll be damned," he said, mostly to himself. Then he sat up again abruptly and looked at Twyman again. "How about the houses on Coventry? It would have had to drive up Coventry. Were they all questioned?"

"Yes, sir. The ones that were home. No one saw a thing."

"That guy Parker. Isn't he one of 'em that lives close to where the car was found?"

"Yes, sir."

"And he couldn't help you at all?"

"He says he was asleep until noon. He didn't see anything unusual, sir," Twyman said. He found himself desperately wishing he could say something that would please his Chief.

Chief Thomas rubbed his eyes with both hands, then put them in his lap and looked at Gus Foster, who was concentrating on his jelly beans. "You got any questions Gus?" he asked.

"Nope," Gus said, without looking up.

"You can go Twyman. Good work. Sometimes there's just nothing there," the Chief said disconsolately.

Twyman stood, stepped dramatically back behind his chair, and then saluted his Chief before turning sharply and marching out of the room.

"All your men act like that?" Gus asked after the door closed. He was looking for the last of the black jelly beans.

"No. Just Twyman. What are we gonna do Gus?" Chief Thomas asked plaintively. "I mean, you're in charge here, and we've got all this help, but…"

"Nothin' till we know something," Gus answered, cutting him off. "This guy's smart, but he's getting careless, I'm telling ya. Driving that car back in broad daylight? That's nuts! We'll catch a break Rodney. It's only a matter of time. He'll come to us."

Darrin came back to see Jon at a little after 5:00 that afternoon. He had a 12-pack of Bud Light with him. "I brought dinner," he said when Jon opened the door.

"Don't you have to work tonight?"

"Nope. Worked all day. I got to go to the big meeting with all the big shots. They've got no clue, that's for sure."

Even with the temperatures climbing again it was pleasant out on Jon's deck in the late afternoon, under the shade of the Maple tree that virtually bestrode the deck's west side. There was a soft breeze blowing from the south into their faces, and the view, as always, was spectacular.

"You've been writing," Darrin noted, nodding to the legal pad, pen and various scraps of paper on the table. "I hope it's gonna be a book about all this crap. You'll sell a million copies."

"Actually, that's the plan," Jon said as he cracked open his beer and put his feet up on (not under) the table. "I've been writing an outline of all this. Putting down notes. It's a start. I just don't know how it ends yet."

The two of them drank in silence and looked out at the pasture, and the beautiful but now so ominous looking woods for the next few minutes. For Jon, the drinking was a welcome diversion, a way to finally relax for a few minutes; even if he had been doing way too much of it lately. He had spent the whole afternoon writing, thinking, and trying to get a handle on things.

He was aware that he needed to make some decisions, and

soon; the most fundamental of which, was whether he going to leave or not. Possibly writing a book about it all was one thing, but this "adventure" was beginning to affect his health, at least his mental health. He had to decide how much more, if any, he was going to take.

For Darrin, this was a time for gathering his thoughts, because he had come up with a wild theory that he knew Jon would think was nuts, but he felt compelled to run by him. But perhaps…in stages. It was too much to take all at once. Jon was smart, he knew. Terrified, but smart; and he was just the sort of guy he needed right now. On the long, meaningless patrol that he was assigned to the previous night, he'd had a lot of time to think, and he decided on a few things. And everything that he'd discovered in his research that day had confirmed it.

"The cops are all wrong on this case, Jon," he said to begin.

Jon looked over and said, "Well that came out of the blue."

"I'm serious," Darrin said. He put his beer can on the table, turned his chair toward Jon, bent over and rested his arms on his knees. "I want you to listen to me for a few minutes, OK? You may think I'm nuts…"

"I already do."

"Very funny. Just listen, OK?" Jon was grinning, pleased with himself, but nodded. "Sometimes, at least this is my theory, police, or homicide investigators, or whatever…they get stuck in patterns. Teachers probably do that too. Like, if I did it this way before, and it worked, then I'll do it the same way next time, and forever, because that's the way to do it. Do you know what I mean?"

"I don't know what the hell you're talking about," Jon said, looking bored. "But go the hell ahead."

"OK, I'll cut to the chase," Darrin said. He took a deep breath. "We're looking for all the wrong things, with all the wrong methods. Look at the evidence we've got: a big, fat, nothing. Zero! I'll bet you anything they don't find a single fingerprint in Melrose's car, except for his. Whoever this is, whatever this is, isn't going by the regular rules."

"What do you mean 'whatever this is,'" Jon asked. Darrin had his attention now.

"I mean, well, you were the one that got me thinking about this. You were the one who went to see the old widow first. You were thinking 'outside the box,' like they always say. I just followed the path you were taking."

"What are you getting at, Darrin?" Jon asked. He slapped at a mosquito that had landed on his leg, much harder than was necessary, as if to relieve his stress, and to emphasize to Darrin that he should get to the point at the same time.

"I went through the records today. There's no death certificate for anyone from the Meredith family for anyone but Chester, and that was the old man, the husband, in 1985. There's a birth certificate for a Chester William Meredith from 1957, and one for David Meredith from 1964, but that's it." Darrin sat back in his chair to let it all soak in, before continuing.

Jon was looking out toward the pasture. He had been listening intently, and was fascinated, but didn't show it. He was still not sure about where Darrin was headed. "Go on," was all he said.

"Suppose this Chester kid didn't die, like the old lady babbled. Suppose, because of whatever was wrong with him, the old Chester really did just put him away somewhere. Their story could have been that he died, for their younger son's sake, because they were ashamed of it. People used to be ashamed of mental illness, and that kind of thing back then, right?"

"I guess…I don't know. What are you saying, Darrin?"

"I'm saying that whoever is doing all this, this murder, and this seemingly impossible stuff…is crazy, but smart crazy. Somebody who knows the land. Knows all the tricks. What if it's the young Chester Meredith?"

Jon looked from the pasture to Darrin. "Can I say that you're nuts now?" he asked dryly.

" Listen, didn't the young son, David, tell you that his old man told him to stay away from those woods? Didn't you tell me that he had a feeling that something bad must have happened up there?"

"Yea…but you're the one that threw cold water on it," Jon argued. "You're the one who said I was on a wild goose chase, or snipe hunt, or whatever you said."

"Now I'm taking it back. Now I'm saying you and I can find out for sure." Darrin said, then sat back for a moment. He took a sip from his drink, then added, "I've got some ideas, but I need a partner."

Jon looked hard at his friend, then turned to look out at the peaceful pasture again. "Why in the world wouldn't you work with Dick, or some other cop on this? I wouldn't know what the hell I'm doing," he said sensibly.

"Because you're smarter than any three of those guys put together," Darrin said. He had been expecting this question, and hoped a little flattery would help. "Plus," he added casually, but ominously, "a couple of the things we're going to do are a little, well… illegal."

Chapter 30

At 6:30 P.M., on the button that Monday evening, Fred, Pete and Rory met in Fred's back yard, where they couldn't be seen by any wives (especially Pam). They had agreed to meet at that time every night for the foreseeable future, to assess the possibility of setting up their own trap for the deranged killer. "The way I see it, as soon as we get to a night when there's no cops back in the field, it's a go!" Fred had said, thrilling the other two with his confidence and command.

Now they met in relative secrecy to go over the plan, just in case.

"What do you think Fred? No cops yet!" Rory said excitedly.

Fred raised up a hand for silence, and then peered around the corner of his house. Jim Burgett, who lived across the street and down a few houses on Coventry, was mowing his lawn with earphones on, undoubtedly listening to the Cubs game. He waved to Fred, so Fred waved back. "I don't trust that guy," Fred mumbled, "I swear, he knows what you're thinking before you can even think it." He looked at his two men, "If he comes over here, the meeting's over," he told them.

The other two had no idea what Fred was talking about, so they nodded and waited for instructions.

"Pete, you're the man that makes the call," Fred said. Pete smiled. "You can see that pasture and the woods just taking a few steps into your back yard. The first night, and it could be tonight…that there's no cops stationed back there, you give us each a call, by 10:00, and it's on, for 2:00A.M., like we discussed."

"What if Pam answers the phone?" Rory asked worriedly.

"Simple. He'll ask if Rory can come to the phone!" Fred said irritably.

"She'll want to know what you wanted, why you called me, Pete."

Fred sighed, and peaked around the corner to make sure Burgett was still mowing. He was. "Tell her he asked if he left something over at your house; something like that."

"Pete's never been inside my house, Fred."

"Then tell her he wanted something else! I don't know! You two come up with something!"

"OK," Rory said. "Pete, you and I can have a meeting after this meeting to decide, OK?"

"Sure," Pete answered.

Fred peaked around the corner again… no Burgett. "OK, remember the plan. If there's no call by 10:00, it's off for the night," he said hurriedly. "You men remember your positions once we get out there?" They both nodded. He peaked around the corner again. No Burgett. "OK, meeting's over. As you were, men."

"But Pete and I need to have another meeting, remember?" Rory reminded him.

"Go hold it in your yard! We can't be seen together any longer!" Fred whispered fiercely.

The others started quickly walked away, and Fred scurried into the back door of his house, afraid that Jim Burgett might be coming.

Detective Foster, Chief Thomas and the other various law enforcement luminaries decided on a different, more covert type of strategy for that Monday night. Only one marked police car would be stationed on Devonshire itself. Other officers and several detectives were to be placed surreptitiously in what were thought to be key observation posts around the neighborhood, and bordering the pasture and woods. The consensus was that being "too visible" had perhaps made it "too easy" to avoid detection. Everything, excepting the one obvious cop, was to be hidden.

Dick Blackwell had again drawn the short straw assignment, at least in his opinion. He was instructed to park anywhere he wanted on the little Devonshire cul-de-sac, and to make himself "obvious." So it was Dick who had to brave all of the queries in the first hours of nightfall from what neighbors remained in the emotionally scarred neighborhood.

Pam Frey was the first, and the worst. "Do you mean to tell me that the Highland Police Department is only sending one man to protect that little boy up there?" she demanded as she pointed to her portly son Robert, who was busily and happily finishing off some unidentifiable ice-cream snack as he sat on his porch steps. "How in God's name can you defend that!" she cried.

"I'm just doing what I'm told to do, Ma'am," Officer Blackwell said. He was trying to avoid looking at Pam in the eyes. He found her black eyes frightening, and she seemed one who would be prone to violence. Instead he chose to calmly stare off toward her feasting, corpulent boy.

"Well, I'm calling the Mayor! I know him, you know. Just where are all the other cops, anyway?"

"I'm not at liberty to say, Ma'am."

"You refuse to cooperate? You won't answer a simple question from a citizen who helps pay for your salary?" she screamed. "Is this that fat pig Detective's idea?"

Like Rory and many others before him, Detective Blackwell learned quickly that the quickest way to weather the storm was to silently wait it out. He eventually quit answering, and she eventually went away.

He also talked to Bruce Ellsworth and Dick Korte, who also protested the lack of manpower, albeit more politely. The fact that both of their wives were absent tempered their objections.

His last conversation of the evening was the oddest. Fred Knotts walked out of his house and approached him right before 10:00. He was smiling and friendly. "They leave you out here all alone tonight, bud?" he asked, offering him a handshake.

"Apparently so sir, though I'm not at liberty to say," Dick answered.

"Well, I'm sure they know what they're doing," Fred said. "I admire you guys, I'm telling ya. I have faith in you, sir!" He warmly patted Dick on the back, then turned away smiling and walked back home.

At the same moment Fred was walking back into his house, Darrin stood up from the comfort of the deck chair at Jon's. He stretched, yawned and said "I better get going, old buddy."

Jon was glad to hear it, but not in any kind of spiteful way. They had talked, speculated, and argued for hours, until there was just about nothing else to say. They had, in fact, been talking about baseball for the last half hour, just to give themselves a break.

Jon stood and stretched too. "Thanks for the beer, man. My treat next time," he said.

Darrin helped Jon pick up the several empty cans that were strewn about them, and within a few minutes they were inside and walking toward the front door. "Keep your doors locked tonight Jon," Darrin said, "and remember, I pick you up at 10:00, and we head to Meredith's."

"How could I forget?"

Darrin stopped at the door and turned to face him. "I really appreciate this, Jon. I know you aren't completely buying into it, but…it's just something we gotta try. Besides, what else are we gonna do?"

"I know, I know. Now I've gotta take a piss, so will you please go?"

When 2:15 A.M. came and went without incident; when absolutely nothing happened that was the least bit unusual, Dick Blackwell was so relieved that he became almost instantly sleepy.

It had been a long night already. Besides defending the Department to the residents of Devonshire, he had had to leave his post three times because of an upset stomach. Each time he had to call another car in so that he could leave, and it had been embarrassing as well as painful. The incident from the previous night was also more on his mind than he would even admit to himself, and the tension had built steadily until the magic time had passed.

So at 2:45, with both his stomach and his mind feeling better but his eyes growing heavier, he decided to get out of the car and take a walk up and down Devonshire to get some air.

When Dick's car door slammed Rory came instantly to the alert. It was a still, moonlit night, and from where he was hiding he couldn't tell what had made the noise. He could see Fred, barely, out in the middle of the pasture, dressed in black, crouching down close to the ground. He couldn't see Pete, who was up hiding at the edge of the woods, at all.

Fred had heard the door slam too, but he knew it was a car door slamming, and he guessed that it was Officer Blackwell (who else could it be?). Fred was on alert too, but it wasn't because of the car door. From where he was he could see Pete, but barely. What disturbed him though, was that he had also seen something else, intermittently, something white, moving between the trees. At the moment the car door slammed he saw it, then it was gone. Then he saw it again, closer to Pete, and then it was gone. He had no idea what it was. He was aware that he might be seeing some sort of mirage, but was on full alert anyway.

Pete also heard something right then, but it wasn't the far away car door. It was the crackling of branches, as though someone or some animal was nearby. It wasn't a steady sound. It was like a heavy footstep, then nothing, then another heavy footstep, closer, maybe ten seconds later. Pete faced the woods with his gun ready, and held his breath. It was very quiet. Then, very close, there was deep, gurgling laughter.

A shot rang out just as Dick got to the end of Devonshire. Then another. Then four or five in a row. Then a shout and another round of fire. Then more shouts.

Dick called it in and drew his gun as he sprinted all the way down Devonshire, through Jon's yard and around his house to the pasture where the shots had come from. He saw at least three flashlights converging on the scene, and could hear at least one person, no two, yelling in pain. Not having a flashlight himself, he proceeded to run into the fence that he had forgotten was there at full speed, and when he thumped to the ground his own gun went off. This caused all the flashlights to whirl toward him, and he heard the command "Drop your weapon!" repeated several times while he was lying on the ground, trying to get his wind back.

Jon may have saved his life at that point by turning the deck lights on. It was easy to see then that it was a policeman on the ground tangled in the fence, and the flashlights turned back to the business of finding, and arresting, the wounded.

Chapter 31

It was a miracle that no one had been killed. Though it would take days of ballistics tests and interviews to confirm, the three wounds were in fact inflicted by Fred, a hidden Illinois State Policeman, and Rory.

It was Fred's bullet that brought down Pete, hitting him in the leg after Pete had screamed and fired hysterically several times into the woods. It was the State Policeman who shot Fred's hand (it could just as easily have been his head), when Fred kept firing aimlessly toward the woods. And it was Rory, panicking in his hidden position in the weeds, who shot himself in the leg, leaving him writhing in pain and screaming for help during the bulk of the action.

All three were hospitalized briefly with minor wounds, and all three were officially arrested during the process.. Chief Thomas, who was having trouble sleeping anyway, arrived at the hospital at the same time as the victims, and insisted on interviewing all three before even their families could see them. Even after having his initial hopes dashed (there was no evidence that the killer had been shot), he wanted to see if any of these guys actually saw something during their soon to be legendary misadventure.

When he finally got the doctors OK to talk to them, it was disappointing. All Fred wanted to do was complain that his rights had been violated, and that he was going to sue somebody, though he wasn't quite sure who.

Rory was moaning in pain even though it was a minor wound, and was calling continually for his wife, Pam. When the Chief finally got a question in about what he had seen, he said it was too dark. Then he started crying.

Pete Vanderberg, however, was a different story. He was lying on his back on the stretcher, hazel eyes opened wide and staring at the ceiling. He was trembling from head to toe, even though his flesh wound had been patched, and he had received medication. Chief Thomas had to ask him if he had seen anything three times before he could give an answer, and even then it was a stuttering, halting one.

"It…it was hor…it was horrible!" he said with much effort.

"What was horrible Mr. Vanderberg," Thomas asked.

"The…the face…I shot right…I shot right at him!"

"Did you shoot someone, sir?" Thomas asked. Could someone, maybe the killer, still be out there, he thought excitedly.

Pete seemed to be shaking more all the time. Chief Thomas picked up a blanket lying on the back of a chair and spread it over him. "Th…thank you," Pete stuttered.

"It's OK. Mr. Vanderberg. Who did you shoot at, sir?"

"It was…all white. His face was smiling….he was smiling at me. Laughing…I shot him. I did…"

"Did you miss? Did he run away?"

"He…kept smiling…horrible red… red eyes!"

Then Pete shut his own eyes, and didn't answer any more questions… because he couldn't.

David Meredith gave Jon a 10:30 appointment. He sounded reluctant on the phone, so Jon hinted that he might be interested in buying the property behind his house after all. That got him revved up.

Darrin insisted on not going in with him, even though Jon had asked him to several times. "He might know I'm a cop," he'd said, "and then he might clam up. You gotta better shot by yourself."

Jon knew he was probably right, but was really not looking forward to it. Meredith gave him the creeps.

"How are you this lovely Tuesday!" was Meredith's happy greeting a few minutes later. "Come on in! Hey, I hear ya had more trouble out there last night. Makes ya wonder, don't it?"

Jon didn't get a chance to answer that question, or even get a word in until well after he'd sat down, because Meredith kept babbling on, jumping from one subject to another. He was clearly excited about the possibility of doing some business, and he wouldn't shut up. It wasn't until he had told a long, unfunny joke about a mailman, then put his feet up on his desk while he was laughing that he gave Jon an opening. "What can I do ya for?" he asked.

"Well, sir…"

"Call me Dave!"

"Well, Dave, like I told you on the phone, I've been thinking about, maybe, making you an offer on that land behind my house, and…"

"And you want to know what'd cost ya?"

"Well, yea, but, in light of everything that's been happening around my neighborhood…"

"Ain't that somthin? They aught to stretch that guy from the highest tree when they catch 'em. That's what they ought to do."

"Yes, sir…Dave. But before I make you an offer, I have a few questions, about the history of the land."

"History?"

"Yes. Last time you told me that you were told, by your Dad, never to farm that land, right?"

"That's right," Meredith said with a frozen smile on his face.

It was a hard, grizzled face that gave Jon the strong impression that he'd better not say something wrong.

"And you have no idea what the reason for that was, right?" Jon asked.

"That's right."

"But, you put some kind of crops, what was it…winter wheat or something? You put some rows of that on the south side of the woods not too long ago, right?"

"That's right." He wasn't smiling now.

"Well, can I ask why you did that?" Jon asked. Then he waited nervously as Meredith put his feet down on the floor. He glared right into Jon's eyes.

"If you're worried about that, I can sell you that piece too. It don't amount to much," he said.

"No, no. I was just wondering why you planted on that land after all these years?" Jon asked. Meredith's expression was growing more dour by the second. It was making Jon nervous.

"Well, for the life of me, I can't see what that's got to do anything. What business is that of yours?" Meredith scowled. Jon could easily see that he could be a very intimidating man when he wanted to be. He'd hate to have to really do business with the guy.

"Because stuff started happening not long after you planted," Jon said as firmly as he could. "I know it doesn't make sense, but…"

"You're right. It don't," he said. "Now are we gonna talk business, or what?"

"Did you do it to spite your old man?" Jon asked, then cringed. He was certain Meredith would explode at that, but he didn't. He just stared quizzically at Jon, as if he couldn't quite figure this boy out.

Then he suddenly leaned back in his chair again, put his boots up on the desk and his hands behind his balding head. "I don't have an answer to that," he said after a few seconds. "Tryin' to prove somthin to myself, I guess."

It was clear to Jon that that was as much as he was going to get, so he readied himself for the tough part. "Dave, I have one more thing to ask about, and it won't seem relevant to the land sale either, but I'd like you to answer. If you do, we'll get down to the brass tacks about me buying the land. I promise."

Meredith looked at him suspiciously, but kept his non-threatening posture. "Shoot!" he said, and nodded once firmly.

"You had an older brother. Do you know what happened to him?"

Meredith glared at him. He sat motionless for a long moment. The literary term "pregnant pause," actually went through Jon's head. "You're not here to buy land, are you?" Meredith asked at last.

Jon felt himself beginning to sweat. "I have a friend. He's a cop. He has this theory that your brother…that he never died. That something was wrong with him, and…"

"I never saw my brother," Meredith said calmly but firmly. "He died before I was born, in an accident, and I have no idea why you're asking these questions, but it stops now." He put his feet on the floor again, very deliberately, and pointed toward the door while glaring at Jon. "Get out!" he practically roared.

Jon got to his feet quickly, and did as he was directed, but when he got to the door he turned and saw that Meredith hadn't followed him, at least yet. That made him feel safe enough to say something else. "There's no death certificate for him, Dave. There's no record that your brother died."

Meredith gave him a confused look at first, which abruptly turned to one of red-faced anger within a few seconds. He stood up threateningly and started walking around the desk.

"Do you know where he's buried Dave?" Jon asked, but when he saw the man's face he knew he wasn't going to get an answer. In fact, a beating seemed much more likely.

Jon stepped quickly out the door, slammed it, and jogged

over to where Darrin's car was waiting. He looked back over his shoulder for Meredith before getting in, but he wasn't coming.

"He said he saw the guy, and shot him, but the guy just stood there smiling at him," Chief Thomas told Detective Foster. "He said his eyes were red, Gus."

"It was dark out, for Chrissakes!" Foster said irritably. "He couldn't see shit!" Gus Foster was frustrated for several reasons, not the least of which was that there had been no doughnuts for the morning meeting, and now it was close to noon and he was starving. It had been Rodney's turn to bring them, so it was his fault. He was also frustrated that the three bozos from the neighborhood had ruined his trap the night before, and that the forensics lab was so slow and unhelpful. Also, his hemorrhoids were back.

"I don't know Gus. I'm beginning to think this is bigger; stranger than we can handle. There's something so…different about all this. I mean, we got nothing! Nothing! All these computers and labs and extra help, and all those people expecting us to do something. I just don't know," the Chief said with resignation. Unlike Gus, he wasn't hungry. He had rarely eaten, for days now. He'd lost the five pounds his wife had wanted him to, and then some. He was living on coffee and worry.

Even sitting in an uncomfortable position, and even with all that he was aggravated about, Gus could see that Thomas was becoming unglued by it all, and he felt a fair measure of sympathy for the Police Chief. They were in a hell of a predicament, he knew. What "clues" they had didn't make a lick of sense, and the bravado and confidence he tried to show everyone was only an act that was wearing thin now. He didn't even believe it himself. The fact was they were, literally, clueless.

"All we can do is keep trying, Rod," he said as sympathetically as he could manage. "This guy is smart. Real smart. Some of the worst killers out there are, and sometimes it takes years to catch 'em. That Uni-bomber guy, for example. The FBI looked for that sucker forever, remember? And they still didn't catch 'em. His own brother turned him in!"

"Yea, but this is Highland, damn Illinois," the inconsolable Chief responded, "and it's all taking place in one neighborhood. And it doesn't make sense. It's like its haunted, or something."

Detective Foster smiled, shifted uncomfortably in his chair, and said "Well if it's haunted, we ain't never gonna catch him, are we? Come on, let's run out to the restaurant. Come on Rodney. You can't worry about what you can't control. Nobody has ever been able to do that."

Chief Thomas nodded solemnly, but didn't respond.

"Come on to the diner with me," Foster said as he got to his feet, "I got a few new ideas to run by you… And you're buying, by the way."

bean fields dotted with the occasional hill, farmhouse or barn. They met no traffic, and if it hadn't been for where they were headed, Jon would have enjoyed this drive on a beautiful day. Walking around cemeteries though, even in the middle of the day, had never been his idea of a good time.

The cemetery was right next to a church that looked like it had been built a hundred years before. It was mainly old, rusty brick, with a lot of fancy stone work in the front, beautiful painted glass windows, and a steeple that seemed a mile high when you stood next to the building. The cemetery itself was marked only by a rusty iron gate facing the church that said "Be Blessed in My Arms" or something very similar, as the letters were badly faded by the years. Beyond that were dozens of tombstones, all looking like they had been out in the elements for decades. It was obvious from the weeds everywhere and the tall grass that this was the home of many, long neglected dead.

"Are you sure this is where they buried him?" Jon asked as they looked over the stones. "It looks like it's been completely abandoned. Besides that, it gives me the creeps, even in the middle of the day."

"Yep. There were graveside services. Right here… somewhere." Darrin answered. "Let's get started."

"Get started doing what?" Jon asked suspiciously.

Darrin glared at Jon. "We get started finding his grave, dip shit," he said.

Without another word Darrin walked toward the east after waving Jon toward the west end of the cemetery to start reading the stones. Jon felt terrifically uncomfortable, like he was invading the privacy of all of them. He wanted to get it over with quickly and get out of there, so he worked as quickly as he could. He kept looking for cars to go by and see them wandering around suspiciously, but none did. He went down each row reading as quickly as he could. He noticed that all the stones, at least in his section, told of births and deaths from a long time ago.

Chapter 32

"He's buried in Evergreen Cemetery down by Aviston," D[arrin] said. "At least I think so."

Jon looked at Darrin in astonishment. He could not be[lieve] what was happening. "You really are nuts, aren't you?" wa[s all] he could think of to say as the car barreled down a country [road] that Darrin had told him was a short-cut to their destinati[on.]

Darrin was filling Jon in on his "theory" only a little [at a] time. The purpose of doing so was simple: to keep Jon on bo[ard.] So after Jon had scurried back into the car and filled him i[n on] his conversation with Meredith, Darrin just drove and list[ened.] They were already well out of town before Jon asked him w[here] the hell they were going, that Darrin told him. "We're goi[ng to] see where old Chester Meredith is buried," he said, as th[ough] it were an everyday occurrence. "I want to see if the grav[e has] been disturbed."

"What? Why? What for?" Jon asked.

But Darrin had said nothing more, ignoring Jon's que[stions] and protestations, until this mention of just which ceme[tery] was they were headed for.

"What did you mean when you said the grave mi[ght be] 'disturbed'?" Jon asked.

Darrin looked over briefly at Jon. "Just a hunch," h[e said.] Then he smiled.

This bastard is actually enjoying this stuff, Jon thou[ght.]

They drove for five more miles past mainly flat co[untry]

"Here it is!" Darrin yelled. "That didn't take long!" he said enthusiastically.

His noisy exuberance startled Jon. It seemed to him like it should be against the rules to yell in a graveyard. He trotted quickly over to where Darrin was standing in front of a large tombstone, hoping he wouldn't yell out again.

"What do you notice?" Darrin asked once he'd been there for a minute. He spread both his hands out and waved them in a way to indicate it wasn't just Chester Meredith's grave he was talking about, but the whole area. He was way too excited.

"I just got here. What's to notice?" Jon asked.

"Two things," Darrin said happily. "First, do you see his son's grave anywhere around?"

Jon quickly looked at the stones on either side of Meredith's, as well as the one directly behind it. "Well, no. So what?"

"Maybe nothing, but if you had lost a son in a farm accident, wouldn't you want to be buried in the same cemetery?" Darrin asked.

"Yea, I guess, but…what are you saying?" Jon was very nervous, but becoming intrigued.

"We'll check the rest of the stones to be sure, but there's something else unusual here. Can you spot it?"

Jon looked around again, but saw nothing unusual at all. "Why don't you just tell me, Sherlock," he said sarcastically.

"Look at the grass in front of the stone," Darrin said. "It's sod. It's dead grass, but it's sod, and none of the other graves have that. They're all covered in regular grass and weeds." He reached down and pulled at one of the pieces. It came up fairly easily. "And it didn't have time to take root!" Darrin shouted triumphantly.

Jon took a step back. He was still confused, but beginning to see where Darrin was going with this. "Exactly what are you saying?" he asked anyway, "I need to know. Right now."

"The body you discovered," Darrin said, "it's got the forensics people all confused, right? They say it appears to have been dead for a long time. Maybe a real long time. 'The mummy,' they call it. If Chester Meredith's boy didn't die, and if he was crazy, maybe he'd be crazy enough to dig up his old man, and mutilate him, just like he did to Melrose and those pets. It's got to be the same person, we know that, so why not Chester Meredith Jr.?"

Jon stood looking at his friend with his mouth hanging open in amazement. It was so ridiculous that it actually kind of made sense, if you completely suspended your sense of disbelief. But it was almost too much to comprehend. A crazed killer who would dig up his own father?

"How, how are we…how are you ever going to know?" Jon stuttered. He was beginning to feel like he was in a bad dream, and he wasn't sure he really wanted to hear Darrin's answer.

"Easy," Darrin smiled. "We dig up the casket and see if old Chester is in there," he said matter-of-factly. "That's the illegal part I was telling you about. You check the rest of the tombstones for any Merediths, I'll go get the shovels out of the trunk."

Darrin walked away, while Jon found himself holding onto Chester Meredith's tombstone, to try to keep himself from fainting.

"It's the worst thing I've seen in my life, Margie," Pete said. He felt a sob welling up in his throat, again, and he bent his head down and hugged himself to try to keep it down. He and Margie were standing out in their back yard, looking at the pasture and woods to the southeast, behind Jon's, as they talked. "We've got to get out of here honey," he added solemnly, when he could speak again.

Pete had been told to stay home from work for a day or two, and to elevate the leg with the flesh wound. He had found that to be nearly impossible. He just couldn't do it. The only thing he had been half-way comfortable with had been sitting out on his back porch, or standing where he was now. He had just been staring out there, and thinking, all morning and now into the afternoon. Margie had brought him his lunch outside, and now, checking on him again, she had found him out here at the corner of their lot, all alone, like a man looking for something that he was very afraid of finding. Margie was very worried. He was pale, continually trembling, and his hair seemed to have turned grayer overnight.

And he was not following the Dr.'s instructions.

Margie searched for the right, comforting words to say. She reached out to pat his arm. "I know losing Bubo was hard on you too, honey," she said cluelessly. "We can always get another dog."

Even in his misery, Pete found himself turning to look at her. Her words would have made him snap like a dry twig just the day before, but now he only felt sympathy for her; and for everybody else. They didn't know. They just didn't know.

"It was there, Margie," he said softly, shifting his gaze slowly back toward the woods. "It was the thing that's been doing all the killing. We have to leave. Tonight."

Margie just nodded, and patted his arm affectionately.

It was the hardest damned work Jon could ever remember doing. Digging a six foot hole in the hot July sun for a guy that could barely jog half a mile without stopping was, as he told Darrin repeatedly, nuts. "Friggin' nuts!" to be exact.

And it wasn't just the work. It was the anxiety. Darrin had told him that doing this in the light of day was exactly the right time to do it. "No one suspects you when the do the crime right in front of them," he had said. "Wave to the people when they drive by. If we did this at night, we'd get busted in the first half-an-hour."

But Jon didn't buy it, and every time a car drove by (three times, but it seemed like more) he cringed in fear, once even diving into the hole they were digging. Darrin got a good laugh out of that one, and waved merrily at the passers-by.

It took them an hour to get the job done, even though the ground was relatively soft. It was an hour where Darrin never seemed to take a break, and Jon needed one every five minutes. It was an hour where Jon's objections grew less and less stringent, but only due to an increasing lack of breath to voice them. And it was an hour during which his anxiety grew with each shovel full of dirt.

At the end, it was Jon's shovel that hit the coffin first. His reaction was to almost throw up, and to crawl urgently out of the hole as fast as he could. He let Darrin do the rest. He couldn't make himself look a few minutes later, when Darrin actually opened the coffin. It got very quiet when he did. Then the coffin closed, and Darrin came up clutching something in one of his hands. He sat down by Jon, and got his breath. Jon didn't even want to look at him.

"I was right. Empty," he said. "except for this."

He handed Jon a piece of paper. It was a drawing, Jon saw. A picture a kindergartner might draw. They were childishly drawn stick figures of two people. The small figure had a frown, and what appeared to be large blue tears coming down its face. The large stick figure was standing by the little one, with both eyes scratched out, wildly, in bright red crayon.

Chapter 33

"We've got to tell the investigators about this. You know that, right?"

Darrin didn't answer. His eyes were on the road and his lips pursed in concentration, his thoughts were a thousand miles away from Jon's frantic questions. He was speeding down a country road back toward Highland, trying to balance the adrenaline high he was feeling with what the next logical step should be.

"We've got to report this, even if we get accused of being grave robbers," Jon pleaded. "You figured this out, man! You're a genius! I admit it! But we've got to tell the people in charge, Darrin."

Darrin snapped out of it long enough to glance over at Jon, then looked back at the road. "Tomorrow," he said.

"Tomorrow?! Somebody else could be dead by tomorrow! We know who the damned killer is, Darrin!" Jon shouted.

"Easy, easy. You're going a little apeshit on me, partner. We're in the same car. I can hear you," Darrin said calmly. "Let's go to your house and have a beer. We deserve it. Then we'll talk it out."

"Talk what out? We can't just sit on this! Are you friggen' nuts? And don't you have to work tonight, anyway?"

"Personal Day," Darrin smiled. "We get two a year, and I took one for tonight."

"Personal Day? What the hell is that? Why?'

Darrin looked at Jon again as he slowed the car. They were entering the Highland city limits. "You're beginning to hurt my feelings," Darrin said. "It almost sounds like you don't want me to take off! Don't you like my surprises, dear?"

Darrin looked over at Jon, smiling, but quickly saw that Jon was in no mood. He quickly changed gears. "I took a day because I thought we might find what we found out today. There's a couple of things I... we, still need to do. Take it easy. I'll go see the Chief first thing in the morning. I swear."

"What do you mean '*we* need to do'? 'We' my ass! We already broke the law, you dumbass!"

Jon was a little perturbed, at this point.

"The place is haunted," Ben Wilson said matter-of-factly. "Strange stuff's been happening in that patch of woods for years Rodney. There just wasn't anybody that got killed, that's the difference."

Ben Wilson was as highly respected a citizen as Highland had. The bald, 79 year-old long-retired lawyer and city council member had sought out Police Chief Thomas for "a cup of java," and they sat now in the 8th Street Café in the late afternoon, doing just that.

"I know the word 'haunted' sounds a little strong," Ben went on, "but I'm telling you, there's a reason they haven't developed that property."

Chief Thomas was fascinated by what he was saying, but had to wonder if the old-timer wasn't finally losing his marbles. Still, the fact that it was Ben Wilson made him listen…closely.

"What kind of things happened out there?" the Chief asked.

"Oh, goofy stuff," Ben said dismissively, "Halloween type, scary stuff. Kids would wander back there and get the hell scared out of 'em, and never go back. They claimed there was some kind of monster out there, or ghost. One parent actually brought it up at a City Council meeting once, but we laughed it off. It was nothing like now. Nothing at all."

Thomas thought about Pete Vanderberg at the hospital the night before. He'd had the hell scared out of him too. Could someone be playing the same game, though now in a much deadlier way?

"Doesn't David Meredith own that land?" the Chief asked.

"Well yea!" Ben looked surprised. "You mean you haven't talked to him yet?"

"There's been no reason to," Thomas answered. "We've searched those woods again and again. There's nothing there."

"That's kind of my point. There's nothing there…but there's a legend there. Sometimes legends hold a grain of truth. David's old man wouldn't touch it either. I'd talk to him, Rodney. You ain't getting anywhere anyhow. Might as well."

"Just do two more things with me, and I'll walk right into the station and tell the Chief. Deal?"

"How stupid do you think I am?" Jon answered. "I've got to hear what the two things are, and if they're illegal, I'm out."

Darrin and he were out on the deck, sipping the best beer they'd ever had (after downing two glasses of ice-water apiece). Jon could already feel soreness setting in all over his body from their frenzied digging. He couldn't imagine what he would feel like by the next morning.

"I'm thinking that there are a couple of simple things we could do that might, just might, clarify this case a little bit," Darrin began. "Knowing who this guy might be, and catching him, are two different things. If the younger Chester Meredith, who'd still be pretty old, is really behind all this, nobody's seen him yet, so…"

"I've seen him."

The words had come from just off the west side of the deck and down the hill, just past the base of the towering Maple tree. Darrin and Jon both jumped a little, and Jon let out an involuntary gasp of alarm. Then he saw who it was.

"Damnit Pete! You scared the hell out of us! What the hell are you doing?" Jon demanded.

Pete's face was chalky and expressionless. He looked up at Jon as if trying to make up his mind about something. After a moment of indecision, he started walking, limping, toward the steps of the deck. Jon thought he looked as pale as one of the zombies he'd seen in a movie recently.

"What do you mean, you saw him?" Darrin asked as Pete struggled up the two steps to join them.

Pete didn't answer right away. He came over to where the two were sitting, sat down heavily into a chair facing the two men, and then looked at them solemnly. He struggled to get his breath, and his head trembled as he spoke. "I saw the thing out there. Last night, before I was wounded. You're not going to catch him."

Jon and Darrin exchanged glances, then looked back over at the stricken neighbor. He looks like he's aged ten years, Jon thought.

"What did you see, Pete?" Darrin asked.

"It was laughing. It wasn't there, and then it was," Pete said. He was having trouble being coherent. His breathing was still labored. Jon wondered if he'd been drinking. "…right next to me," he continued. "He was white, like he was already dead. I shot him. Twice. He just smiled at me. It was horrible Jon! You've got to get out of here. That's why I'm here. Everybody's got to get out of here! You need to help me tell everyone."

Jon could feel the hair on his scalp and back of his neck tingle. There seemed to be a knot in his stomach and his throat at the same time. Pete was so absolutely convinced about what he had seen that it was impossible not to take him seriously. He was so devastated.

"Did you see him run away?" Darrin asked. He was leaning forward, studying Pete intensely. He looked to Jon like he wasn't the least bit shook up by Pete's story.

"No. He just... disappeared. His eyes were so red. Did I tell you that? I can still see those eyes, Jon."

Chief Thomas decided to stop and pay David Meredith a visit after having coffee with Ben Wilson. Meredith was meeting with a banker in town, so he had to wait. Meredith kept looking over at the Police Chief as he listened to the banker's proposal. He seemed nervous about getting a visit from someone in uniform. It's a little like driving down the street and noticing that there's a cop car in your rear view mirror, Riggs thought. You're always wondering if you did something wrong.

When the banker left, Chief Thomas introduced himself, and as Jon had done earlier, was invited to sit across the desk from the wealthy farmer and look at the bottom of his boots.

"What can I do ya for, Chief?" he asked with his usual greeting.

"I'm here to ask you about that land you own behind Devonshire. The plot with the pasture and the stand of woods?"

"Join the club. You're the second one today to ask me about that. First one was a rude son-of-a-bitch though."

Chief Thomas' curiosity was aroused. "Who else was here," he asked. His immediate suspicion was that it was Gus Foster, who was rude to everyone.

"It was that young teacher at the high school who lives at the end of the cul-de-sac. Uh...Jon Parker, or Parkland."

Chief Thomas knew who that was. "How was he rude?" he asked.

"Oh, he acted like he might want to buy the land. He really

just wanted to ask a lot of personal questions. I have no idea what he was after," Meredith said.

Chief Thomas' instincts told him a guy like Meredith absolutely knew what Parker was after, but he decided to let it go for now. "We have a neighborhood that's pretty much terrorized down there," he said, "and we've had some terrible things happen, as I'm sure you know."

"Yes sir. I'm sorry about that cop."

"The residents all seem to think that whoever is doing these things… they're coming out of your woods to do it."

"Who says that?" Meredith asked defensively.

"Everyone who lives there, Mr. Meredith. I'm not accusing you of anything, sir. You don't need to get defensive with me."

Meredith said nothing, but he wore his bullying sneer on his face.

"Have you ever known, have you ever noticed, or heard about any strange activity taking place on that land?" Thomas asked.

Meredith relaxed a little bit. He was beginning to think that he better not shoot too much bull with this fella. The guy had a tough side. A cool kind of tough. Besides, he didn't know much he could tell. Give them what they want, and they'll leave sooner that way.

"I know about how kids think it's haunted, if that's what you mean. I've heard that since I was a little boy. But I've never had no trouble, or had squatters, or nothing like that. Besides, you guys have searched them woods enough, haven't ya? You know there's nothing in there."

"How do you know we searched?" Thomas asked.

"Cause they're my woods, Mr. Police Chief."

What an arrogant son-of-a-bitch, thought Thomas. Used to getting his own way. Arrogant.

"An old-timer told me that your Dad wouldn't mess with that land. Is that right?"

Meredith sighed. "Yea, that's true, but he never told me why. He just told me not to ever go in there, or farm any of it."

"Did you?"

"What?"

"Go in the woods, or farm any of the land."

"No!…Not for years anyway. I put a little wheat down there on the south end a few weeks ago, but it's nothing," Meredith said. He had turned red. It seemed to Thomas like he realized he had made a mistake, or was embarrassed about something. Something wasn't right.

He decided to press him. "You farmed where your Dad told you never to farm?"

"That's my business, not yours," Meredith huffed.

"You're wrong about that Mr. Meredith. I don't know what the hell is happening here, but when dead people start showing up, it's my business," Thomas pointed out calmly. But the truth was, he didn't have a clear purpose in his questioning, and he had no idea where to go next. Arguing with some farmer over a few rows of wheat wasn't going to get him anywhere, but he thought he could sense something. Something was wrong, for a guy to be this defensive.

"Mr. Meredith, I'm just going to ask you one more question: Do you have any idea, any idea at all, about what might be causing all this to happen, or who it might be that's killing these people?"

Meredith smiled for a second, then swung his feet down to the floor, leaned over his desk, and looked at the Chief soberly. "I have no idea whatsoever, Chief," he said.

He's lying, Chief Thomas thought. For some reason, he's lying.

Chapter 34

"David Meredith is lying," Darrin said as they walked back to Jon's deck.

They had had to take Pete home. He had become more of a mental and physical wreck with each minute that went by on the deck, and was crying like a baby at the end. It shook Jon badly, and even bothered Darrin. They ended up taking him home to his Margie, each helping support him with an arm, and helped get him into bed while his wife called the doctor. It had been a sad, and alarming sight to see.

"What are you talking about?" Jon asked irritably. "We just saw a guy fall completely apart right in front of us, and you're thinking about David Meredith?"

Darrin didn't answer until they were back on the deck. Jon asked him if he wanted another beer, and he agreed to just "one more." After they'd sat in silence for a few minutes, each looking out at the woods with their own thoughts, Darrin broke the quiet.

"Meredith has to know something. He has to," Darrin said.

"Why go there now?" Jon asked. "You don't think he's the killer, do you?"

"No. Probably not."

"Then what's the difference?"

"Because he might know who the killer is, that's why," Darrin said. He looked at Jon, who he knew was becoming more recalcitrant with each passing minute, and said, "OK, we'll just do one more thing, and then I'll call Chief Riggs. What do you say?"

"Is it illegal?"

"Yes...technically," Darrin answered.

"No."

"Come on, hear me out, Jon! We might be able to stop all this!"

Jon looked at Darrin and frowned. He felt like he was almost at the end of his rope. He'd veered between numbing shock and being outright terrified for too long now. The grave robbing had been about all he could take, and Pete...well, it was horrifying.

"The way I figure it," Darrin began, figuring he had nothing to lose with Jon, "Old Chester Meredith had made some kind of deal with the Devil...probably his first son, young Chester. Now just suppose, and you've got to stay with me for a minute Jon; suppose the kid was flat crazy, like the old lady said."

"She didn't say that, exactly," Jon interrupted.

"Just say he was, OK?" Darrin demanded. "Now, say old Chester, with another kid on the way, finally decides he's got to do something with the kid. So he takes him out in the woods, and...I don't know, leaves him out there. Chains him up or something."

"Jesus Christ," Jon said impatiently.

"Stay with me!" Darrin said. "Christ, I don't know what happened, exactly, but open your damn mind up for a minute!"

Jon shook his head, but didn't say anything. Darrin continued.

"So say, however it happened, that there was a deal struck. Between the two Chesters. 'Here's your piece of land, I'll stay off it, but you can't ever leave it.' Something like that. Then David Meredith, years after the old man's death, decides to violate the agreement. 'What the hell,' he figures, 'it's my damn land now.'"

"So young Chester, who lives where nobody can find him,

gets pissed off and starts killing everything," Jon interrupted sarcastically.

"Almost," Darrin answered. "Young Chester's crazy, see. He doesn't know his old man didn't do it. So the first thing he does is to dig up the old man and mutilate him. When that doesn't work, he starts killing everything he can find."

Darrin stopped, and took a big swig from his beer. He knew that Jon's first reaction would be dismissive or sarcastic, so he wanted to let it all soak in and get it over with. Jon's first words surprised him.

"Why wouldn't he kill his brother David?"

"Cause he can't find him," Darrin said. "Except for old Chester, he's only killed things that wandered into his territory."

Then the two were quiet for a few minutes. Jon thought that actually there were aspects of Darrin's story that held at least a degree of plausibility. He had been right on about the empty grave, and parts of this wild theory he'd just heard had a, distant… ring of truth to it. But his head was swimming with all kinds of possibilities; all kinds of grisly pictures.

"Why did he put Melrose's head on my porch?" he asked Darrin quietly, playing along.

"Maybe he thinks you're his younger brother…or maybe he's just trying to scare everybody away. I don't know."

Jon looked at Darrin, "What do you think Pete saw?" he asked.

Darrin took a deep breath and sat back. "I don't know, Jon," he said, "but I'll bet anything he saw something. It was real to him. I've never seen anybody more shook up."

Jon closed his eyes and tried to imagine what Pete had described: something so horrible, so beyond what we know to be real, that it changes you forever. It was just too hard to really accept.

"What is it that you want to do?" he asked Darrin when he opened his eyes.

"We can't afford it," Detective Foster told Chief Thomas, "The state won't back us up. The news has died down a little, and they're pulling some people out already."

They were sitting in Chief Thomas office in the late afternoon, discussing what strategy to try next. Thomas had suggested going back to some sort of saturation coverage and Foster was delivering the bad news.

"The State guys are as frustrated as we are, Rodney," he continued. "They want to work on something that has clues." He reached over and grabbed a handful of jelly beans. "Hell, half the neighborhood's gone anyway. Might do just as well with just a couple of men out there."

Foster was so unemotional about everything; so nonchalant, that it was beginning to really bother the Chief. What they were involved in was the most serious thing that Highland had ever seen, would probably ever see, and Gus acted like he'd just as soon be fishing.

"We've got to keep working on this, Gus," he said forcefully. "We can't give up!"

Detective Foster looked at him coolly as he chewed the candy from across the table. "I'm not," he said.

Thomas looked at him for a long moment, then sighed and sat back in his chair. "Had a couple of interesting conversations today," he said. "one with a guy that told me the woods are haunted and I should talk to Dave Meredith. So I did."

"Haunted, huh. Who's Meredith?" Foster asked.

"He owns all the land behind Devonshire. Owns half the county. He told me that his Dad told him never to farm that land. That's why it's just a field and woods."

"And?"

"He was lying to me Gus, about something. And there

was no reason to. He was defensive as hell. I think he knows something he's not telling anybody about."

"Maybe we should bring him in. Push him a little bit," Gus said.

"Maybe," Chief Thomas said as he leaned back to study the ceiling.

"You've got to be kidding!" Jon cried.

"Nope," Darrin replied, "I think it's worth a try. I'll go do it alone if you're chicken. Course, it'll take me twice as long."

Darrin had just explained what he had in mind to do late that afternoon, and that night. Both parts sounded absolutely insane to Jon.

"First, while it's still light out," Darrin had said, "7:00 or so, when everybody's home for dinner - we drive out to the south side of the woods, see where that winter wheat is planted, and we pull up or destroy as much of it as we can. That's the illegal part." Jon had just looked at him, open-mouthed, in astonishment. "Then," he had continued, "I call Thomas and tell him everything, except maybe the crop damage part, and the grave digging part, like I promised you. After that, we wait for it to get nice and dark, and we make our little trip."

"What trip?" Jon asked incredulously.

"The trip into the woods. Armed, of course. We call Chester out. We tell him the crops his brother planted are gone, that he's got his land back!"

Jon got up and started pacing up and down his deck, obviously upset, and trying to think of just where to begin his answer. "This...this isn't a game, Darrin! Pulling up crops?! You actually think the killer is going nuts because of a few rows of winter wheat?"

"I don't know," Darrin said calmly.

"Call Chief Thomas right now or I will!" Jon yelled. He had

stopped pacing and was pointing his finger at his seated friend for emphasis.

"I can't until I do the crops thing," Darrin said evenly. "I have to do that first."

"You don't have to do anything! We just dug up a coffin! Isn't that enough excitement for one day?" He began pacing again.

"Look, it's wild, I know. But I think we're onto something, Jon. Like I said, I'll do it by myself, if you want out. But no one will see us. It's close to the woods, and we can hide in them if we hear a car coming."

"Yea! Oh yea! That would be safe, wouldn't it? Hide in the woods. Jesus!"

Darrin watched his agitated friend for a few moments, then said, "They've tried everything else, Jon. It's a shot."

"It's a crazy shot!" Jon shouted back.

"We've got a little over an hour before we go. Just think about it." Darrin said.

"I don't have to think about it! I'm out! No way!" Jon shouted defiantly.

Chapter 35

"I can't believe I'm doing this," Jon mumbled disgustedly, more to himself than to his partner in crime.

He and Darrin were indeed in the mysterious field under the darkening evening shadows of the south end of the woods, each with a hoe in hand, walking systematically down the last two rows of winter wheat, killing the innocent, just emerging plants with each step they took.

"Another five minutes and we'll be done," Darrin said. "Quite a day so far, huh?"

Jon couldn't think of a good enough sarcastic answer, so he just kept working. He was having a hard enough time keeping up as it was, and he was also, for the second time that day, sweating and nearing exhaustion. So he saved his breath.

The two men worked steadily, gradually moving into complete shade as they smashed and dug up the last of the plants; the ones closest to the trees. When they were down to the very end, Jon stopped and leaned on his hoe and tried to catch his breath while watching Darrin take the last few whacks.

When there was one plant left, Darrin raised his hoe dramatically toward the woods and screamed out "Here it is Chester! The last one! May it, and you, rest in peace!" Then he brought the hoe down on the helpless plant with all his might, crying out a mighty "UUGGHHH," in the process.

He turned then, with a grin on his face to see if his gesture had met with Jon's approval. Jon was lying, face down in the dirt and not moving, almost 20 yards away from where he had just been standing.

Darrin looked at him for a long moment, his smile gone, trying to comprehend what had just happened. How did Jon get that far away that fast?

Then he grinned again, and yelled "Very funny Jon! You are very damned funny, you know it? I get it!"

But Jon didn't move.

"You can get up now..." Darrin said, more uneasily this time.

Jon still didn't move. He was lying face down, and was motionless.

Darrin threw down his hoe and dashed through the soft dirt to where his friend was lying. He turned him over. "Jon! Jon, what happened?"

Jon's eyes were closed, but Darrin saw his chest moving a bit. He was breathing, but irregularly. Darrin slapped softly at his face. "Jon! Come on buddy. Wake up buddy!" He reached for his water bottle (Jon's was empty), unscrewed the cap, and poured what he had left onto Jon's head and face. Jon's eyes started to flutter, he coughed, then he blinked and gradually opened them. He looked up at Darrin, then seemed suddenly to realize where he was, and in panic, tried to rise to his feet.

"Hey! Hey! Hold on!" Darrin said as he struggled to hold Jon's arms down. "You're all right, man. You're all right," he told Jon, "a little too much sun...My fault, Jon, my fault."

Jon's face was beet red, and his blue eyes were wide open in alarm. "I didn't pass out!" he screamed at Darrin, "I got attacked!"

Darrin let him go, and Jon immediately sat up. "What the hell do you mean?" Darrin asked.

"I got...picked up! Thrown! Oh my God!" Jon cried. He looked, wide-eyed past Darrin and into the woods, then quickly scrambled to his feet. "We gotta get outta here!" he said.

Jon's eyes were hysterical enough to cause Darrin to turn from his knees to try to see what he was looking at. At first, he saw nothing but a lot of shadow and tall trees, but after a few moments, he saw something else. Jon's hoe was at least 10 feet off of the ground with its blade embedded in the trunk of a huge oak tree, as though it had been thrown with tremendous force, at least 30 yards from where he and Jon currently were.

Darrin rose slowly to his feet. "What the hell?" he said, and started walking slowly toward the oak.

"Leave it!" Jon yelled with as much force as he could muster. "This time, you're listening to me! Let's go! NOW!"

July in Highland, and in all of North America for that matter, means that the days start becoming, incrementally, shorter. Most people, busy with the normal pursuits of work and summer recreation, hardly notice. Excepting the occasional relaxed and informed evening comment made from a thousand places (inevitably, with cool drink in hand) that usually goes something like: "You know, it doesn't seem like it, but the days are getter shorter now," there is hardly reason in the hottest of months to mourn the shortness of days.

The residents of Devonshire, with the remarkable dark week that they had experienced, were the dramatic exceptions. The setting sun was like a mournful bell that tolled the end of peace, and the beginning of long, tumultuous night; night they had once known, and taken for granted as Heavens' reward for the labor of day. It seemed long ago now, and everyone, whether still at home, or far away, knew exactly when the sun would set.

The cul-de-sac that Jon and Darrin drove back into that early evening was a far different one now than back then. Three men were nursing gunshot wounds and shattered psyches, caused by their own self-inflicted foolishness. They also no longer had guns. Two wives and four children had been sent away. Spontaneous vacations had now claimed three families, as the Closters and the Carmines had joined the Bensons in seeking retreat. For Sale signs were about to ring the tiny neighborhood, though only one, standing alone in front of the Ellsworth house, had made its initial presentation. Indeed, Devonshire Street would be as dark that night as it had ever been.

Pete Vanderberg knew he could not spend another night at 333 Devonshire. He was also not well. Not having the means or the vacation time in hand to escape, he made a decision that was, in effect, the embracing of his second worst nightmare to avoid sleeping with his first: he told Margie that they were going over to her Mother's house to spend the night. Perhaps many nights. For Margie, this was wonderful news.

Dick Korte had made a similar decision. He missed Ginger far too much to spend another night alone.

The restless and haunted Bruce Ellsworth had decided to stay, and was at his living room window, as was his firm habit of late, when Jon and Darrin arrived home just before a purple and gold sunset began. He made the immediate decision to break his self-imposed isolation to walk over and visit. Anything was better than watching the sun gradually leave his forlorn and darkened neighborhood to night. There would be solace in company.

Jon, who was still in somewhat of a state of shock, and Bruce sat on the deck while Darrin went inside to make his promised phone call. Chief Thomas' wife Mary answered the phone, and seemed to be reluctant to hand it over to her suffering husband, especially after Darrin identified himself as a police officer. "Can I tell him what this is about?" she asked archly.

"It is in regard to an important case we're working on

Ma'am," Darrin answered. He felt nervous calling the Chief, and didn't want to mess around.

"All right then," she said, but it was a full ten seconds before his boss picked up the phone, and Darrin could hear what he took to be arguing on the other end.

"Yes Crandle, how can I help you," Thomas said crisply when he finally picked up.

"Chief, I need to talk to you," Darrin said quickly. The way the Chief had answered gave him the feeling that he didn't have much time.

"Can't it wait until morning Crandle?" the Chief asked irritably.

"No sir. It involves the Devonshire murders, sir. I think I know who did it, and I think I know the identity of the first victim, sir." In the ensuing silence, Darrin imagined his career spiraling toward the earth as fast as Bobo had.

Rodney Thomas found himself dumbstruck. Disorganized thoughts, along with a thrill of excitement, competed for his tongue. Wasn't Crandle off today? Should he call Gus? Could this kid really have something? First victim's identity? From a rookie cop?

"Sir?...Are you there sir?"

"Yes...yes I am. You bet I am. Can you come over here, to my house Crandle?"

"Sir, I'd prefer you to come over here, to the Parker residence on Devonshire, if that's OK. There's another person, maybe two, that I want you to hear from, besides myself. And sir, I would really prefer it if you didn't bring anyone else, sir." By that, he meant Detective Foster, of course.

There was another long pause, and Jon was about to ask again if the Chief was there, when he finally answered, "I'll be right there Crandle. Put the coffee on."

Darrin closed his cell, then slid open the door to the deck. Jon and Bruce both turned in their chairs to face him with anxious school-kid like faces.

"Put on a pot of that crappy coffee you make," Darrin said. "The Chief is on his way. Bruce, I'm going to need to talk to Jon for a minute alone. No offense. We just have to get our facts lined up, OK?"

Chapter 36

"God damn that's hot! What'd ya do, boil it?" Chief Thomas had spit out his first sip of Jon's coffee onto the kitchen table, and after the aforementioned slur, was now rubbing his burnt lips with one hand and fanning himself with the other.

"I should have warned you. Sorry," Darrin said. "I found out the hard way too. You gotta give it a minute."

Darrin and Jon had talked briefly while Jon was making coffee and Bruce was still outside, and they had a plan on how they were going to play things. They didn't think Bruce should be around for the sordid details, so the plan was to switch off. Darrin would do his part while Jon stayed outside with Bruce, then vice versa. They had determined on their ride back into town just what they were going to tell the Chief, and, just as importantly, what they weren't going to tell him. Nervous Bruce didn't need to hear it all. It was as simple as that. And besides, it had occurred to Darrin that maybe they could use him.

"OK, what do you got for me, Crandle," Chief Thomas asked. He blew on his coffee while raising his eyes to the rookie cop.

"I'm pretty sure that the first dead body is Chester Meredith, David Meredith's father," Darrin said flatly. "I think if we could get some DNA somehow, maybe from the old man's house, we could prove it."

Chief Thomas forgot about blowing on his coffee. He sat slowly straight up, staring at his young patrol officer in wonder.

"How in God's name do you know that?" was all he could think of to ask.

Darrin, who had been standing nervously behind the kitchen chair opposite the Chief, quickly sat down in it. "I, well, Jon and I…have been trying to apply a different kind of logic to an illogical situation, I guess you'd say." Chief Thomas just looked at him. Darrin continued. "Chester had a son before David, whose name was also Chester. The legend is that young Chester got killed in a farm accident, but there's no record of it. I went way back. I'm not saying I'm the greatest researcher ever, but I don't think he died, Chief. I think he's our killer."

Darrin stopped here to let the Chief grasp the enormity of what he was saying. He was determined to tell his story without revealing where he and Jon had crossed the legal line if possible, as per their agreement made earlier, but only if he could accomplish his goal of getting the Boss on board. He could already tell from the expression on the Chief's face that it was going to be difficult.

"How the hell do you know all that?" Chief Thomas asked. He looked a little like a man who knew he was having his leg pulled, but couldn't quite figure out how it was being done. And he didn't like it.

Darrin told him about the nursing home visits to Lilly Meredith, about Jon's visits to David Meredith (one of which the Chief already knew about), and about the strange, silent understanding the Meredith's had about not farming the land. He tried his best to paint the picture as he theorized it, without including everything.

Some of this, of course, rang true with Chief Thomas, because of his recent conversation with the suspiciously arrogant David Meredith. But a lot of what he was hearing seemed a stretch too. It was about to get worse.

"There's something else about all this that you should know," Darrin said a while later. "This Chester Meredith, the young Chester…" he paused here to try to come up with the right wording. It was difficult to talk to your boss this way. He might get laughed out of the room, and out of a very short career. "He's, uh...he might not be real. Not in the way we think of it."

"What do you mean?" Chief Thomas asked. His strange interview with Pete Vanderberg went through his head.

"Some things have happened, really all these things... they seem almost, supernatural, I guess you'd say." Darrin felt himself beginning to sweat, even though they were sitting in a comfortable, air-conditioned house.

Thomas didn't respond, and Darrin couldn't read anything on his face. Darrin pointed out to the deck. He was changing his game plan a bit. "Both those guys out there, and that Pete guy next door; they all had things happen to them, violent things, that don't make sense. But I'm sure they happened. I want you to listen to their stories, Chief. Please. It'll only take a few more minutes."

Chief Thomas moved from his hunched over, intense listening position to leaning back in his chair. He took a deep breath and looked up to Jon's kitchen clock. It seemed to Darrin like he was trying to make up his mind. It was a nerve-wracking few moments.

"I've already talked to Pete," the Chief said finally. "He told a strange story all right, but he'd just gotten shot, Darrin. He was hysterical." He looked again at the clock, then pulled out his cell phone to check for messages, and thought about it. It had been a strange day, from Ben Wilson's words about haunting to his brightest young patrolman telling ghost stories. It certainly wasn't a logical day. That was for sure.

"Sure, what the hell," Chief Thomas said, in a bit of a disparaging manner, "Bring in your witnesses, Crandle."

For the next 45 minutes, Chief Thomas listened.

First, it was to the reluctant Bruce, who had had no idea

when he came over for a little male camaraderie that he would soon be testifying to the Police Chief about something he didn't want to think about while sober, much less talk about. His story of the mysterious encounter in the woods from only a few days before left a lot to be desired, as far as Darrin was concerned. He kept using qualifiers, such as "it seemed like…" and "I'm not sure…' and it seemed like he was embarrassed even to talk about it.

"All I know is you were terrified enough to immediately put your house up for sale," Darrin added pointedly after he had finished. Bruce had nothing to say to that, and headed back out to the deck to drink beer.

Jon was next, and he was far more impressive. Still in at least partial shock, and woozy, from what had happened to him just a few hours before, he wanted to talk.

"…something picked me up and threw me. It knocked me out. My hoe was pulled out of my hands at the same time, like some super force had grabbed it, and then it was thrown it into the woods. The blade was actually buried into a tree…" he testified, speaking so fast that Darrin twice had to ask him to slow down.

"Can I ask what you guys were doing in the woods?" Chief Thomas interrupted.

Jon shot a quick glance to Darrin, who answered "We were just looking around. Looking for clues."

"With hoes?"

"Yea. You gotta have something to knock the brush and stuff away," Darrin said.

The Chief leaned back in his chair and folded his hands behind his head, as though he was in his office. "I don't understand, guys," he said, "You're telling me these stories about how there might be something, something beyond human out there…and then you go out poking around with hoes? You see what I mean here?"

Darrin felt like he was losing the Chief. He felt like he had to do something. Something more. "Jon, go get the drawing," he said calmly.

Jon looked at Darrin with a mixture of panic and confusion. "Drawing?" he asked innocently.

"You know what I mean. Get it."

Jon slumped reluctantly out of the room, then returned a half minute later with the child's drawing. He handed it to Darrin, dreading what was coming next.

"We went out to where Chester Meredith was buried today," Darrin said to his boss.

"Sounds like you boys had a busy day," the Chief said. He was beyond surprise now, and he was smiling as he said it.

"Yea. We did," Darrin said. "You should know that it looks like the grave is fresh, the one he's supposedly buried in. It looks like someone dug him up not too long ago. Maybe days ago."

Chief Thomas leaned forward with interest again. Keen interest. "Are you sure? Are you sure it was his grave?"

"Yes sir. It was his. And someone left this on top of the grave," Darrin said.

He handed the drawing to Chief Thomas, then looked over at Jon while the Chief studied it. Jon did a pantomime of himself passing out, and Darrin had to bite back a smile. Jon's relief with Darrin's lie was clearly evident.

"Oh my God! Oh my God!" Rodney Thomas exclaimed softly. He looked up from the drawing. "You've…the two of you…you've got something here!" He said in astonishment.

The deck door slid open violently, and a panicked looking Bruce stuck his head in.

"Come out here! Quick!" he whispered as loudly as he could. The three of them hesitated in surprise, then bolted as one for the door and the deck. A few seconds later they were all standing against the railing in the new night's darkness, and they looked and listened in the direction that Bruce was pointing; the foggy pasture and the black woods.

They stood motionless, but heard and saw nothing

immediately. Moments went by, and when he couldn't take it anymore Jon broke the silence by asking "What happened," in a fierce whisper to Bruce.

And then it was there, shattering the stillness of the night. It was the laughter. Hideous, bone-chilling witch-like laughter. It was very clear, and seemed very close.

Chapter 37

Darrin knew that no one would want to accompany him into the woods that night. He didn't even want to himself. First, it had been a long, hard, traumatic day. And that was nothing compared to the incredible, hair-raising, other-worldly incident that they all four experienced, including ("Thank God," Darrin had thought) Chief Rodney Thomas.

The whole thing had probably lasted less than a minute, but like a Fourth of July fireworks display, the awe it inspired easily tricked the mind into thinking that it must have been five times as long. The laughter they heard seemed almost simultaneously close, then very far away, then close again, as it had the other times, but more definitively. Once it seemed to come from way up above them, in the Maple tree just to the right of the deck, and they all four were ready to run for their lives, but it stopped. It was absolutely terrifying, but it wasn't the worst of it. The white wisps were.

All four thought it must have been an optical illusion, so no one cried out, or pointed, or screamed "Did you see that?" or anything of the kind, until it was over and they were able to talk again. They saw floating, fleeting wisps of white that were there, and then gone so quickly that the mind could barely comprehend the sight. Two of them (Jon and Bruce) saw a quick glimpse of an upright floating body, white arms dangling by its sides, with its ghoulish face twisted into a horrifying smile. It had been right in front of them in the pasture, coming their way.

But it turned into a white wisp, and then was gone, well before a scream could rise from either of their throats. It was a sight so horrifying that neither of the two brought it up afterwards, when memories of the event were being shared between the four of them. It seemed too much like an admission of insanity to do so, and so would remain only in their nightmares.

Then it was all gone. Four pale, stunned fully grown men were left in the wake, each seeking solace in the eyes of the others; each praying that they weren't the only witness to what had just happened.

For minutes, no one spoke. They didn't even move at first, and only eventually went numbly to the chairs on the deck to sit. Each struggled with what to do, or say. It was Bruce, who had been the most nightmare-plagued, and who was now wondering in panic if he'd ever sleep again, who eventually broke the silence. "Did, did…" he cleared his throat, "…did anyone see what I just saw?" he croaked out haltingly.

And then it was a cacophony of confession. All talked at once at first, then when the important realization took hold that everyone had seen it (and no one was crazy) they re-established order and each shared what they had heard and seen with the others. All was told, excepting the floating, ghost-like body that the two witnesses kept to themselves.

Police Chief Rodney Thomas went home three quarters of an hour later feeling (no… knowing) that his life had changed. As upsetting, and then terrifying as the night had been, he found himself in a deeper peace than he had ever known. Professionally, he now knew what to do. The brilliant Crandle kid had made it all clear. But that wasn't the important part of the night as far as he was concerned. He felt that ultimately, deeply, this night had, once and for all, confirmed the Faith of a nominally religious man who had in truth been a life-long doubter. If what he and the others saw was true, then his Faith was true. They had glimpsed Hell, and for him, that confirmed

Heaven. For reasons that were finally clear to him, he couldn't wait to get home to his family.

Bruce Ellsworth was hardly comforted that he wasn't the only witness to the awful laughter and white visions. He felt even more of a loss of control than before; even more afraid of the wild ruminations of his own mind. After telling only some of what he saw, and listening only partially to the others, he was the first to go home. He didn't even think to say goodnight. He went into his house, packed a bag, and got into his car. He spent the night at the Holiday Inn Express right there in Highland, looking out the window at the well-lit half empty parking lot between fitful snatches of sleep. He would head to Wisconsin, and Barb, at daybreak. He would never go back to Devonshire again.

Darrin and Jon were left to talk well into the night. They too felt an inexplicable sense of peace. The truth was closer, no matter how awful that truth was.

At around midnight, after a long silence that neither of them had noticed, Darrin offered a reason for what they were feeling.

"I think it's almost over, Jon," he said. He was silent again for a moment, and then added, "I think we did good today."

Jon looked over at him. He could barely make out his face in the darkness of the night. He felt blissfully overwhelmed, both physically and mentally, and could barely get any words out, "Why do you say that?" he finally asked. "*How* can you say that?"

"Because that…that thing could have killed you today. And it didn't." Darrin answered. "And tonight, I'm seeing that as a warning. A spectacular warning, I'll grant you, but a warning."

"To stay out of the woods?"

"That's right," Darrin said, "That's why, just to be sure, we're going up there tomorrow night. I want the Chief to see…that it's just about over. "

Jon could only chuckle sardonically at that. He was too tired, too sore, and way too overwhelmed with what he'd seen to do anything else.

"That's why we're meeting him at the morgue," Chief Thomas said. He and Detective Gus Foster were finishing breakfast at the Cypress Restaurant, or rather, Gus was. Thomas was too wound up to do anything but drink coffee. Rodney knew that the best way to get Gus to listen, to really listen, was to buy him a meal. The Cypress was becoming Gus' favorite spot, so it was easy.

The Chief had waited for the food to arrive before starting, and then warned Gus to listen, and told him the whole story from the night before. And Gus had listened, usually with a mouth full of pancakes. Even when the more unbelievable parts of the story were told, or when Thomas said something that interested him, he would only look up briefly, then dive back into his food. Chief Thomas ended his talk with the fact that he had called David Meredith that morning, informing him that he could voluntarily come in for questioning, or that they could pick him up. Meredith had agreed to come in.

"You're going to take him into the morgue and show him that mutilated body?" Foster asked after swallowing the last of his buttermilks covered in syrup.

"Absolutely," Thomas answered.

"Does he know that's what you're going to do?" Gus asked.

"Nope."

Gus smiled at that. He reached for a toothpick. "Ought to be fun," he said. "You really think that could be his old man? Seems like a long shot to me."

"It's not a long shot, Gus," Chief Thomas said confidently.

Detective Foster chewed on his toothpick and looked closely at Thomas. He belched, then said "You seem different today Rodney. Can't quite put my finger on it, but you're, I don't know, happier, maybe?…More confiden?."

"I'm on top of the world, Gus," Chief Thomas smiled.

Jon woke up at 9:22 A. M., his precise little clock told him, more sore and more excited than he could ever remember being before. The soreness from the grave robbing, field vandalism and from being tossed into the air and knocked out by an apparently supernatural being was understandable. His excitement was wholly from a dream.

Jon had dreamed his book. He had seen the pages and chapters vividly. He had lived the story. He was still living the story. As his strained and aching body struggled to even get out of bed, his face held a smile. The book he had always dreamed of had come to him as a wonderful finished miracle in his sleep.

All he had to do now was write it down. Suddenly, nothing else really mattered. As terrifying and disorienting as it had all been, as much as he had been shaken (both psychologically, and now, physically), by the events of the previous days, Jon felt something inside him was changing. His dream was part of it. Maybe part of it was Darrin pushing him, too. Maybe part of it was being forced to face his fear. It wasn't all clear, yet. He knew one thing for sure that morning though. What he had gone through (was still going through) made all the other things he had faced in his life look very small. Being afraid to take chances, being afraid to commit to a relationship, always playing it safe…it was all so very small.

He got up and stretched, then made himself stretch again, as painful as it was. He took a hot bath first, and soaked in it for 20 minutes. Then he shaved, even though his shaving arm hurt each time he brought it up to his face, got dressed, and was out on his deck with a cup of too-hot coffee, his writing materials, and his cell phone by a little after 10:00. He put his feet up the way he used to without thinking of looking for cut-off heads. He checked his cell. Two calls from Mom, and a call from Darrin. He had an overwhelming feeling of wanting to share his idea; the dream that had come to him the way "Kublai Khan" had come to Coleridge… with someone. Anyone, who would understand.

He looked out at the sunny green pasture and dark woods and thought about how few people there were, now, that would welcome a call from him; that would really be interested in what he was going to start on today. "Too much lost love," he said wistfully and out loud, and to no one…

Then he called his mother.

The morgue had only one occupant. It was a body that had been tested and dissected in every way, and was now quickly becoming a corpse that nobody really knew what to do with. The sole worker in the morgue seemed happy to see Chief Thomas and Detective Foster, especially after he heard that they were bringing someone in to I.D. the body.

"Worse looking corpse I've ever seen," he had said. Chief Thomas was sure that it was.

He and Foster now stood on the sidewalk outside the hospital building, waiting for David Meredith to show up. He was five minutes late already, and that was enough to make Detective Foster irritable.

"That bastard better show up," he scowled. "It's too damn hot out here to wait around, Rodney."

"He'll be here," Thomas said calmly. "This is just his style. Make the customer wait. Make him anxious, and you'll get a better deal."

"I ain't dealing with him, I'll tell you that," Foster muttered.

They waited for exactly three more minutes, and then

Meredith turned the corner and pulled up to them in a shiny blue Cadillac. He smiled and waved to them as he parked his car.

"Remember, I take the lead on this one Gus. I've got a plan," Chief Thomas said as the smiling, ever confident Meredith walked toward them.

"Yea. Whatever. Looks like a used-car salesman." Gus mumbled. He had already decided he didn't like the looks of the guy.

"Well, I'm here! What can I do to ya, boys?" Meredith said jovially as he offered to shake hands. Thomas did, Foster didn't. Thomas told him who Foster was anyway.

"Thank you for coming Mr. Meredith."

"Call me Dave!"

"OK, Dave. We won't take too much of your time. There's a few questions we need to ask, but there's something I want you to see first," Chief Thomas informed him.

"See?" Meredith asked. His smile was slowly disappearing. Detective Foster's was just beginning.

"Please follow me sir," Thomas said, and abruptly turned and went into the side door that had been unlocked for them.

David Meredith looked at the smiling Foster nervously. Foster made an elaborate "after you" gesture, and they both followed Thomas through the door.

The three men walked 30 feet through a narrow corridor with claustrophobic lime green walls. It was barely wide enough for Foster to fit through. Then they turned left and went down a much wider, newly carpeted hallway, walking past busy looking offices on either side. They came to an elevator at the end of this hall, and Chief Thomas stopped there and pressed the button to go down.

"Can I ask where we're goin?" Meredith said.

Thomas turned casually and said "The morgue," and turned back to face the door again, as though this was an every-day event.

"The morgue?! Why, for God's sakes?" Meredith cried. He didn't look like a cool businessman anymore.

Thomas turned to look at him again, "To look at a body," he said, and then turned back.

The elevator door opened and both Thomas and Foster stepped in. Meredith didn't move.

"Aren't you coming?" Thomas asked casually.

Meredith hesitated. He turned and looked back in the direction they had come from, then back at the men in the elevator. "Do I have a choice?" he asked.

"Sure, but we'll just come after you with a warrant if you don't," Chief Thomas said matter-of-factly.

Foster almost smiled again. A warrant to look at a body? Good one.

Meredith got in. He paced around the elevator for the whole short ride. When the doors opened, they could see Bobby Miller, the sole man on duty, standing by the covered body he'd brought to the center of the room. He was smiling idiotically, and to Thomas' mind, unprofessionally.

"We'll take it from here. Thanks Bobby," the Chief said. Bobby's smile disappeared and he skulked out of the room without a word.

Thomas walked directly over to the covered corpse, then turned to address Meredith. Both Meredith and Detective Foster had hung back a few steps. "David, I want you to come over here in a minute and look at the face on this body. I want to warn you, it's not pretty. The body was mutilated recently, and has apparently been dead for a long time. David, listen to me...There's the possibility that this body could be your father, Chester Meredith."

Meredith stared at Chief Thomas with utter astonishment. He was having trouble fully comprehending the words that the Chief had just spoken. "What?...How?" was all he could manage to get out.

Thomas put his hand on the sheet by the head of the corpse.

"Come on over and have a look, David. You might as well get it over with."

Meredith swallowed hard and looked at Foster beside him. Foster had a scowl on his face and his eyes glued to Meredith. He would be studying his reaction the whole way.

"Come on, David," Chief Thomas repeated a little more forcefully.

Meredith slowly walked over to the table. As soon as he was by Thomas' side, the sheet was pulled down.

Meredith looked at the face for a full five seconds. Then he started visibly shaking. He put his hand up to his mouth, took two quick steps back, and vomited on the cement floor of the morgue.

Chapter 38

"I want to go with you," Jon said forcefully. "I'm going." He was talking to Darrin after having had a long conversation with his Mother and an initial wonderful hour and a half of writing. He had finally called Darrin back while taking a short break. This was more than a friendly call-back, however. He had just informed Darrin, several times, that he wanted to go into the woods with him that night. It seemed like an unexpected, puzzling about- face to Darrin.

"I'm just telling you what the Chief told me this morning," Darrin repeated. "Just him and me. That's what he said. He doesn't want to put any citizens at risk. I thought you'd understand that."

"So I was a good enough partner up to now, but now I'm just a 'citizen,' that needs to be protected?" Jon asked.

It's not me, I told you. Chief Thomas made the decision. It's nothing personal, man," Darrin pleaded.

Jon felt, rightly, that he was getting nowhere fast. So like his friend Darrin had the night before, he decided to take another angle. "I know you'll have trouble understanding this, but I've got a great book in me now, Darrin. I'm writing already, and it's beautiful. I've got to be in on this. I've got to see what happens. Nobody…nobody that's still alive, has been through more than me. I found the first body. I'm the one who had a god-damned head on my porch! I put my bare feet on it! I'm the one who got knocked out, not you, not the Chief. You tell the Chief that if I'm not allowed to go, I'll go by myself. How safe would that be?"

And he hung up the phone.

"It wasn't Papa. It couldn't be Papa." The weathered, heretofore tough-guy David Meredith sounded more like a little girl now, Detective Foster thought.

The three of them were sitting in an office that Chief Thomas had asked for, for the post-viewing interview. They had left Bobby Miller with the vomit to clean up and the body to be put back in the cooler, while Meredith took the lead in summoning the elevator to deliver them from the dank basement morgue. Meredith had been ready to flee the hospital altogether, but Thomas had reminded him on the way up that were still questions to be answered.

"How do you know that's not him?" Detective Foster asked.

Meredith was still very shaken...more than shaken, as Thomas had hoped he would be, and it took him an inordinate amount of time to answer. "That body...was so little. My Dad was bigger than that," he said absently. Then he looked up at Chief Thomas. "What happened to the eyes? That was so terrible! The eyes were missing."

"I know, Dave. Did you see anything at all, anything, that would give any indication that it could be your father," Thomas asked him.

Meredith rocked back and forth, slightly, in his seat. His arms were folded at his chest, as though he was cold. "The hair...maybe. A little. I don't know!" he cried out as he began rocking harder.

Thomas and Foster exchanged a glance. Thomas dropped his voice down some when he started talking again; "David, there's something you need to know. One of my officers, a very good young officer, tells me that your Father's grave has… has recently been, well, disturbed."

Meredith kept rocking, but a little less so. Despite the state he was in, he was listening. He looked up at Chief Thomas. "What do you mean?" he asked in a soft voice.

"It means that it's possible, just possible, and, excuse me for saying this sir, that someone could have dug him up. Your Father could be the first body…the one we haven't been able to identify."

Meredith looked at Chief Thomas uncomprehendingly for a moment, then looked down and started rocking harder again. "Oh Jesus… Sweet Jesus!" he said. Meredith looked helpless now.

Thomas looked at Foster again. He was grinning, and nodded at Thomas. He was signaling that it was time to move in for the kill.

"Dave, you had an older brother. We know that. We want to know, we have to know, that you will answer this next question honestly. Do you understand?"

Meredith nodded. He was still looking down at his lap, and rocking.

"Do you know for sure that your brother died? That he got killed in some farm accident? Do you know that for sure?" Chief Thomas asked.

Meredith rocked. He didn't answer.

"What do you know Dave? It's very important that…"

"He's dead. I know that he's dead," Meredith blurted out. "I'm not sure how." Thomas could see a tear run down his left cheek. He kept rocking like a little kid.

"What the hell does that mean?" Gus thundered. To Thomas' astonishment, Gus stood up, and then over, Meredith. "Answer the question!" he shouted.

Detective Foster's display had no apparent effect on David Meredith. Anyone else would have at least flinched, Thomas thought. He was tempted to tell the ineffectual Detective to sit down, but thought it would be better to let him realize it himself, and keep a little dignity. His threat just wasn't helping, like so much of what Gus had done.

"Dave, tell us what you know about your older brother, Chester," the Chief said calmly.

Meredith looked up at Thomas. The emotion on his face made him look a far cry from the tough guy he'd met the previous day. "I grew up being told that he died in an accident, like everybody says, but…" He choked a bit then, perhaps trying to bite off a sob, and continued his rocking, though more slowly now.

"But what?" Chief Thomas asked. Detective Foster saw that he was being completely shut out by Meredith, as Thomas had hoped. He sat down.

"Mom said something…but she's, she's gone senile ya know. You can't tell when she's remembering something, or when she's imagining something…but she said once, when we first put her in the home, that Daddy had to put him away…'like a dog gone bad,' she said." Then he stopped, and looked down at his feet. The rocking stopped too.

Thomas and Foster looked at one another. It was hard to know whether to prod for more, or to give him time. Thomas chose the former. "Did you take that to mean that your Dad had to kill him?" he asked as gently as he could.

Meredith looked up at Thomas again. He started slowly shaking his head. "I don't know," he answered softly. Then, for the first time in the interview, he looked over at Detective Foster. "Honest to God, I don't know," he said.

The relentless July sun had regained its rightful place of dominance over the busy, if distracted, city of Highland. "Hot enough for ya?" once again became the standard greeting in shops, banks, and at the inevitable yard sales. The mighty storm and the accompanying cool front from just a few days before was already fading from the collective memory. Everywhere, once again, air-conditioners hummed, construction workers suffered and dawdled, and children played indoors while their abandoned dogs panted outside in what shade they could find.

An observer, or an assigned recorder of events taking place that day on the Devonshire cul-de-sac would have had a terrible time trying to stay awake. The street was as abandoned and lifeless as a ghost town. Not a single resident, with the exception of Jonathon Parker (who would have been difficult to observe, as he was on his deck in the back yard, writing), was home all day, and less than a handful would be there that night. Not a single car or truck entered the cul-de-sac until 3:05 that afternoon, when a jittery mailman made his obligatory rounds. Not a single stray cat or dog ambled down the street, and to even see a bird in the sultry blue sky would have seemed remarkable that day.

At a little after 5:00, with the heat at its peak, Pam Frey came home after picking up Robert at his friend's house. She pulled right into the garage and shut the garage door immediately, before she would let Robert out of the car. They stayed inside the house with doors locked, until Rory came home that evening.

Fred Knotts came home a few minutes after Pam, and followed the same pattern for safety's sake, although he did brave a trip to the mailbox. Being unarmed, as well as chastened and discredited by police and family alike, he had taken the precaution of sending his wife and daughter away, while he sulked and worried alone.

No one else entered the cul-de-sac until almost 8:00, at the beginning of the cool of the evening. It was then that the first of two police cars pulled up to the curb in front of Jonathon Parker's house. He had been anticipating their arrival, and was standing in his front yard in his jeans, t-shirt and hiking boots, hoping (and yes, praying) that he was physically and mentally ready for whatever the night would bring.

Chapter 39

Officer Darrin Crandle was in the first vehicle that arrived.. He got out of his car and had walked up to where Jon was standing, just as the second car was pulling into the cul-de-sac.

"Good news and bad news," Darrin said. "Chief says you can walk with us if you want to assume the risk. He says he can't stop you."

"What's the bad news?" Jon asked with relief.

Darrin turned to look at the police car that was now parking behind his. "The bad news is that fat ass is coming to… something about him being in charge, or some such bullshit."

Police Chief Rodney Thomas and Detective Gus Foster got out the second car. Thomas and Darrin were in uniform, and Foster was wearing uncharacteristically casual attire. Jon, who had never seen Foster without a tie on, noted how odd the fat man looked in oversized jeans, untucked Hawaiian shirt and white tennis shoes that looked like they'd never been worn. They walked up to where the other two were standing.

"Mr. Parker, do you know Detective Foster?" Chief Thomas asked.

"We've met," Jon answered, and the two shook hands.

"Mr. Parker… Jon, I've got to emphasize that what we're going to do tonight, based on the murders that have taken place, not to mention what we all witnessed last night, it…it could be very dangerous," Chief Thomas said, "I am hoping you may have re-thought this?"

"I want to go, sir," Jon said.

"Well, understand that you are to stay with us, in our protection at all times."

"Yes, sir."

"We have to assume that there could be someone out there who means to harm us, even though Officer Crandle here may not think so," Thomas said. He smiled at Darrin, then continued, "You aren't armed, are you son?"

"No sir. I don't own any firearms," Jon answered.

"Good," Thomas said. "Despite the, uh, adventure you two have been on, and despite what you may have done up until now," he gave a sterner look to Darrin, "our purpose is clear: to catch the killer, and to stop these crimes. Tonight is a stakeout. We're going to confront whatever's out there. We have reason to believe, or at least we can hope, that things might be different out there tonight. We can only hope so." He looked at Darrin again, like they were sharing some secret, when he said this. It made Jon wonder just what Darrin had told the Chief to get him to cooperate like this, and what the Chief had in turn told Foster to get him to come out here to traipse around in the dark. Whatever it was, it had worked. "Does everyone understand?" the Chief asked in finishing.

Both Jon and Darrin nodded. Foster grumbled something that was inaudible, and undoubtedly negative.

Jon invited them to come in, and offered iced tea and soda that he served them out on the deck while they waited for it to get closer to dark. Twilight was still a half an hour away and complete darkness would take almost an hour. While it was still humid, it was much better temperature-wise now that night was closing in. Only Foster appeared to be uncomfortable. It took only a few minutes outdoors for him to sweat through his shirt. The men sat on deck chairs (Jon thought Detective Foster would surely break through his, but it held) while they waited, and Thomas used the time to go over a few rules with Jon, and then asked both Darrin and Jon to go over their stories again, for Detective Foster's sake. Foster actually acted interested in Darrin's investigative work, even asking him questions at certain points. It was evident that he was clearly impressed, even though he didn't buy into Darrin's whole theory.

"You've got a real up-and-comer there, Rodney," he said to Chief Thomas afterwards. Thomas winced once again at being called by his first name.

When the sun began to sink, Thomas stood up and announced that it was time to take off, and the other three got up with flashlights in hand (Jon's, which he couldn't resist playing with, was on loan from the Police Department) and filed off the deck, then walked into the yard toward the pasture.

"I feel like we need to be carrying wooden stakes to drive through the hearts of the vampires," Darrin joked to Jon. Jon gave him a forced grin.

The fence between the yard and pasture was their first trouble. Detective Foster simply could not get over it, despite repeated, comical looking efforts to do so. Darrin had to bite his lip until it was almost bleeding, to keep from laughing out loud.

"Is there any way around this damned thing?" the already exhausted Homicide Investigator eventually asked.

Jon explained that the fence ended past the Vanderberg's property, about a quarter of a mile west, and Foster reluctantly headed that way. He rejoined them several long minutes later at the top of the initial hill in the middle of the pasture. They had had to wait for him, and he was covered with sweat and breathing hard by the time he got through the thick grass.

"Why …why doesn't somebody…why doesn't somebody mow this shit?" he sputtered out as he fought for breath.

Thomas looked at Foster and declared a five minute rest, much to Darrin's disgust. Jon was in no hurry. As he knew he would, he was beginning to question his own judgment in making the trek. The sun was already gone, and an eerie twilight had set in. There was an ominous fog-like mist in the trees ahead; a mist that was moving; floating above the ground even though there wasn't a hint of a breeze where they were resting. Jon felt the beginning of the now familiar feeling of cold fear his stomach. But he was determined to fight through it.

"How far into the woods are we going, Chief?" he asked, as he watched the mist uneasily.

"I don't think we need to go in, actually," Thomas said. "I don't see what good it would do. Whatever, er… whoever's out there, they'll know we're here, don't you think, Darrin?"

Darrin was flattered to be asked, but had no idea how to answer. "I have no idea," he answered.

"Well, let's get to the trees, and then we'll play it by ear," the Chief said. "We better get going."

The four walked down the slight hill, then up another one, and the huffing Foster quickly started to fall behind again. "Shit, I hope we don't have to run," Darrin whispered to Jon, "Old Tubby there would be lost for sure."

The five minute walk they had left to get to the woods edge took a full ten minutes. When they arrived it was nearly dark. There was just enough light to see twenty feet or so into the woods. The four of them stood and looked into the misty darkness for a few minutes before Chief Thomas spoke.

"That undergrowth is so thick we'd have trouble making it in the daytime," he said. "We'll stay right here."

"Thank God," Foster huffed.

"We need to spread out a bit, but not too far. Parker, you stay with Crandle. Don't use flashlights until and unless you actually see something. No one draws or fires their weapon unless it's clearly self-defense. We don't want to shoot each other up like those clowns the other night."

"Darrin, take Jon and go no further than 30 yards that way," the Chief continued, pointing to the east. "Gus, no further than 30 yards that way. We've got to be able to hear each other. Keep low, and take care," he said.

And so they went where they were assigned, with Gus Foster grumbling, and Jon and Darrin openly wondering whether they were doing the right thing.

"Excuse me for asking, but just why are we doing this?" Jon asked Darrin when they were safely out of earshot.

"Beats me," Darrin answered. "I don't know. To me, we just walk in and ask ol'Chester to knock it off," he half-joked. He said nothing else though, and walked with his head down, seemingly distracted by other thoughts.

The men were in their positions within a minute. It didn't take half an hour for all four of them to find a semi-comfortable place to sit in the tall grass, and simply wait. Standing while looking into the black woods half the night was out of the question.

The minutes went slowly by. There was nothing to be seen, even though it was a bright, starry night, and there was nothing to hear but the monotonous, sleep inducing insect and frog cadences of the summer evening.

An hour later, Jon and Darrin were startled by the sudden appearance of Chief Thomas. He was checking on them.

"See anything?" he whispered.

They both whispered "No!" at the same time.

"OK. I'm going to check with Gus now," he said, "Be careful," and he trudged slowly away.

Another quiet, still half an hour went by. Jon was starting to get cold. Temperature aside, there was a damp chill in the air. He had debated with himself about bringing a sweatshirt, but it had seemed absurd when he was thinking about it in the middle of the sweltering afternoon. "Wrong move dumbass," he mumbled to himself.

Darrin was getting edgy. In one way he was relieved that everything was quiet and normal. But in another way, he wanted to make something happen. He was afraid of something happening, and he was afraid that nothing would.

He let another half an hour of quiet go by, with the darkness ever deepening, before he leaned over to Jon and whispered. "I'm going to talk to the Chief. I think you're supposed to go with me."

Jon was more than happy to get up and stretch, and move. It didn't take long to get to Riggs.

"Chief," Darrin said, after they'd initially scared the hell out of him with their approach, "I want to try something."

"What are you talking about?" Thomas snapped. His heart was still racing from the surprise.

"I want to call him out. Chester, I mean. I know it sounds crazy, but yesterday, when I called out his name…well, that's when Jon got attacked. It seemed like when I yelled, it evoked a response."

Chief Thomas was getting cold too, and discouraged. He had been second-guessing himself for some time now. He realized that it would be midnight before long, and despite what he'd seen the night before, it seemed increasingly evident that nothing was going down tonight. He had been entertaining thoughts of when he should call things off. He thought about the implications of what Darrin was requesting. It could be a terrible mistake if the killer was anywhere near, whether human or something else. On the other hand, if Crandle called out and nothing happened? Maybe the way to end a disappointing night. What the hell.

"OK," he whispered, "but we've got to tell Detective Foster first. We don't want him to come out blasting."

"I'll take care of it," Darrin whispered back.

He left Jon with the Chief and trotted over to find Foster. He was easy to find, even in the dark. He was snoring loud enough to wake the dead. "Jesus Christ," Darrin mumbled disgustedly while shaking the big man vigorously. "Wake up, you slob!"

Foster woke up in a panic and tried to rise to his feet too fast. He slipped and fell back down hard.

"Easy!" Darrin said, "Take it easy! You were asleep! It's OK!"

Foster stopped struggling and asked "What the hell happened?" from his position lying on the ground.

"Nothing happened!" Darrin scolded. He couldn't help being disgusted with the guy. He wanted to get this over with. "Look," he said, "I'm going to try to communicate with the guy, or that thing in the woods. You're going to hear me yelling. The Chief told me to come over and warn you so that you wouldn't panic and shoot me…or yourself."

Foster sat up and rubbed his eyes. "Communicate? With your ghost?" Then he laughed. "What? Are we gonna have a séance now?"

Darrin just walked away. He went back to where Jon and Chief Thomas were. He found them crouched down and alert, both staring intently into the dense woods. Darrin crouched down with them. "What's up?" he whispered.

"SSHH! Jon saw something!" Thomas whispered back.

Darrin wanted to ask Jon what he saw, but figured he'd get shushed again, so he peered, on edge, into the blackness with the other two.

A minute went by. Nothing. Not a sight or a sound. Then another minute. The tension the three of them felt seemed only to mount with the waiting. It was the waiting, the not knowing, that was the worst part of fear, Darrin thought.

Then they heard the sound of a branch falling to the ground from somewhere not too far away, in the woods. All three held as still as possible, and listened. There was the snap of a stick, as though someone had taken a step. It was very close, but they couldn't see anything. A few seconds later, another crackle. It seemed even closer.

Then nothing more. Minutes went by. They all strained to hear even the tiniest sound, but there was nothing.

"I'm going to try calling him out," Darrin said suddenly, startling the others.

"Are you sure? Something's close!" Jon whispered frantically

Even in the dark, Darrin could see how pale Jon's face was. Whatever he had seen had scared him badly.

"Yea, I'm sure," Darrin said confidently as he stood up. "OK Chief?"

Chief Thomas was still crouched and staring at the woods. His weapon was drawn. "Go ahead," he said.

Darrin took a few steps toward the woods. A sudden, cool breeze hit him. It was strong enough to make his shirt sleeves and uniform pants flap, and caused him to temporarily stop dead in his tracks. Then, again very quickly, it was gone, and it was a still summer night again. So still in fact, that he and the others knew something was different. Something had happened, or was about to happen.

They all listened. There was absolutely no sound. That's what was different. No insects, no tree frogs; nothing. A complete absence of anything.

Darrin couldn't wait any longer. He cupped his hands around his mouth. "Chester!" he shouted, shattering the perfect silence, "Chester, it's all right now! It's all over now, Chester!" Darrin tried to sound as strong, and as authoritative, as he could. He dropped his hands and listened. All he heard was laughter. Laughter that was coming from Detective Foster, 30 yards down the way. He sounded like he was really getting a kick out of it all.

"Oh Chester?!?" Foster mocked in a high female-type voice, "You're late for supper Chester! Your Mommy's calling you Chester!" and then he laughed uproariously again.

"Shut up Gus, will ya!" Chief Thomas yelled, but it didn't help much. Gus was having too good of a time. It made the other three feel silly; silly to be doing what they were doing. Jon thought of Darrin's story of the snipe hunt.

Despite it all, they waited it out for another hour and a half. There were no other mysterious sounds heard, nothing else was seen, the mating insects started calling again, and even Gus quieted down. They assumed he'd fallen asleep again.

Jon and Darrin stayed with Thomas, and as the tension gradually subsided, they talked more and more, eventually without bothering to whisper. Jon had seen only a quick glimpse of something white, and as sure as he had been at the time he saw it, he began doubting himself as time went by, and under the questioning of the other two.

Darrin confessed to Chief Thomas (under the cover of darkness?) that he had destroyed Meredith's new crops, and he told him why. He left Jon's name out of it.

"It sounds nuts, and I know it was wrong, but I think that may stop the killing," Darrin had explained.

"I thought that's what happened," the Chief said coolly. "I have a hunch Meredith won't be filing a complaint." He was smiling when he said that, but the other two couldn't see it in the dark.

It went on until 1:45 in the morning, when Chief Thomas decided that enough was enough. "Let's pack it in boys," he said. He turned on his flashlight for the first time that night, which temporarily blinded all three of them, and waved it in Foster's direction. "We're calling it a night Gus!" he yelled out.

When there was no immediate answer, Darrin said "I had to shake hell out of him to wake him up the first time. He snores like a grizzly bear."

The three of them walked over to Detective Foster's stakeout position. "Gus! Wake up Gus!" the Chief yelled.

With all three powerful flashlights blazing, they could all see that he wasn't where he was supposed to be before they even got there. The grass was still matted down from where the big body had been sleeping, but no Gus Foster.

"Gus! Where are you?" the Chief called out irritably. The three of them stood where Foster had been, and used the flashlights to do a sweep search in every direction. They came up empty, and, inevitably, the tension started crawling back into their guts.

"Do ya 'spose he gave up and went in?" Darrin asked as he took a few steps and shined his light into the woods.

"I think he'd tell me. I know he would," Chief Thomas said. He was shining his light on the pasture to the west, where Gus would have to go if he wanted to walk around the fence.

"Oh my God! Oh my God!" Jon screamed. He had walked about ten feet into the woods without the other two really noticing. Now they quickly ran through the grass and underbrush to where his light was shining. When they got there, they stopped dead.

Jon held the picture in his flashlight, which he held with both hands, that none of the three would forget until their dying day. Detective Gus Foster was sitting with his back up against a tree, like someone who was taking a summer nap by a stream while waiting for the catfish to bite. But his head was gone, and he was sitting there on top of a rapidly spreading pool of blood.

"Oh, Lord Jesus! Oh God..." Chief Thomas cried in a choking voice, "Oh Gus!"

Darrin walked slowly over to where Jon was standing like a frozen statue, holding his flashlight with shaking hands, shining it on what was left of Detective Gus Foster. Darrin stopped by Jon's side, patted him gently on the shoulder and then walked over to the body. He bent down over it, careful not to step in the blood, and flashed his light in a tight circle around the sitting body and behind the tree he was leaning against, looking for footprints, a weapon...anything. He felt a drop of moisture land on the back of his head. Then another. Confused, he looked above him up towards the starry night, right as another drop hit the side of his face. He wiped at it, stood straight up and shined his light on his hand. It was blood.

Darrin jumped back quickly and pointed his flashlight up the tree. There, impaled on a branch directly above the body was Gus Foster's now eyeless head, with blood smeared up both sides of his lifeless mouth, as if a child had painted on a smile.

Chapter 40
Epilogue To A Haunting

"It's been three months now," Jon wrote, "Three months of wondering, waiting, praying, and trying to embrace life again in some form, knowing that it will never, ever be the same."

He put down his pen, picked up his cup of coffee and looked out at the pasture and woods, now clothed in the glorious, radiant garments of fall. It was the kind of crisp but still warm mid-October Saturday that makes a person feel grateful to be alive, and, for once, to be living in the Midwest. There was no wind at all, but still there was that sweet smell; that mixture of harvest and decay that only autumn can create after a long, hot summer finally ends. There wouldn't be many more days like this. Jon knew his deck days were numbered.

He breathed in deeply as he looked out, and thought. His book, thank the Lord, was almost done. He had told a terrible, true story, as clearly and honestly as he could. It had been a necessary, at times tortuous, but ultimately cleansing ordeal for him. Now it was almost over. But the end of anything is always tough. He closed his eyes for a moment, then picked up his pen again.

"Time is our survival mechanism," he wrote. "I've learned that. Only three months ago, there was almost no one left on my street. Two police officers had been mutilated, as well as a cat, a dog, and a dug up corpse. The terror was palpable, the tension unbearable, day after day. Now, already, memories are fading, or shut out altogether. We are a weak species, I think; but a species that somehow knows that remembering, fully… would be devastating. Now, except for having new neighbors in the Vanderberg house, and having the Ellsworth house still standing forlornly empty (I'm trying to talk Darrin Crandle into buying it), everyone else is back, and we are living life normally…almost. It is incredible, what the mind can do; what the mind can shut out.

"Yes, we are still wary of the night, but we sleep now. Yes, there are more nightmares than there used to be, but we know that they are only nightmares. As a neighborhood, we are closer than we used to be. People seem kinder; more concerned. Faith and caring for each other seems more real; more genuine. We are better grounded, somehow. We are survivors. We have come to realize that we need each other; that we can help each other."

Jon put his pen down again. He read over what he had just written. So-so, he thought. It was so hard to describe; the aftermath. He sipped his coffee and breathed in the wonderful air and tried to clear his mind a bit. He needed to finish this for the day. He had papers he should be grading, even now. He was a better teacher this year. Better by far. He never seemed to get behind anymore. He cared more about his kids. He wasn't sure why, but he just did.

He finished his coffee, then picked up his pen again, looked up at the warm southern sun, and wrote a little more.

"They never found any clues. None. And we all know they never will. I, none of us, will ever go into those woods again. I dearly hope, in fact I pray, that no one ever does. Those woods are haunted. I know what being haunted is now, and they are haunted. Whether you want to call it a ghost, or a demon, or some kind of witch, makes no difference to me.

"Someone, probably Chester Meredith, was kept up there, and was probably killed up there. The exact details aren't important. They really aren't. What's important is that Pure Evil exists. There comes a moment, when you go through what we did, when you realize this fully and completely. It is there. I have seen it, and on some nights, I can still hear it. It is living Hell, and it will punish those who push too hard, or are too curious, or who give in to a dare, or temptation. That's one way of putting it."

Jon put his pen down again, and got up to walk around his deck. He was getting nervous again. He needed to get this over with. It was amazing to him how upsetting it still was to think about and write about it all; especially the end…because he couldn't tell it all. He couldn't tell the whole truth, as he had up to this point, here at the end. He didn't dare. It was too dangerous… too dangerous for everyone.

Even if he had made his own separate peace, it was too dangerous.

It had happened to him on a late August night, about a month after Detective Foster's grisly, horrible death. It was weeks after the police, who had endlessly searched the woods day after day and night after night, had finally given up. It was at the end of the first month of relative normalcy for the scarred but slowly healing Devonshire neighborhood. Enough time had passed in peace that it all seemed to be gone.

His now close friend Darrin had been over that night. They had talked, for the first time really, about things other than unexplained murders and mysterious hauntings. They had talked about real life, and Jon had opened up to Darrin about things ranging from failed relationships to secret ambitions and his progress on his book, and Darrin (whenever he could) talked about a girl that he had met that he was actually excited about.

In fact, Darrin going home to call his girl was the reason

the night ended early, and the reason Jon was out on his deck when it happened.

He had only gone out for a breath of air on a cool, late summer evening. He was going to be out there only briefly, and then head back in to watch some TV. He didn't even turn the deck lights on, and didn't even sit in his favorite chair. Instead, he leaned against the rail, and looked out over the pasture, while feeling a bit sorry for himself. He was thinking about how guys like Darrin would always get the girl, while guys like him were always trying to write books, but by themselves.

The feeling came over him quickly and hard. His mind, in alarm, snapped him away from his idle thoughts and back to where he was like a shot. He knew, just like that first morning when he had woken suddenly after Barb's scream, that something was wrong. Something was very wrong. Someone was watching him. He knew it. For sure.

Jon's first instinct was what almost anyone's would be; to go inside quickly and lock the door. But he waited, not moving. He didn't even look from side to side, or call out, or go back and turn the deck lights back on. He simply waited, holding onto the deck railing tightly, breathing shallowly, when at all. He was tired of being frightened away. He stared out at the pasture and the distant woods and waited.

Less than five minutes later, and very suddenly, he saw it. It was a long ways away, up by the woods, but it had a glow that dark night that made it unmistakable. It was a person, or at least appeared to be, dressed in some kind of white shroud.

Jon tried not to move. He tried not to breathe hard. He didn't want to do anything that might make it go away. For several long minutes he just watched the motionless figure, squinting to try to see it more clearly over the long distance. He thought of walking off of the deck, and down to the pasture fence to get at least a little closer, but felt that, somehow, if he moved, it would go away. So he waited, and watched.

When it first started to move toward him, Jon thought it

must be an optical illusion. It was far enough away that he thought he was surely imagining it. But within half a minute, he knew that he wasn't. It was moving.

It was floating just above the ground and it was headed straight in his direction. It seemed to pick up speed, slightly, as it got closer. As it got to the top of the last small rise 50 yards before the fence and his house, it stopped suddenly, and Jon could see it fairly clearly, again because of its strange, incandescent glow.

It was the size of an adolescent boy, with unnaturally long arms dangling at its side. The head, from that distance, appeared to be bald. The face was too far away to see. It's robes flapped in the gentle wind.

Jon was trembling slightly, but for some reason, he wasn't terrified. He didn't know why, but as he watched, he was conscious of the fact that he wasn't afraid. At least not like before. This time, it seemed different.

Some of that surety began evaporating when it started moving, floating, toward him again. It came down the hill rapidly, still just above the ground, and stopped abruptly just on the other side of the fence. It was now less than 15 yards from where Jonathon Parker stood, in awe, on his deck.

Jon stared down into the bright red eyes of a face more horrifying than he could ever have imagined, on a little boy. If it is possible, in any life, to feel at the same moment total horror combined with the natural empathy one feels for the young, it happened to Jon Parker then. Revulsion, fear, compassion and sympathy are uncommon bedfellows, and Jon saw and felt it all in an instant. A boy in communion robes, and a monster beyond description and understanding, all together. What he was looking at was beyond horrible but at some level, vulnerable. An infant terrible.

The white, ghoulish head twisted slowly downward to an impossible, almost upside-down angle, but the red, pupil less still looked up at Jon with a primal, canine-like curiosity. Its long tongue flicked out and then back in several times, as if testing the air for prey.

"I'm not afraid," Jon said in a low voice to himself. It wasn't true. Not now. He was now terrified, but had somehow gotten the words out. He was trying to hold his ground with all his might. He would only realize later, much later, that he was also trying to understand; trying to comprehend. And that he was passing through a barrier.

The powdery face then twisted slowly into a horrid smile, the same one that would haunt Pete Vanderberg for the rest of his days, and strongly resembling the one that appeared to have been painted in blood on Gus Foster only a month before. The head twisted back upright, the gray hands dangled like useless appendages at its sides. A deep, chuckling gurgle came from its smiling but unmoving mouth. It was a sound that seemed the very embodiment of Evil, and Jon felt it permeate every cell of his body.

The danger was here now. It was hair-raising, palpable, and unmistakable. But what Jon did next, instead of running or screaming as most would, was something new for him. He had no way of knowing it then, but it would give him something he had never had before.

He tightened his hands on the deck railing to assure himself that this was really where he was, and this was where he was going to stay. No matter what. Then he gathered all the courage he had left deep within him, and spoke.

"Chester?" Jon asked with his voice cracking. "Are you Chester?"

The boy-monster's smile disappeared, and the red eyes seemed to open wider as it glared. Several interminable moments of silence followed. Jon held his ground.

Then, suddenly and with great force, it growled, without opening its mouth, so deeply that it seemed to be coming from inside the earth itself. It was a growling howl of evil and pain that Jon would remember always.

Jon closed his eyes tightly and prayed, and held onto the rail and shook, until the interminable sound finally stopped. It took all he had to open them again, and when he did, he saw that it was still facing him, but floating backwards and away. Its face was expressionless and dead. Its arms dangled aimlessly at its sides. It hesitated at the top of the hill, just as it had when it approached him, but then floated slowly away.

In a minute it was gone, and there was only distant, horrible laughter coming from somewhere deep in the woods.

Jon looked at his watch as he paced, trying to decide if he should quit for a while and do something else. It was 2:07 on Saturday afternoon. It was October 25th. Halloween was a week away. "Oh God," he said out loud (glad for a chance to think about something else), "Halloween."

He sat down to write just a few more lines that he'd fit in somewhere, later. He grabbed his pen, and took a deep breath. Just a few more lines, that's all.

"Halloween used to be one of the biggest nights of the year on Devonshire," he wrote. "Hundreds of kids came to see Jim Burgett's Haunted House; the adults of the neighborhood built fires in their driveways and visited, and trick-or-treaters were everywhere. It was wonderful here in Highland; here on Devonshire.

"I can't imagine that anymore. No one will come here, or anywhere near here, unless they don't know. And they all know. Halloween has been taken from us."

Jon put his pen down for the last time that day. Enough was enough. "At least I won't have to buy so much friggin' candy this year," he said out loud.

It was time to move on. Time to do something else… both today, and with the rest of his life. He would always teach. He would always write. But there was so much more out there; so much that he hadn't had the courage to do before.

He sat back in his chair and looked out for a moment past the still, now gold and yellow pasture, and out to the woods beyond. And out there, he could see them – the beautiful trees, wearing their yellows and oranges and reds for one more day in the dying season, dancing in the distance to a mysterious breeze of their own, on an otherwise windless day.

Printed in the United States
151148LV00002B/5/P